With her law career becoming more nerve-wracking by the day, Rory must decide once and for all whether to leave it for her true twin passions – dance and her partner, Sasha. As she and Sasha begin to train for the largest competition in the world, Blackpool, their partnership, and their very lives, are threatened by Rory's returning anorexia that had haunted her as a child ballet dancer, one of Sasha's jealous and vengeful former students, and, most seriously, demons from Sasha's past.

This is part two in a continuing three-book series.

Praise for writing by Tonya Plank

"Swan Lake Samba Girl" (blog):

"Tonya Plank is one of the blogosphere's freshest, liveliest, least predictable, and most pleasing voices. Long may she samba!" Terry Teachout, author, "All in the Dances: A Life of George Balanchine."

"Tonya Plank [is] one of New York's most precious assets…" James Wolcott, Vanity Fair online.

"Swallow" (novel):

"Hooks you from the opening pages with its breathless urgency and captures what it's like to live in NY now, with money worries and ambition and myriad obligations breathing down your neck… give it a try." – Vanity Fair Online, James Wolcott, January 15, 2010

"Plank has a knack for combining philosophical opinions, hard-luck family stories, discount shopping triumphs, and gently slapstick humor into a book that makes readers laugh, think, and swallow hard in sympathy." –ForeWord Reviews

"Chatty and engaging. A great beach read." Gotham Gal

"Unlike any novel I've ever read before, and I loved it from the first sentence to the last." Blue Archipelago Reviews

"…I was happy with the way the story turned out and delighted in watching the main character grow. I liked the message of the book also as I think it's an important one for all of us."– The Cajun Book Lady

"Wow! This book was a revelation! Tonya Plank's writing style is captivating and natural, Sophie is a very likable girl-next-door character, Swallow is truly a great surprise novel. would recommend it to everyone." Ex Libris

"Read it instead of seeing 'Sex and the City.'" Christy Leigh Stewart (YouTube video)

"Very unique and different, and a wonderful story that was a pleasure to read! I can't wait to read more by Tonya!" Hanging Off the Wire

"Essentially, Swallow is a coming-to-grips-with-who-you-are story. And it's a good one." Basil & Spice

# FEVER

A Ballroom Romance

Book Two

## INFECTIOUS RHYTHM SERIES

Tonya Plank

ISBN: 978-1-942289-01-2
ISBN: 1-942289-01-4
ISBN Kindle: 978-1-942289-04-3
ISBN epub: 978-1-942289-07-4
Library of Congress Control Number: 2015906777

Edited by Julia Ganis, Juliaedits.com
Cover design by Marisa-rose Shor, Cover Me Darling

For all the Latin ballroom dancers who, over the years, have inspired, entertained, intrigued, and captivated me.

# CHAPTER 1

"So." Sasha placed his hands on his hips. "I have…" He spoke slowly and deliberately. "…a prrroposition for you."

His uber-sexy Russian-accented rolling r's and inviting tone made me weak in the knees. Very weak. He had to know that by now. He had to know what those rolling r's did to me.

"Uh-huh," I squeaked, so simultaneously startled and elated by his presence I didn't know what to say. Or do.

"Would you like to sit in the courtyard area to talk? Or the Coffee Bean down the street? I would prefer not to be in a very public place, though. I mean, not near the school. If you don't mind."

That impeccable English grammar made me smile. He was back to his old self, his tone a one-hundred-and-eighty-degree difference from yesterday. He seemed concerned about me. It sounded as if he had something important to discuss, not that he was still flaming mad about our prior fight.

"Would you like help with those?" he asked, pointing to my groceries.

"Oh. Yeah." I looked at my paper bag, now dripping from the ice cream.

He took the bag from my hand and stepped aside so I could access my lock.

"Oh, come in," I said, when he remained standing on the doormat as I walked toward the fridge. As soon as he walked through the doorway, I immediately began stressing about when I'd last vacuumed, cleaned the toilet, dusted the TV. But those thoughts stopped abruptly as I focused on his words. Why didn't he want to be in a public place or near the school? Was he here secretly? Was he embarrassed of me? He stood in the middle of the living room, gazing at my walls which were mainly bare, save for a giant drawing of Rudolf Nureyev I'd gotten at a discount one year in Massachusetts near a big dance event, and a few photographs of favorite contemporary dancers I'd ripped out of coffee table art books and had framed.

He took it all in, nodding, a dimpled smile lighting his face, then eyed the poppy red two-cushion sofa—the only real place to sit down I thus far had in my living room—well, in my entire apartment.

"Oh, have a seat, please," I said, extending my hand toward it. It was a love seat, so we'd be sitting quite close together. I would have to get some chairs in the future. "Do you want anything to drink?" I asked, right before I sat down. Jeez, this man was really making me forget all the niceties of social discourse.

"No, no thank you," he said politely, extending his palm toward the cushion next to him, indicating for me to sit.

I sat next to him, trying to keep my butt as far to the outer edge as possible, hugging my armrest. Polite as he was being, I truly didn't know how I felt about him anymore. I mean, other than the maddening white-hot animal attraction. I guess it would depend on what he had to say in apology or explanation, if that's what this was. He'd called it a *prrrrrroposition*, after all.

"So," he said when I finally got myself all adjusted. His voice had that hyper-sexy cocky tone to it. So, now, did his smile.

"Yes?" I said, squeaky-voiced.

"I think I have told you about the Blackpool Dance Festival coming up in just a few months' time."

*Ugh.* I thought I'd made it crystal clear the night of our fight that I absolutely did not want to do any expensive and annoyingly political pro/am competitions with him. Was he really here to pressure me now? Did the studio pressure him to pressure me?

"Yes. Well, actually not you, but Mitsi told me about it. And, as I told you before, I have no intention of doing any competitions. I simply can't afford—"

"I know, I know, I know," he said, nodding rapidly. He held his finger to my lips as if to shush me. It smelled of caramel.

I wanted to lick it. Instead I breathed in his scent. Deeply. He smelled of fresh, crisp outside air and pine trees. He quickly moved his hand to my forearm, as if realizing touching my lips was too much at this point. His hand was warm, soft, silky. His fingers brushing my skin sent tingles down my spine.

"Just listen, okay?"

I nodded.

"I know the studio is expensive. That's why I insisted you no longer take the private lessons."

"I don't understand. How would I do pro/ams with you if I didn't take lessons from you? Oh, you want me to compete with someone else?" My heart sank. I only wanted to dance with him.

"No." His lips curled into a sly smile. "There are no pro/am competitions at Blackpool, or in Europe at all. Or, actually, anywhere outside of the U.S. That I know of. Those are strictly an American thing."

"Oh." So there were no Lunas and Cheryls in European competitions. Interesting. That was a plus for Euro comps. "Oh. Okay?" I still didn't understand what he wanted.

"Rory." He turned his body more toward me, inched a little closer. His eyes widened. "Arabelle and I were set to compete at Blackpool together, in the regular pro Latin. But she and I are…how do you say it…not seeing eye to eye."

"I kind of noticed," I said, looking down, trying not to be judgmental like Samantha.

"So, I was wondering if you would like to take her place. Be my partner."

The room suddenly grew very still. My eardrums seemed to adjust so that it sounded like his voice was echoing. Like I was in a parallel universe.

I shook my head. "I'm sorry. What?"

"You would be taking coaching with me. I would pay for that. The comp fees are already paid for. The sponsors pay for the costumes and hotel and airfare and all. There wouldn't be any charges for you."

I sank into the love seat cushion, feeling like a child in a chair made for an adult, aka Alice. I really was in Wonderland.

"The only thing I would need from you," he continued, now brushing this thumb over my forearm, a little more firmly than he had his fingers, "is a commitment to learning and practicing. As much as you possibly can."

I looked him straight in the eye for the first time today. He had pleading, puppy dog eyes. But he nevertheless looked shock serious. He wasn't kidding. "Your real partner?" I sounded like an infatuated schoolgirl.

He chuckled. "My real partner. It will of course be a great deal of work," he quickly added. "A lot of work, Rory." His smile lines disappeared and his eyes grew wider and more austere.

I'd wanted this more than anything. I had my job, but that was all I had going on in my life outside of dance. And, other than the one low-level felony trial Gunther gave me, I'd hardly had any work. The mambo team didn't seem to be a time-hog, and the hours I spent doing that were devoted to dance, so it was a kind of practice. Yes, I could handle this, I thought.

Then I remembered seeing him with Xenia, with Arabelle, Xenia yelling at him in the studio, Arabelle crying in the studio, at the competition, the countless others he'd tried out with in the studio being scolded by him, by the coach, all of them always on the verge of tears, storming out the door. Was this what I wanted? Of course it was.

"Yes," I said with such heartiness I nearly spit on him.

His face broke into a dimpled smile. This was his sincere smile, I now knew, not his seductive one.

"I can't believe you think I'm that good!" I shouted, full of excitement, now getting an inkling as to why he wanted to speak in private. "But, I mean, I know from the O.C. competition how hard it is for a newcomer to get anywhere very fast. And I have so little experience."

He flashed that sly smile that always melted me. "Are you questioning my choices, neglecting to trust my expertise in this matter, Ms. Laudner?" he asked with a cocky flirtatiousness.

"Of course not, Mr. Zakharov." I giggled.

"Good. Don't you ever do that." His playful smile belied his dictatorial tone. "Seriously though, please stop thinking about the O.C. The American pro/am competitions are totally different from the professional international ones. Another set of judging standards entirely. I think you will be...refreshing to the judges. And since you are new, you haven't developed any bad habits yet. And you'd better not." This he said with a sly raise of the eyebrows. "Plus, you have innate... Oh, don't make me spell it out, Rory. You obviously have potential. Stop doubting yourself and stop doubting me." His smile dissipated; his eyes bored into mine. He really seemed to be getting angry at my questions. "But, regardless of potential, as I said, there will be a great deal of work. A great deal."

"Yes, I know. So why don't you want me to take your group class? Isn't it still good for practice?"

He frowned and his eyes began darting around the room. I'd caught him off guard. "Rory," he eventually said, gaze stopping to focus on some obscure point off to the side of my head. "When you implied that I encourage women to compete with me just for money, it really...it really angered me. I don't make most of my money that way. I make it through choreographing for professional live shows and television and film, and by performing all over the world and winning comps—my own professional comps. We are paid by our sponsors for wearing their costumes and accessories. And we are paid, quite well, by the people who put on the shows. I just..." He trailed off, his lips pursed and jaw clenching as it had before. His hand was still resting on my arm and I could sense that internally he was getting worked up again.

I didn't want to relive that conversation right now. And there was no need to. He wasn't trying to get me to be a Cheryl or a Luna. "It's okay. Let's not rehash that right now," I said, patting his arm gently.

"I just don't think that's a good environment for you," he continued. "With all those women. Too much competition. I don't want your mind...wandering." His eyes connected with mine briefly, then he quickly looked away.

I still wasn't completely sure I understood what he was saying, but I sensed a tension forming between us and I wanted to get as far away from that as possible right now. I didn't care, anyway. I'd have him all to myself for hours every day. I didn't need that badly to be in one hour-long group class with him.

"Okay, okay, don't worry. I'll stay away. I promise," I said with a giggle, which turned into an outright cackle.

I was Sasha Zakharov's professional partner!

\*\*\*

My doorbell rang at nine on the dot the following night, the exact time Sasha said he'd be by to pick me up. He was going to be out of town for several days as he and Xenia had another show dance performance in Tokyo. He'd explained to me before that they'd been invited to perform together since they were world finalists in the last championship, but I did notice he was going to Tokyo a lot. He wanted to arrange an initial practice session at his house before he left. At his house, I wondered? Did he have space to practice there?

"It's in the hills, not very far from your apartment," he'd said.

"You're so prompt!" I was slightly surprised, since he always seemed to have a hard time getting away from his studio groupies.

"Yes, I am always on time. Almost always, anyway," he said with a sly smile.

He led me to a black Porsche parked along a narrow, secluded side street. He opened the passenger-side door for me. "I don't think there's anything on the floor," he said, peering in first.

"This is your car?" I said, slightly out of breath from the sight of it and the knowledge I'd be riding in it. I remembered the car from the night outside the Chateau Marmont. Either he borrowed it a lot or it was his.

"Yes, do you like it?" he asked, a sincere expression on his face.

Yes, the question was laughable. This was a total sex-mobile if there ever was one. "Of course! It's gorgeous!" I hoped I didn't sound too shocked like when James and obnoxious Mitchell had insisted an artist could never afford such a car. This was way the hell nicer than James's Lexus, anyway.

The ride was smooth and fast, as I'd imagined it would be, and Sasha handled the gears with a virile mastery that made me want to melt into the low, black leather seat. He drove fast but not too fast so as to scare me. I hated it when guys did that. We wound around a maze of twisty, turning streets, snaking this way and that, up, up, up, high into the Hollywood Hills. So high my ears popped. I was so glad he was driving because I'd never find my way out of here. Finally, he pulled up to the top of what seemed to be a small cliff. He stopped in front of a line of tall bushes and pushed a button on the top of his car, which caused a black gate I hadn't even noticed to slide open. He pulled into a long, oblong horseshoe-shaped driveway, and parked near the front door. I hadn't seen the house from outside the gate because of the bushes. It was two stories and was made mostly of rock, or at least it appeared to be rock, and kind of reminded me of a Frank Lloyd Wright design—organic and looking as if it were part of the earth surrounding it.

He opened his car door and came around for me. I hadn't even thought to open my own door, I was so in awe of the house. I couldn't tell exactly how big it was since there was so much shrubbery and cacti framing it, but it was really, freaking cool-looking.

We walked up several marble steps, then into a large living room with a black leather L-shaped sofa sectional set across from an enormous wall-mounted big-screen TV with surround speakers. I initially felt embarrassed about my own lack of an entertainment system, about my own lack of a gorgeous house. But I definitely didn't feel he was judging me. There were floor-to-ceiling black velvet drapes hanging on the wall to the left of the sofa. I wondered if they covered a huge window and, if so, what it overlooked.

To my left, on the other side of the sofas and that magnificent entertainment system, was an area with a more homey feel. Two large, comfy-looking lounge chairs covered in a plush blood-red velvety fabric with matching ottomans surrounded a black and white marbled fireplace. In between them was a long rectangular coffee table that appeared to be made of oak, or some substantial polished wood. Beside that was a winding staircase that led up to, I supposed, the second floor.

"You can put your things down on the chairs, or anywhere you like. Then come back here," he said, walking past that increasingly intriguing circular staircase, something about which was a little Hitchcockian in a way that simultaneously thrilled and unnerved me. The same drapes covered the opposite wall, which I assumed must be another floor-to-ceiling window.

I followed him through a doorway into a big, beautiful kitchen, with everything a five-star chef would need. Across from the cooking area was a large nook with bay windows. In the nook was a big kitchen table made from the same dark polished wood as the coffee table. The bay windows were huge and the curtains covering them were pulled back, so I could see out a bit. But it was dark and I could only see black and what appeared to be lots of little lights coming from afar. Stars, perhaps?

Sasha kept walking, past a long mahogany bar, with hardwood stools lining each side. There was an aisle, then another bar, also set with stools. That bar had an opening section, which led into—wow—a gorgeous, huge, hardwood-floored studio. Each wall was lined with ballet barres except the back wall, which was covered by yet more black velvet drapes. How many floor-to-ceiling windows were in this place?

"Oh my gosh, you do have a studio!" I said. "What's behind the curtains?" I was unable to contain myself. I needed to know. Suddenly, the black velvet began parting.

I looked back at Sasha, who now stood under a large raised stereo speaker pointing a remote toward the curtains. They slowly opened to reveal a long patio door that opened out onto an absolutely breathtakingly beautiful backyard area. Immediately behind the patio door was a wood floor under an awning, under which sat several tables and chairs looking out over a set of steps. I peered through the glass to see that the steps led down to a colorful red-rock-covered area which contained a Jacuzzi to the left, and to the right, an immense swimming pool. In the distance, I could see the same lights I saw from the kitchen. I couldn't wait to see his view during the daytime. I imagined he must have a spectacular view of the canyon.

"That is for relaxing. After the hard work is done." He emphasized the word "after" and pointed to the hot tub. "Not every day, of course. Only special days, when we just…click." He snapped his finger. His sly smile was back, sending an electric shock to my belly.

"Of course," I tried to say. But all that came out was a crackle. I was so stunned. I couldn't believe he lived here. I tried hard to keep my mind from fixing on Rajiv's words: *mafia money.*

"Would you like something to drink?" he said, walking back to the kitchen. I hadn't noticed when I first passed, but at one end of the aisle laden with barstools was what looked to be a full liquor cabinet.

"Are you going to play bartender?" I laughed.

"We should probably just have water for now. Or energy drink. Cocktails are another thing that should wait. That should wait for the hot tub." The roguish smile returned.

I imagined myself sipping champagne in that hot tub with him overlooking the canyon. Of course I'd have to see how my bikini looked. It had been a while since I'd worn it. My mind flashed to Xenia in that hot tub. Or maybe Arabelle with her perfect little body. I felt a volt of panic shoot through my center and my chest tightened. My breath caught and I took a sharp inhale.

"Are you okay, Rory?" His voice was deep and commanding, but soothing, like Godiva liqueur.

I caught my breath and nodded, trying to laugh it off.

"Good. Would you like sparkling water? Or still water? Or juice? I have some green juices made of kale and celery and green apple? Or regular fruit juices. Orange and cranberry." He'd walked from the bar to the kitchen and was looking in the refrigerator.

I could see from the side door, the entire thing was lined with various juices. *Holy crap.* This man wasn't kidding about nutrition.

"The green juices are actually quite good. And not many calories. Honest. Here, I think you will like it. A small one to start?" He looked back at me with pleading eyes.

I immediately wondered why he mentioned the calories. Did he think I was too fat? Or did he read my mind, currently addled with images of myself in a bikini, alongside his exes?

I nodded.

"Good." He pulled out a small green bottle and walked back to the bar, opened a cabinet and pulled out a champagne glass. "I will make it pretty for you," he said, slowly pouring the green liquid into the elegant, long-stemmed glass.

*Mmmm.* It was actually pretty good. Just as much apple and celery as kale. And it felt light going down. I hated feeling bloated and like my stomach was a balloon when dancing in that leotard.

"You like it!" he said, boyish dimples spreading across his face. His genuine, happy-boy smile.

I laughed. "Yeah, it's pretty good. Did a friend of yours make these or something?"

"I'm sorry?" He looked confused.

"I just mean, you're so into pushing them."

He frowned and shook his head, looking taken aback. "Pushing them? No. I just want you to have energy, Rory. We have lots of hard work ahead."

I nodded again, and drank some more. The way he kept saying my name and the way he said "lots of hard work" made my heart pump faster.

He walked out to the center of the ballroom floor. "I would like to start by getting a sense of your body weight."

*Body weight?* I looked down at my stomach. Was it flat enough? Was I thin enough? Was I light enough? Ugh, talk about déjà vu. My ballet psyche was rearing her ugly head.

"Um...I haven't weighed in a while. I, ah..." Last time I weighed myself, about a month after starting dance again, I'd lost about ten pounds, making me then about a hundred and fifteen. But that was a month ago. I didn't really like announcing my weight, anyway. Didn't guys know this?

"Rory, I don't need to know the number of pounds," he said, reading my mind. "I need to feel you.

Come." He extended his arm toward me and motioned with his fingers for me to go to him.

My insides began to melt. I managed to get up off the barstool. I set my drink down and walked to him.

"Good. Now, I want you to lean into me. Just stand before me and let yourself go. Don't hold yourself up."

This was also vaguely familiar. I remembered advanced partnering class in ballet, wondering if I felt to the boys who tried to lift me as heavy as I felt when I saw the girl in the mirror. I'd started ballet a cute, sprightly, carefree little girl, but those feelings slowly morphed into major insecurity as I sloughed toward puberty and began to feel like a whale amongst goldfish as my body developed, became more womanly, before the other girls' did.

Ugh, I so didn't want to be in that mental place again. Oh just do it, Rory, I said to myself. *You're an adult now. You're supposed to look like a woman.* I subconsciously sucked in my gut and did as he asked. I leaned into him. He reached out and held me with his arms.

"No, lean into me completely. You're still holding yourself up. I can feel it in your tight muscles."

He could tell a lot about me by feeling me. I tried to loosen my muscles a little more.

"You're still holding yourself, Rory. Come on. Fall into me."

*Okay, fine.* I made myself relax, pretending this was like that game of trust, where you completely fall backward into the arms of another, trusting them to catch you.

"Yes, good, good," he said, his solid biceps flexing as he held me. "Now, I am going to lift you a little bit. Put your arm around my neck. We're just doing a cradle lift. So you plié and jump and bring your legs in and I'll put my arms around your legs and hold you like that."

I nodded and inwardly cringed.

"Okay, plié."

I bent my knees and did a little jump. I pressed my arm that was wrapped around the back of his neck down so as to hold myself up in his arms, which were now wrapped tightly around my legs. I pulled my center in, trying to make myself as weightless as possible.

"Please don't do all that," he said, feeling my thoughts again.

I relaxed, loosened my arm.

"Not enough. That was just your arm. I want you to let it all go. Like a rag doll. Like a child."

"Are you sure?"

"Yes! Of course. I will not tell you something I am not sure about."

*Okay.* I forced myself to breathe out, deflate myself. I wiggled my toes. Fluttered my fingers. Pretended I was a little girl again, in a large, protective man's arms.

His center didn't waver a bit. I felt no difference in his ability to bear my weight.

"Thank you. See I am very, very strrrrong. I can hold you, no prrroblem." He said this without any emotion whatsoever, as if he didn't at all realize what those rolling r's could do to a person. Not at all. He was oblivious to the workings of his accent.

I was unable to stifle a giggle.

"Okay," he said placing me back on my feet. "That was good. But enough of that. For now."

I was simultaneously glad and a bit sad. It was fun to be lifted by the man of your dreams. But I really needed to overcome my issues. I knew that logically, though it didn't mean my subconscious would be in sync with that logic. I knew from before that anorexia spectrum disorder was a mind game you played with yourself.

"Now, we will learn all of the main characteristics of each of the five dances on the competitive Latin syllabus," Sasha continued. "You with me, Rory?"

He waved a hand in my face, then snapped his fingers off to the side of my cheek. How did he know when my mind wandered? Damn, this man could really read my thoughts.

"Okay, good," he said. "You must concentrate? No scrrrewing around. We don't have time." The intensity in his eyes kept me from swooning over the r's this time.

I nodded.

"We start with paso doble. Spanish dance. Man is bullfighter, woman is bull. Or cape. Varies. Mood is fighter, intense, sometimes with flamenco undertones."

He wasn't paying close attention to his grammar now at all, leaving out all the articles. I could tell by now that meant either he was frustrated or was concentrating more on dance, on getting it right, and was getting a little worked up over that desire. He could read my mind through the way I held my body, the way I clenched my muscles. And I could read his emotions through his lapses of grammar. He proceeded to explain the character of all the dances, and show me the basic, first-level steps of each. Since I'd now had a few months of rumba, with that dance we managed to get through not just the first level but the entire syllabus, all the way through to the open gold level.

"Okay?" he said, eyeing the clock.

I felt my head spinning worse than I had after finishing the California bar exam. I'd taken in such a huge amount of information. I glanced at the clock as well and stumbled in my tracks.

"Oh wow," I said. It was nearly midnight. I had to get up early for work the next day. I hated getting a poor night's sleep at the beginning of the week. How had the time gone by so fast?

"I know," he said, again reading my thoughts. "Don't worry, I will get you home in no time."

With that car, I could imagine.

"I will be back next Sunday. We will meet again at the same time?"

"Oh yes." I nodded. Probably with a bit too much vigor.

"Good." He flashed me a devilish grin and my heart missed several beats.

"Next time we will take videos so you can study. For this week, just continue to prrrrractice as much as you can. I hope you will be able to retain most of what I gave you. Also, I want you to meet with Greta, the coach, while I am gone. I will arrange one or two practice sessions with her. I will text you which days. You will show her everything we did today and she will teach you the rest of the syllabi in the other four dances. So you will know all the basic steps when I return." His face turned shock serious again, the intensity in his mind palpable, radiating outward, almost.

*This man and his moods.*

# CHAPTER 2

Fortunately, my lack of sleep Sunday night didn't much affect my workday Monday. I had a lot of busywork, but it was of the easy but brain-numbingly boring kind. Gunther gave me a small research project for one of his cases, and Edward, the partner with the wills, continued to keep the top left corner of my desk stacked with files from which wills were to be drafted. I didn't get all the wills drafted, and I assumed it was okay to leave for the studio each day by five so I wouldn't be late for my first classes of the evening. I assumed the wills could wait since none of our clients were on their deathbed. At least none that I was made aware of. Plus, with the frequent dearth of work for me there, I was always worried I'd have nothing to do the next day and wouldn't be able to meet my requisite billable hours. It was better to leave work for myself each evening, I thought, instead of doing a rush job and having nothing to do.

\*\*\*

I remained in such a state of shock over Sasha's proposition, I didn't tell anyone about it that whole week. Not Samantha, not Rajiv, Pepe, Mitsi, Paulina—no one. I simply continued to go to the studio and take my regular classes.

I had my make-up private lesson with Bronislava, as Sasha had commanded. I have to admit, I cheated a little and had her go over the entire first-level syllabi of all dances with me, same as Sasha had done, so I'd get a little more practice and instruction before seeing Greta later in the week and Sasha the following weekend. But talk about head-spinning confusion so great you felt like you'd been slapped upside the head repeatedly. She corrected so many teensy tiny things, there was always, and I mean *always* something more to add to each millisecond of timing, each millimeter of movement. I felt when I left that I didn't even know the steps. I'd lost the forest for the trees with her. Time would tell, though, how much better she'd made me in one hour.

Cheryl didn't come to the studio at all the week Sasha was out, but Luna did. She eyed me curiously throughout my lesson with Bronislava.

*** 

*Hello, Rory*, read the beginning of Sasha's text to me informing me of my upcoming meeting with Greta. The longest text, I might add, I'd ever received, which was hilarious given that English was a second language for him. And of course all spelling, all punctuation was perfect.

*Greta will meet with you this coming Wednesday, in the studio's private practice area, in the back room, where we had our lessons. She will meet with you from 8:00 to 9:00, the same time I have my group class that you are no longer attending. We will all meet together next Sunday evening after I return so that I can see what progress you have made.*

It was so cute how he enunciated every word so carefully, even in writing. I could totally hear his voice.

*I am excited for the two of you to meet. Have a good lesson and a good week at the studio and at work. I will be happy to see you next Sunday.*

I was practically bursting with nervous energy for my first lesson with Greta. The woman was a ten-time Blackpool champion. Ballroom royalty, basically. After Sasha had told me we'd be working together, I realized where I'd spotted her before—on the DVDs I'd bought of Sasha at WorldTone. So, in preparation for my lesson, I watched the videos again—the early ones. She and her partner, Dean, had retired early on in Sasha's career. So I'd watched the ones where Sasha and Micaela won the junior championship and where he and Xenia placed second in the pros. In the second video, Greta and Dean announced their retirement, leaving the crowd to give them roaring standing O after roaring standing O. Wow, it didn't take a genius to see why she was so beloved by the crowd, and why she'd been a champion for a decade. She consumed the entire floor when she moved. More than Micaela, far more than Xenia. She and Dean created magic.

What do you wear to your first lesson with a legend? I chose my best leotard and tights, leg warmers, and practice shoes—the ones that hurt in the heel after wearing them for too long, but the ones I knew most of the professionals wore. I had my hair pulled neatly back into a bun. I wanted to emanate "serious dancer" as much as I possibly could.

She wasn't in the back room yet when I arrived. But the door was unlocked. So I let myself in, turned the lights on, and used the ballet barres to stretch out. As I slid my leg along the barre to stretch my adductor muscles, I spotted Luna. She stood in the center of the practice room. But instead of looking at herself in the mirror, she was staring straight at me, squinting her beady little eyes, then frowning, probably in confusion as to what I was doing there in Sasha's absence.

The front door to the practice room opened and in breezed Greta. My stomach immediately filled with butterflies. Luna turned to follow my gaze, and watched as Greta approached the door to the private room, where I was. Luna's eyes widened and her mouth fell open. I could see her out of the corner of my eye. I was far too nervous about Greta and what she would think of me, the neophyte, to worry about what was going through Luna's crazed mind.

"Hello, Rory!" Greta sang out right as she passed Luna. She waved her arm about in such a dancerly way, she looked like a swan.

Many people stopped what they were doing to look at her, probably out of surprise as to what she was doing there since Sasha was busy. But probably more just because she was a star, and still had the kind of presence that commanded attention.

"Hi," I said shyly as she walked into the back room.

Though she'd aged a bit since her competitive days, she still carried herself like a consummate dancer—upper-body tall and proud, feet pointed slightly outward, walking with the heel of her foot lightly touching the ground first followed by the ball then the toe, making her appear to float across the floor. So elegant. I so hoped she'd rub off on me. I immediately straightened, pushed down on my shoulders, lifted my center, and turned my feet out at a forty-five degree Latin angle.

"Thank you for that," she said, noticing my alteration, waving her swan-wing-like arm up and down my body.

I felt myself blush.

"Okay, let's get to work. Sasha said you have been going over the basics of each dance so far?"

"Yes."

"And that you are very new at ballroom?"

I now knew from the Blackpool emcee's introduction that she was German. And I could detect an accent. But, like Sasha, her English pronunciation and grammar were quite good. "Yes. I have a ballet background, but have only been taking ballroom for three months."

She raised her chin, along with her eyebrows, in thought. "Well, good," she said after a moment's reflection. "That means you have general dance skills but will also be someone he can mold. He's never really had that before. That should work out well for him. He found a real tabula rasa—at least in body, if not in mind." She said this matter-of-factly, eyebrows still raised and head still cocked.

I wasn't sure what that last sentence meant. I was a blank slate? Completely blank, as in nothing? Hmmm, we'd see about that. At any rate, it seemed she knew him well and thought we'd be a good match.

"Now. Show me what you know. Starting with rumba."

I nodded, took a swallow, and positioned myself at the beginning of the first step Sasha had given me. She said nothing as I went through the bronze-level syllabus. It felt very weird, to put it mildly, to be dancing ballroom, by myself, doing only the ladies' movement, without music, and while having a former world champion scrutinize me.

"Should I go on to the silver syllabus?" I asked her when I'd finished, and she had yet to utter a word. She held a cherry red-fingernailed index finger to her right jawbone. After a couple seconds, she slowly nodded, eyes narrowing. I couldn't read her at all.

"I want to see everything you know about rumba."

Everything I knew. And with that, I suddenly felt like I knew nothing. Not a single thing. I took another breath, another gulp of air, and tried hard to remember what Sasha had taught me, and Bronislava had followed up with. I tried hard as I could to remember each pattern as I went along. I knew I left out a few steps—or parts of steps—but somehow I got many of them.

"Okay," she said after a deep breath as soon as I'd finished. "I think you have a good sense of the basic rumba syllabus for each level. Now let me see the others. Start with cha-cha."

"We've only gone through bronze for the others," I said, my voice sounding squeakier than I wanted it to.

"That's okay. Again, show me everything you know." She crossed her feet elegantly at the ankles and clasped her hands together in front of her, while cocking her head to one side as if in contemplation.

Ugh, I really wasn't sure I'd remember every dance. I only knew rumba because we'd done it so many times. Well, I could only give it my best shot.

Which I did. I could feel myself leaving things out and totally messing up the steps, which got worse as I went along. Jive was the worst. It was the one we'd practiced least.

"Sorry," I said when I finished.

"No need to be sorry. You did as I asked and showed me what you knew," she said.

I wasn't sure how she meant it. She seemed neither impressed not dismayed.

"Okay, so you know many of the basic steps, but definitely not all. You can count beats, which is huge. You have a natural ease with movement and it's obvious you have dance training, so you understand the importance of a strong center and a finished line, etcetera, etcetera, etcetera." With the last three words, she flicked her wrist as if she were an orchestra conductor waving an invisible baton. "But," she said sharply, raising her eyebrows and pointing the invisible baton right at me, "you don't have a strong sense of the character of each of the Latin dances, and how they differ from each other. So you can't convey the proper emotions. And you are still dancing much like a ballerina. For example, your hands are soft, as if you're holding a teacup, and you have a light, feathery look. It's as if someone told you that's the way you always must dance; that that's what dance IS. We have to cut those habits." She emphasized the "cut" and sliced the baton through the air.

I nodded like a good, docile student.

"You also don't seem to know…how do I say…" She looked up, in search of the proper English word. "How to be a woman." She now looked at me straight on, one eyebrow shooting up so high it practically hit her hairline.

*Excuse me?* I felt my eyes widen.

"Yes," she said as if she were arguing against me though I hadn't actually said anything. "Maybe in your…other dance background, you were taught so much technique at the expense of showing a story with your dancing. Or maybe you were just taught to be sexless in that other dance. Or perhaps you were just young when you danced previously."

I thought about this. I was in my mid-teens when I left ballet. And, yes, to say there was an enormous emphasis on technique there couldn't be overstated. And, I guess ballet is perhaps a bit sexless, if that's the proper term… The main characters—female characters, anyway—are often young girls or girl-swans, or just abstractions if you're in a Balanchine ballet. I raised my eyebrows and nodded but seriously wondered how the woman in me was lacking.

"Let's focus on rumba. Rumba is the dance of passion, of lust, of seduction, of sex. That saying that dance is a vertical expression of a horizontal desire— well, rumba kind of epitomizes that. Okay, so you are seducing the man in this game of cat and mouse. He is impassioned by you. There is sexual angst, sexual urges."

She now made motions with her fingers as if she were kneading something and I wondered how that figured into it. She was into gesticulation, which I guess was a dancerly thing.

"Okay, so now you show me that."

I must have looked at her as if she were nuts and she must have read my mind.

"I know it is odd doing this when you are alone," she said, "but that's all we have right now. I want you to pretend he is here."

Oh my, this took more than dance technique. It took serious acting skills. I tried to perform the same steps while imagining myself dancing with Sasha. I tried to play the tempting seductress as well as I could with every step. But then I'd get caught up in being Miss Sexy Temptress and would forget the steps. And who was I kidding? I wasn't a sexy vixen! I sucked at seduction. I barely got through the bronze syllabus before having to stop and have a good laugh at myself.

"It's okay," Greta said, seeming to agree with me on how horrendously bad I was. "You know, seduction isn't really about making sex faces, which can sometimes appear a bit…ah, goofy."

*No, you don't say?*

"It's about the movement itself. The thoughts, the emotions should be in the body—the legs, the way your foot brushes the floor, the way your hip shifts direction, the way you expand your rib cage—not on your face."

Oh, that made much more sense. And good; I was perfectly happy to give up the sexy-face thing.

It took me a while—most of the lesson, actually—but eventually I did begin to consciously move my body in accordance with the emotions I was trying to evoke. The way I'd trace my toe on the floor in a forward walk toward him, and think of tracing it on his back; the way I'd move faster on the second beat in approaching him as if I urgently wanted him; the way I'd flick one foot in front of the other, then shift weight before doing a quick, sassy spiral turn. It was weird, feeling I'd had some kind of sensual conversation with him without him even being present!

"Good, good," Greta pronounced, making me happy she could read my thoughts through my movements. "Okay, we'll go back to getting the technique down. But I want you to always be conscious of the emotions you are conveying as you perfect the technique. You understand?"

I nodded. I did. I understood her approach now. This was so different from ballet.

She was an amazing coach. We went through basic rumba movement, Greta teaching me not just which part of the body moves when but why the body moves as it does—physically, I mean—the way the legs compel a movement in the rib cage, which in turn compels movement in the hips. I soon realized why some people—like the one, I couldn't help notice in my periphery, who kept peeping in on us—looked so superficial when they danced. They just moved the legs, or the shoulders, or the butt, without understanding the organic flow of the movement of one body part into another.

Anyway, I couldn't wait to for Sasha to get back so I could practice my sensual conversation with him in person!

*** 

Sunday afternoons had become my favorite time at the studio. Mambo team practice was simultaneously challenging and nerve-racking, yet caused us continual fits of gut-grabbing laughter. We were now trying to do these crazy little lifts, with the guy on his knees and the girl passing over his head on her stomach. It was a step Pepe had seen Baryshnikov do in a snazzy Twyla Tharp number and he badly wanted to incorporate it into our routine. But of course there were no Baryshnikovs on our team. We watched the move again and again on video. It looked like the easiest thing in the world, and was truly romantic to boot. No wonder Pepe wanted to include it in the slow, sweet section. But whenever any of us went to try it, it just didn't seem humanly possible. Baryshnikov bent down on his knees as if he were about to propose. His lady held her hands to her heart, in a prayer shape, and lowered herself to him. He caught her in his arms, then seemed to lift her and propel her body over his head. She floated above him for a few glorious seconds, then continued over and beyond his head, and, as he lay her down in back of him, she reached the floor with her hands, and balanced herself on one foot, lifting the other beautifully high in the air behind her, over his charming face.

But when we tried, the guys couldn't seem to get the girls up and over them. And we couldn't understand how to propel ourselves up and over on our own. So, the girl would just kind of hover in the air above the guy indefinitely, looking, after a few seconds, stuck. Not so romantic. And the longer she was stuck, the more pain the guy was in: hands and wrists—not to mention knees balancing on hardwood floors—all began to ache with the hundred and twenty or so pounds they were lifting.

Pepe himself couldn't even figure out the physics of the move. I'd been above his head about thirty seconds, trying hard to hold a bird-like position and somehow move myself forward while having no connection to the ground whatsoever, my abdominals getting quite a workout—when I heard distinct moans coming from below.

"Are you okay?" I asked Pepe.

With one final grunt, he took his right hand from my waist and put it the only place he could find that would help me get over him, then gave me a good, solid push. That place was my crotch.

"There you go, girl," he said.

But with the flimsy leotard I was wearing, his fingers went, let's just say, quite a ways through the fabric and up into my nether regions. Definitely was one of the weirdest feelings I can say I've ever had. A gay man basically fingering me in a completely non-sexual way in front of twelve other people.

The penetration freaked me out so much that I screamed, and fell to my hands on the floor, bringing my groin straight into his face, falling over him, both of us crashing to the ground. When we landed, his mouth was now where his fingers had been. I quickly got on my hands and crawled crab-like over his face, spreading my legs as wide as I could so I wouldn't put any more body parts on the poor man's nose and mouth and eyes.

After I'd gotten completely over him, and was fully on the floor, I turned onto my back. I looked around at everyone else. Everyone had seen what had happened. Everyone had these completely bug-eyed, open-mouthed looks, like they were simultaneously shocked and trying with all their might to stifle laughter.

Pepe jumped to his feet, and looked around the room, not so much at people as out into the air, with an expression that was somehow both mortified and bemused. He looked like he'd just successfully completed a death-defying obstacle course, to his immense surprise.

"Are you okay?" I asked.

"Hmmm," he began after a few moments. "That was…shall we say…intimate." He looked everywhere but at me. His cheeks were tomato red.

At once, the whole room burst into a paroxysm of laughter. Including me. *Sure, I can have a good laugh at myself!*

No matter how much Ron, after cracking up himself, continually warned us we had to move on, we had a competition coming up after all, we couldn't take ourselves seriously for the rest of the team practice.

When I got home, the first thing I did was yank and yank on my leotard and underwear, which I hadn't wanted to do in the studio for fear I'd heighten the…weirdness that had happened, for lack of a better word, or on the way home for fear I'd look very uncouth and might attract unwanted attention walking down Hollywood Boulevard pulling fabric out of my crotch. Man, Pepe had pushed me with such vigor, the cheap fabric had sustained a very noticeably-felt indentation.

After my body cavities were relieved of unwanted objects, I crashed down on the sofa with a bottle of water and a banana. I hadn't eaten much and I was seeing Sasha and Greta tonight. Said body cavity started to pulse all over again thinking about it. I nearly bounced on the couch like a schoolgirl.

\*\*\*

But Sasha was in a dark mood when he picked me up.

"How was your trip?" I said as he stood at my front door. I sensed right away something wasn't right.

"It was fine," he said, the terseness in his voice indicating he didn't want to talk about it. I wondered if he'd fought with Xenia, or if something went wrong during one of the performances. But I didn't want to ask.

"Well, good," I said, not knowing what else to say.

"How were your lessons with Greta and Bronislava? Have you finished all the syllabi?"

My heart stopped. Yes, but that didn't mean I knew them like the back of my hand in one week, I thought, but didn't say. Maybe he was in a bad mood because we'd lost practice time and Blackpool wasn't that far away. I knew it made him nervous to miss practice time. "Yes, we did," I said.

"Good, I'm glad."

"Are you okay?" I ventured once we were in his car. I placed my hand on his shoulder, hoping that wasn't too personal. His attitude was making me nervous, and wasn't exactly impelling me to practice the sensuality Greta had taught me.

"Yes, I'm fine," he said without looking at me, or brushing my hand off. I kept it there for a few seconds.

"Good evening, Rory," Greta sang out when we walked into Sasha's vast living room. I hadn't expected her to be there yet.

"Hi!" I said with an unintentional little bow. I laughed nervously, feeling stupid. Sasha's weirdness really affected me.

She smiled graciously, like a queen kindly bestowing pleasantries on one of her most humble subjects.

Sasha flicked on the track lights, which ran diagonally across the ceiling, to create a rosy hue. The studio was absolutely heavenly when lit like this.

"Okay, guys. Let's start with rumba," Greta said.

Sasha pressed a remote and on came an instrumental rumba. The sound system was simply amazing. He had top-notch speakers, some of which seemed hidden, as rich sound began emanating from all around the room.

"Sorry, too loud," he said, turning down the volume.

Once we started dancing, Greta seemed to be on something too. She wasn't in a pissy mood so much as a perfectionist one. We'd barely completed a basic when Greta began correcting me. And I mean every little millimeter of my body—my upper arms, wrists, fingers, elbows, shoulders, toes, heels, calves—not just the major elements like pelvis, rib cage, and hips. She most definitely corrected those as well. I couldn't take one tiny quarter of a step, I couldn't even shift my weight without her coming over and adjusting my body in some way. She hadn't touched me when I was alone with her, just gave me general guidance on character. Now she was about a thousand times worse than Bronislava. It took us nearly an hour to get through one syllabus. I'd never remember all these corrections, I thought.

After we finished the first, bronze-level syllabus, she directed us to do all the steps again. It was nearing ten p.m. I'd have to get home soon; I didn't want to stay as late as last week. One of the partners at work had warned me she'd have a big document-coding project for me this week. I wanted to be able to get to work early so I'd be able to leave in time to make classes.

Plus, I was tired from team practice earlier. As we went again, I made many of the same mistakes. I felt Sasha's annoyance seep through his pores and into my skin. "Sorry," I said over and over again to him. He'd shake his head either without smiling or with a brief, ever-so-slight curvature of the lips. A fake smile, in other words.

"Stop apologizing," Greta finally said. "You're actually remembering where I corrected you, and you're trying to right yourself."

Yeah, that's because you corrected me every nanosecond, I thought.

"Just keep concentrating," she continued. "So much apologizing takes you away from your attention to details."

After we were about halfway through the syllabus, and Greta was correcting everything again, now for the second time, I lost my ability to focus, or my nerve, or something. Sasha's anxiety-ridden energy was penetrating every pore of my body. Maybe if we weren't so physically connected it wouldn't have, but my confidence was just shot. We were in the middle of a side-swaying *cucharacha* when my hip movement felt superficial. I remembered that she'd corrected that. I went to apologize then remembered Greta's orders and stopped. I could feel his hot breath on my neck.

"I know you corrected this but I forgot how," I said, craning my neck toward Greta.

"It's okay, you're new at this," she said, waving her hand about with her invisible baton again. She approached and made the correction.

This was really the simplest of steps and I couldn't even get this right. No wonder he was pissed. "Can we please record this?" I said, after we'd gone through the whole thing a second time. It was now past eleven. I had to get home. "I'll get my phone." I motioned to my bag in the corner of the room.

Sasha was taking heavy breaths, fuming. But he didn't yell; he didn't say anything. He hadn't said much at all, all evening.

"It'll help me remember."

Sasha released me and turned and walked away.

"No, I don't want to do that, Rory," Greta said immediately, without even considering it. "I don't want to do that because this needs to be in your muscle memory. Not your memory up here." She pointed to her head. "You're thinking too much with your head. You need to think with your body."

"I know," I said. Sasha had told me the same. But I didn't know. Not really. I didn't know how to think with my body anymore. "You said to concentrate. But I need to use my brain for that."

"No, no, no. That's just it," she said. "You need to concentrate with your muscles, with your body. Yes, your mind. But your mind and your body need to work together. I see you thinking way, way, way too hard and it's only going to get worse if you sit there and look at the little screen on your iPhone. You need to be dancing, moving, not watching yourself move. Do you understand?"

Yes, I understood the concept. But I'd been thinking with my brain, learning with my brain since high school. All throughout college, in law school, I'd learned by reading books and lecture notes over and over again, rereading so many times that the information was basically etched into my brain. I didn't know if I knew how to learn and think without reading or hearing words.

"Not really," I said. "But...I'll try my best to...make myself concentrate with my body." I could hear my lack of self-assurance.

"Rory, if you notice, I've been correcting you physically, not with words," Greta said, obviously hearing it too. "That way your muscles will come to remember the correction. You will get this. I know you will. Because you're already realizing when something doesn't feel right. I see you try to correct it."

I could feel tears coming. I was too tired. And I didn't know where Sasha had gone.

"You're on your way, Rory. You've taken the first steps. I'm quite confident you will get it," Greta finished, with a genuine smile and a nod of the head.

\*\*\*

I could hear Sasha and Greta whispering to each other in the living room while he saw her out and I changed shoes and prepared to leave. I tried to hear what they were saying but couldn't.

"It's okay," Sasha said as he drove me home. His nervous energy seemed to have dissipated at least a little. I assumed Greta had calmed him down in the foyer. "Can you do this again tomorrow? I know it's the beginning of your work week, but we need all the practice we can get."

I felt my eyes itchy and clouding over. Maybe dirt or sweat had gotten under a contact lens. As much as I wanted this, as much as I wanted to spend time with Sasha, I didn't know if I could go through this every night. Emotionally or physically. My job, at least currently, wasn't hard, but I still had to be present and alert every day.

"Don't worry, Greta won't always be here," he added. And with that he smiled and placed his hand gently on my knee, which caused a mass of hot liquid immediately to pool in my lower belly.

I looked at him but his eyes remained on the road ahead. My heart raced. Was he implying something would happen if we were alone? Maybe he could just tell that Greta's multitude of corrections overwhelmed me and made me so nervous I couldn't remember anything. He was simply being hopeful I'd be more relaxed, and better, without her always there. That's all he was likely saying.

"Sure," I said, taking a long exhale.

"It is good you are no longer my student, Rrrrory," he said, tracing his index finger ever so lightly over my kneecap, where his hand continued to rest when it wasn't needed to shift gears.

*What?*

I looked at his face. Eyes still focused on the road, no hint of a playfully malicious smile whatsoever. My heart leapt into my throat and lodged there. I couldn't seem to say anything the rest of the ride.

# CHAPTER 3

It turned out that the client corporation hadn't produced their documents in time, so I wouldn't be able to begin my coding assignment until later in the week. I was slightly relieved, since coding was the ultimate boring assignment. But then it meant the stress of having nothing to do all day, yet making myself look busy and trying to figure out how to make billable hours. Will Guy didn't even have any boring wills. Part of me longed for another criminal pro bono case. Part of me thought I should be careful what I wished for.

With nothing to do, I decided to call Samantha. I hadn't yet told anyone about Sasha and it was time I stopped keeping our partnership a secret. Besides, I needed to talk to someone about him, about his behavior.

"Hey, you at work?" I asked when she answered.

"Nope. Just at the studio."

"Oh, go back to practice. I'll call back—"

"No, no, I'm on lunch break. Actually, I have some news!"

"So do I!" I squealed. "But you first."

"No, no, you first. You sound way more excited!"

I filled her in on everything, from our fight during my private lesson following the competition to what he'd said last night to me in the car. "Can you believe it?" When I'd finished my blabbering, I realized she hadn't said a word in a while. "Sam?" I said, hoping we hadn't gotten disconnected without my realizing.

"Yes, I'm here, Rory." She didn't sound at all excited.

My stomach fell. "What's wrong?"

"Nothing's wrong, Rory," she said after a lengthy pause that worried me. "You're a very talented dancer. I always knew that. It's all happening so fast for you. I'm really happy for you." Her tone indicated otherwise.

"Then why don't you sound it?" Part of me wondered if she was jealous. Sam had become my closest ballroom-world friend, other than Rajiv, whom I couldn't really talk to about this. I so didn't want envy to come between us.

"Because…" I could hear her breathing heavily. "I mean, now I'm worried all the more about this…"

"About what, Sam?" I said, panicking. It sounded serious.

"Well, my news that I was going to give you was that my aunt in Tokyo went to his show dance last weekend."

"Uh-huh, he told me he was there with Xenia."

"Yep. They danced several of the numbers. But he seemed just, really in a bad mood, my aunt said. Like really angry. Then, he just stormed out halfway through and never returned. People asked Xenia. She had no idea where he was or what was wrong. He wouldn't tell her anything specific, she said. He just seemed generally pissed. My aunt knows the organizers. They're not happy. They paid Sasha and Xenia a lot of money, for him to just run off like that."

"Wow, that's shocking. Were there problems with the performance? I mean, did they screw up?" I suddenly remembered how he'd been when he first picked me up last Sunday. I'd wondered if that had happened.

"No, my aunt said it was gorgeous dancing. Typical for them. But Rory, that doesn't mean he doesn't fly off the deep end over something he thought was wrong, even if no one else saw it. He's a crazy perfectionist. And maybe something worse. He has a serious temper. Just be careful, honey. Okay?"

*** 

Samantha's words reverberated in my head the rest of the afternoon and that evening, in the studio. He and Xenia were still fighting so badly despite the fact they'd broken up and were only doing these shows because of prior commitments. They didn't even mean anything to each other anymore. And the performances weren't that important, were they? What was wrong? Clearly, the man was just always hard on his partners. I needed to keep that from happening to me, whatever had happened to them. If I just practice hard, if I just keep working, doing my best, I thought, we'll make it. I did wonder what had happened between him and Arabelle that night in Tokyo. I probably shouldn't ask him. The man was moody, that was for sure.

That night I had Bronislava's silver-level cha-cha. Now that I'd learned privately all of the steps in all syllabi from pre-bronze through open gold, I was approved to take all levels of the international classes for extra practice. I knew all of the footwork by now so keeping up wasn't very hard like it had been at first. Instead I tasked myself with remembering Greta's instructions about minute details of the body movement, and moving in such a way that I brought out the character of each dance. Those were the things I used the classes now to practice.

Things were extremely uncomfortable with Luna and Cheryl, who seemed to have become friends with Sveta and the other members of Sasha's Russian contingent despite the language barrier. Now that Sasha was back, Cheryl was back, and taking all the international classes, like me. Weirdly, it seemed worse now that I was no longer taking privates with Sasha. I'd thought he'd put Cheryl back into my slot. Wasn't she happy about that, I wondered? I really felt their angry stares all through class. I tried hard to block them out but the silver- and gold-level classes were a lot smaller. Paulina was still at the bronze level in Latin, so my biggest support was palpably absent.

Even Bronislava was different. She was no longer correcting me, which in a way was good because if something she said conflicted with Greta I would get really confused and my muscle memory would seriously get messed up. But she no longer joked with me either. It was like I was no longer anything special. I actually missed her calling me Swan Lake Samba Girl.

\*\*\*

Sasha picked me up again in his shiny Porsche at nine p.m. on the dot, and whisked me up to his castle in the hills. I was running late from the studio and texted him that I'd just meet him in the lobby, but he insisted he pick me up at home. He wanted to limit our contact at the studio now that I was no longer his student. I didn't completely understand but also didn't ask him about it. I'd wondered if it had anything to do with the no-fraternizing policy but figured that was null and void now that we no longer had a teacher student relationship. And it wasn't like he'd stolen me from the studio since he wasn't going over the studio and charging me for private lessons himself. Who knew? Anyway, we'd agreed that he'd pick me up on the way, near my building.

"How are you tonight, Rory?" he said after he'd closed my door and we were both seated.

His mouth was slightly curled up at one edge. It was sexy and cocky. It made me queasy. He was in his flirty mood, not his crazed perfectionist one. At least right now. I never knew what to expect from this man. And, admittedly, that was part of the thrill of him. I didn't feel he was dangerous though, despite what Samantha said. No one had ever seen him be physically violent with anyone, after all. It was just a matter of being able to deal with his intensity.

I was simultaneously nervous about screwing up in practice and just wanting him to throw his clothes off and pull me into him. Would he ever, though? So far, he seemed all flirt and no action.

"Fine." I squirmed in my plush leather seat that perfectly cupped the contours of my behind. "How are you?"

"Very well, thank you."

*Good, a totally different mood tonight.* And that super-polished English that made him seem so prim and proper combined with that increasingly wicked smile made me squirm even more.

When we walked through the front door, he tossed his leather jacket onto one of the lounge chairs and headed straight toward the back studio. I placed my things on the couch and followed him in. I ran first to the window to look out. The lights from all the houses below glittered. But once he turned on the studio lights, the view was obscured by my reflection, the window becoming a kind of mirror. I immediately straightened on seeing myself. I was forever slouching. I turned my feet outward in third position and rounded my arms into a dancerly *port de bras*. I looked half ballerina, half Latin dancer. I was glad the sweater shorts and sweater top I wore covered the form-fitting leotard, though. I was losing weight, but I still felt so thick around the waist and hips in the leotard alone. My legs did seem to be taking on a little more shaping with all the dancing in heels, particularly my calves. But I didn't want to develop too much muscle; the lean look was far better for a dancer. Okay, stop fixating on your body, I said to myself.

"Rory," Sasha called, rounding the corner from kitchen to bar. "I have made another kind of juice. Come here."

He had, if I wasn't mistaken, a very sexed-up come-hither look in his eye, which became all the more pronounced when he motioned me toward him with his index finger. I wasn't hungry or thirsty, but he was impossible to resist like this. I walked toward him. A little of that light juice wouldn't hurt, I figured. I took the champagne glass from him, held it by the stem.

"Drink," he commanded. "You'll need the energy for tonight." He raised his eyebrows, which shot a bolt of lightning through my lower abdomen. "I think I mentioned last night that Greta won't be here tonight. I figured we could use some time to work on things on our own." His grin seemed to grow more devilish, but it could have been just my imagination.

My knees grew weak. My heart raced.

He raised his champagne glass to his lips and took a very slow sip. "Come on, I made that for you to drink, not for you to stand there holding like you're at a fancy cocktail party."

I glanced up at my hand. I was holding the glass by the stem, in the air. It looked very "Breakfast at Tiffany's." Then I noticed the fluid was light red. "What did you put in here!" I was nervous because of the way he was eyeing me, so my question came out a little more excitedly than I'd intended.

His playfully cocky smile dissipated almost immediately, and turned into a baffled frown. "What do you mean?"

"I mean, what's in it? What's it made of? Cranberries?"

"Oh." His eyebrows lifted and he seemed to lighten up. "It's the beets, actually, that give it the red color. There's also lemon and apple and blood-red orange. It should be sweet."

I moved it toward my lips. *Beets?* How would that taste? And how many calories were in this? The sugars in the fruit could add up.

"Rory?" His eyes grew larger and his frown returned. "You don't think—I mean, the way you said—Rory, I would never try to hurt you. You know that, right?"

I wasn't exactly sure why he was telling me this but relief washed over me. I knew he'd never hurt me. It was as if he knew what Samantha had told me and was assuring me he wasn't a violent man. I had nothing to worry about. "No. I mean, yes, I know that."

He continued to look at me for a few moments, wide-eyed, his gaze shifting back and forth between my eyes and the glass at my lips. I looked back, unable to take my eyes off him. We seemed to be having a bit of a staring contest. I swallowed.

"Good," he said, finally averting his gaze. He walked toward the iPod, picked it up, and fumbled with the songs.

I put my glass down on the bar and walked toward him.

"It's just that you are getting thin, Rory," he said, not turning around. "Weak bones and muscle are much more susceptible to injury, especially when you've put so much stress on them in only a few months. We don't have much time so we have to work hard. I simply want you to have energy and not get hurt."

An instrumental rumba began to sound over the speakers. He turned, looked at me, and held out his hand. But he was all seriousness now, all business. There was nothing the least bit sensual about the way he held out his arm. He kept eyeing the drink.

*Fine.* I took the glass off the bar and drank. It wasn't as sweet as I expected. The beets made it more savory, and hopefully not as calorie-heavy. He was right about the weak bones and susceptibility to injury. I knew he was. I'd seen what anorexia could do to ballerinas.

As I downed the entirety of the glass, his eyebrows lowered and his facial muscles relaxed. I put the glass down and walked toward him. He still held his arm out. I walked into his hold, and he took a finger and gently wiped the corners of my mouth, then traced my bottom lip. His sly smile slowly returned and a jolt of electricity surged through my lower abdomen again.

I went to check myself in the mirror, to make sure the liquid didn't bloat my belly. He seemed to know what I was doing because, as he continued to trace my lip, his hand gently cupped my jaw, holding it in place, making it impossible for me to take a sideways glance at myself.

"Let's not do the syllabi in order this time," he said, his voice low as a whisper, his breath like cinnamon sugar. "Let's just dance, take it easy. Just follow me."

As Sasha began moving, the song changed to a rumba with lyrics. It was a song titled "The Look of Love," which I recognized from the competition. It was a soft, pretty song. The man kept telling the woman, "The look of love is in your eyes." The way he looked down at me, I felt like he was saying the words to me. I wanted to melt into him.

Suddenly he stopped moving and one eyebrow shot up. "You are back-leading," he said, still holding me in close handhold. "You know the steps now and are anticipating what I am going to lead you into, but you still need to let me lead. The judges can see when the woman is leading and they will know it's wrong." His voice and tone were soft, though, not angry.

"Okay," I whispered. "Sorry." But I wasn't sure how to solve the problem since I wasn't aware of it. I would simply try to be more aware.

He began to raise my arm to lead me into a step called a hockey stick. I started to pass in front of him, since that was the step, but suddenly he raised his arm high—too high for me to pass by—and I didn't know what to do. Oh it actually was an *alemana*—an underarm turn, not a hockey stick. I realized this, and tried quickly to alter my direction with a pivot and go toward him fast enough to finish the step in time to the music. But I pivoted too quickly and nearly slipped, catching myself by whacking my hip into his thigh. My lips and nose planted into his shoulder. He was wearing some kind of spicy cologne or deodorant and he smelled quite good. The misstep would have felt kind of kinky, but I was too nervous he'd be pissed that I messed up. I laughed out of nerves, and slowly peered up at his face.

He wasn't smiling. "Do you see? If you were feeling my lead and not anticipating that I was leading you into a hockey stick that would not have happened."

"Yeah, but aren't all of our competition routines going to be choreographed anyway?" I countered.

"Yes, but that's not the point, Rory. You need to learn how to do this correctly. It's part of the technique of ballroom dancing. Of partner dancing. If two people try to lead and no one follows, you're going to be working against each other."

Now he was frustrated, I could tell, but I could also tell he was trying to control that. I could feel him breathing deeply as his chest expanded, filling the space between us. My nipple was about parallel with the bottom contour of his pec.

I took a breath, breathing into him now. "Okay, I'll try again."

We started again. This time he started to lead me into a fan. Now I was anticipating that he'd change it to an *alemana* like the last time, but he didn't, and I hesitated and ruined the step, making us behind the time. This was like trying to read someone's mind.

He didn't say anything this time and started again. I tried hard to take visual cues from his body, from the way he'd turn or the way his chest would move ever so slightly, indicating an arm might soon be raised for me to spin under. It began to feel like a mind game. At the same time, though, it was actually pretty enticing to carefully look for the little subtle twitches in his chest and shoulder muscles.

Suddenly he raised his arm and again I went to dart underneath it. But he pulled me behind him, leading me into spiral where I spun on one foot, wrapping the other foot around it—I loved spirals; they were so pretty—then walked around his back, his raised arm guiding me behind him. Normally, the step, as taught from the syllabus, entailed my walking all the way around him, but I knew now he was trying to catch me off guard to see if I could follow. I caught my image in the back mirror. I looked completely ridiculous, a frightened deer-in-the-headlights look in my eyes, a twisted arm with a bent elbow, feet turned in pigeon-toed. I was trying so hard to concentrate on reading his mind and body I paid no attention to my own execution of the steps. He saw me looking at myself as my eyes made contact with his in the mirror. He frowned, and I thought he was really going to let me have it now that he saw how horrid and undancerly I looked. But then his frown turned into a smile.

"What are you doing?" he said with a laugh.

"Trying really, really, REALLY hard to figure out your cues and not paying any attention to how ludicrous I look," I cried out. He was laughing at me and it was basically his fault I looked so ridiculous. It annoyed me.

He released my arm and I walked away from him, toward the corner of the studio.

"Rory?"

I pivoted around to look at him.

"Don't try so hard. Feel, don't think," he said, softly, reaching out to me again, indicating for me to return to him.

"You and Greta—and everyone else—keep saying that but I don't know what it means." I threw my hands up in frustration and sauntered back toward him.

"It means you are analyzing. You are looking at my hand, trying to analyze it. Why is it where it is? What are all the physical possibilities of what he could want me to do? Where he could want me to go? We are not playing a game of pool or chess. And we are not having a physics lesson."

Okay, that made me laugh. I reached him and placed my hands in his.

His smile was growing loopy. Yet I could tell he was serious.

"Sasha, I'm still not sure what that means."

"Fine. We will try an exercise. Close your eyes."

"Dance with my eyes closed?"

"Yes. You are looking—literally—for cues, as you say. And"—with this he made a clicking sound with his tongue as if chiding me—"You are focusing too much on how you look in the mirror." His eyebrows shot up. His smile was getting more sly and mischievous by the second.

I opened my mouth to protest. I wasn't being vain; I was trying to form good dance lines so as to please him.

But he shushed me, brushing his index finger gently over my lips. "Don't worry about that," he said, reading my thoughts. "I just want you to feel things with your body rather than look so literally for them. Okay. Let's try." With that he took his fingers and gently rolled them over my eyes, shutting my lids.

I really wanted him to just brush his fingertips all over my face all night. "Okay," I said.

Sasha started moving. I felt his body weight veer to my right. I shifted to my right as well.

"Good," he said.

"Don't jinx it!" I laughed.

"Shhhhh," he said, rolling his soft index finger over my lips again. His skin was lightly moisturized. And it felt all silky again. He took his time brushing his finger down past my bottom lip, tracing my chin, before beginning its way down my neck. Just as my breath caught, he stopped, and reached for my hand again.

Okay, concentrate, I told myself as he began raising his hand. I tried to sense where his arm was leading me, the direction his hips and torso were going. Good lord this was hard. Particularly since I couldn't see a blasted thing. And since we were in dance position, I was only connected to him by his hand on my back and the hand I was holding. I couldn't actually feel his chest anymore. As his arm went up higher, I tried hard to concentrate. Was I supposed to turn right or left? Or neither—did he step aside and indicate I was to walk straight, passing him? He was going so slowly, moving in slow motion to, but without slowing, the music. He was like a tease. He raised his arm but I didn't know if I was supposed to turn to the left, to the right, or go past him. I opened my eyes ever so slightly, hoping he wouldn't notice. Of course he did.

"Rory, I see you," he said sternly, his deep voice echoing across the wooden floor.

"Didn't mean to. It's just natural," I said in defense, tightly shutting my eyes again. But I still didn't know what he wanted me to do. I raised my head in the direction of his arm to try to figure out where it wanted me, still trying hard to keep my eyes closed. But I needed to see which way his wrist was turning. I flashed open my eyes, very, very quickly. Just a peek. But it was so fast, I wasn't able to discern anything except the glare of studio lights. His arm moved a millimeter more and without even willing them to, my eyes opened again, longer this time. I caught his gaze in the mirror to my right. His pupils bore into mine. His lips tightened. I was in trouble. He let go of my hand, released his arm from behind my back, and put his hands on his hips.

I mouthed the word "sorry."

The corners of his mouth turned up ever so slightly again. "We are going to have to do this the hard way, no?"

I took a step back. I had no idea what he meant. "No?" I said more as a question than answer.

"I'll be back," he said and left the room.

*Hmmm.* I wondered what he was doing as I heard him climb the winding staircase and tap around upstairs. I looked at myself in the mirror and self-consciously began a rumba basic.

Within seconds he flew down the stairs, holding what appeared to be a large white silk sash. It was quite elegant.

I stopped and turned to him. "That's pretty. What are you going—" I began.

But in a flash, he was behind me. I could see in the mirror that he was pulling the scarf sash thing lengthways and folding it over a few times.

"I'm so glad you think so," he said as he raised it over my head and began placing it over my eyes.

"What? What are you doing? You can't do that," I yelled, pushing it out of the way and turning around to face him.

"Rory, please. Please just try this."

"I need you to understand that I need my eyesight," I said, panicked. "This floor, this room. I don't know it that well. What if I go flying out the—" I pointed to the huge patio door.

"Roryyyy," he moaned, rolling his eyes. "Do you really think I would let anything happen to you?"

I folded my arms in front of me. "I think you would try to prevent something bad from happening. But, but, but, you may not be able to control everything if we get…out of control," I stuttered, trying to come up with something. I just didn't want to be blindfolded.

"Exactly how fast do you think we're going to be moving?" He smiled wickedly, moving toward me ever so slowly.

I took a step back. "Well if we're doing samba or paso—"

"We will do only rumba with you blindfolded. Okay?"

"Well, what's on the other side of that, anyway? A cliff? We never go out there."

His smile grew more wicked and he stepped closer. "We haven't been out yet because it's always been night when you are here and we are practicing. There will be plenty of time for you to see the backyard—and the hot tub—later." He stroked the length of the sash. "It's really very soft. There is nothing to be scared of, Rory." Now the mischievous smile was replaced by a completely innocent-looking grin.

I kept my arms crossed in front of me. "I don't like this," I said.

"Rory, this is just for a few minutes. Just until I show you that your sense of sight shouldn't always control. That you also have other senses, like a sense of touch. Please just trust me." He raised his brows and held the scarf toward me like it was an offering. His innocent grin produced those boyish dimples that made him completely irresistible. "Have I let you down before?" he asked.

I remembered the lifts and the trust holds. *No.* He hadn't. "Fine," I said, uncrossing my arms. "But if I get too weirded out, it's coming off immediately. And don't tie it too tight."

His grin widened as he walked behind me, still stroking the material. "Yes, my dear," he said playfully.

It was silky and perfumed and actually felt cool and comforting against my skin. He was very gentle and he wrapped it around and tied the back. It still freaked me out when he released me and I was standing in the middle of the room with no support.

"That might be too tight. I might get a migraine," I protested.

He chuckled. "It is very loose, Rory. See." He placed a finger between the knot and the back of my head and wiggled it around a bit.

"No, I can't see. That's the problem."

His chuckle turned into a laugh. "But you felt it, right?"

I didn't answer. Right now I just wanted to be stubborn and pout.

"I know you did." He patted my hair down in back as he removed his finger from under the blindfold. Then he walked away, leaving me standing alone.

"Sasha?" I called out. I would have felt more comfortable in my own place. I knew where things were. His dance floor was so blasted huge. It made me anxious when he wasn't touching me.

"I'm just finding the music."

"The Look of Love" came back on, and I could feel the heat of his body moving toward me. I held my hands out, ready to feel him. His fingertips touched mine. He positioned me in our closed handhold, placing the fingers of my left hand around his right bicep and clasping my right hand with his left. Our basic handhold, the feel of which I was now, with no sense of sight, hyper-aware.

"Okay, we will try again."

"Just go slowly. And don't expect me to get everything right." I was perturbed. If he thought he was going to be at all hard on me like this he was really going to get an earful.

He didn't say anything. Instead he just began moving. He shifted his weight to his left, my right, without taking a step, then shifted back to the other side. He was doing a basic *cucharacha*. I did as he did. Then his hand on my back began pressing under my shoulder blade. I felt his body turn to the right and his left arm raise my right one. His hand under my left shoulder blade pushed me into a slight diagonal. Okay, he wanted me to do an *alemana*, underarm turn. I brought my left elbow close to my body so I wouldn't smack him in the chest with it on my way past his body.

"If you get elbowed or stepped on it's your fault," I warned.

"A chance I will take." I could hear the sly grin in his voice. "But you'd better not do it on purpose."

"But how would you know if I did it on purpose or not?"

"I'd know," he said, squeezing the palm of my raised hand. "Believe me. And then I might do something far, far more harsh." He elongated the end of his sentence. I could still hear the grin.

All of a sudden, he released my hand and with both arms whipped me around by the waist. What the—?

"Eeek," I screamed. I stood on one leg, holding the other up with a slight turnout, in an attitude position in back—simply because it was the position that came most naturally to me from ballet. I put my weight as close as possible to the toe of the shoe I stood on so I'd continue turning without stopping abruptly, and so I'd maintain my balance. I held my center in and straightened my back as much as possible and just let him spin me for a few seconds. He kept spinning me around by the waist with his hands. It was a ballet move and I soon realized he knew I could do it. Finally, he stopped me abruptly by grabbing my waist, and brought me toward him, holding me in his arms close to him, both arms around my back.

"Okay, I seriously feel like I'm going to throw up all over you," I said, not exaggerating all that much. I was dizzy from the spinning. Normally, I'd either spot—which I couldn't do with the blindfold on—or, if I'd known the spin was coming, I would have held my head back to try to stabilize my equilibrium.

Surprisingly, he said nothing. Instead I felt his breath on me as he sighed deeply. His lips were very close to mine. My heart began to race as I wondered for a second if he was going to kiss me.

"Don't be such a drama queen, Rory," he finally said, his voice almost a whisper. A sexy whisper. "You're a ballerina."

*Drama queen?* I was being serious. But as he held me still, the nausea dissipated.

"Exactly. And ballerinas spot," I replied, annoyed he was putting me on the defensive. And, okay, annoyed he hadn't kissed me.

"But isn't seeing the room whiz by what makes you dizzy in the first place?"

"It still sets my equilibrium all off. I can feel the room spinning. I don't need to see it."

"Okay. So, why don't you try holding your head back a little. Like an ice skater. That will help stabilize your equilibrium when you spin fast."

"Ugh, I know that," I said, stomping my foot.

"Well, if you know to do that, why are you getting so frustrated, then?" I could hear the bemused look on his face.

*Because you didn't kiss me.*

"Because, uh, I didn't see it coming." I stomped my foot again. Childishly, I knew, but I was frustrated.

He sighed. "But once you felt it happening, why...oh, come on, let's try it again," he insisted. He changed the handhold, now holding me out from him, both hands around my waist. "Lean into my hands and arch your back. Put your back leg in arabesque again. And tilt your head back this time."

I took a dramatically deep breath and did as he said. He moved around quickly in a circle, spinning me with him. I arched back and held my arms out in back of me. They felt like wings. The move felt good; it felt pretty. And I wasn't dizzy.

"Better?" he asked, stopping. He held me into him again, both hands solidly around my back so I wouldn't fall over.

"Blaahhh," I said mimicking throwing up all over him.

He didn't flinch. "Very funny, Rory. I'm serious."

"Okay, it was a little better. But just a little."

He smirked. I could hear his lips part to say something but then the song was over and the music changed into a fast, hip swirling, booty-pumping samba. I waited for him to change the music. Or take the blindfold off.

"Come on," he said instead.

I didn't have time to protest. He flung me out so we were in open position, wrapped his right arm tightly around my waist, his right hip rubbing my left one, and began moving forward in body-snaking *cruzado* walks. I could feel from the way his hip circled against mine that was the step and, since we were side by side, that I was to emulate it. I had no time to think about it, or to be self-conscious as to how I looked—this being my worst dance thus far—as his body tugged mine forward by the entire waist. I had to pay close attention to where he was taking me.

"Sasha, I'm scared. I don't want to run into the window."

Just then he slowed, and moved diagonally behind me, his right pelvic bone touching just above the small of my back. Okay, we were going to do something in shadow position. He reached up and held my right wrist with his hand, lining his entire arm with mine. Samba rolls. My favorite step of all! Not that I could do them at all at this point. And I'd never be able to do them without seeing where his feet were. I'd definitely step all over him.

"Your feet are going to be a bloody mess," I warned. "I mean, I'm wearing crazy-sharp stilettos, you know."

"Yes, I'm familiar with ladies' Latin dance shoes," he said smugly, though I again detected the sly smile in his voice.

Then he bent me over widely, pressing his left hand into my abdomen and circling my right arm up and around with his. Deep samba rolls in shadow position—done well, they were absolutely gorgeous! But I couldn't help but think, with me bent over as such, this was the easiest way for him to feel the rolls of fat on my tummy. He moved faster, as if seeming to sense my self-consciousness, forcing me to concentrate on him, not me.

His right leg darted between my legs and brushed against my right, and his left brushed the side of my left leg. It felt very sexy but it also, I now realized, had the effect of telling me exactly where his feet were so I could control my steps and step next to, not on top of, his feet. I also shifted to the balls of my feet so that if I did step on him it would be with my toe instead of stiletto dagger. Not that he didn't deserve to be gouged right now for forcing me to do a fast dance blindfolded. But I was supposed to be forward-weighted anyway.

The music ended suddenly and on came an old Spanish rumba called "*Bésame Mucho.*" The samba had stopped abruptly so I knew he controlled the music. He'd planned to do that samba.

"I can't believe you did that!" I said, so out of breath I could hardly speak. "You—!" I tried to move forward so I could give him a little smack behind me, but he held my body in close shadow position so my arm was hitting air.

"Shhh." He continued to hold me in that same shadow position while he breathed deeply, apparently as out of breath as I was.

Soon, I felt his breath on my neck. He released my left arm and wrapped both arms tightly around my waist, rocking me side to side to the beat. I could now easily whack him if I wanted to, but I no longer felt the urge. He moved slightly so that he was completely behind me. His pelvis was firm against the small of my back, and I moved in line with his hips. I definitely didn't want to leave this position.

Suddenly I felt more than his breath on the back of my neck. I felt his lips. He'd bent his head and was kissing the hollow just beneath my left ear. It tickled. I gasped. I'd wanted this for so long, I was in semi-shock that it was finally happening. His lips moved back to the base of my head and he spread kisses slowly down the length of my neck, stopping at my shoulder. He drew me more toward him and began moving his lips down the front of my neck. I arched my back and bent my head over his shoulder. He slid his arms around me and circled me so he was now facing me. I could feel his full body and his breath. I cocked my head upward, toward his face, eagerly awaiting his lips on mine. Part of me wanted him to take the blasted blindfold off so I could see his eyes. But part of me found it exciting not to know exactly what was coming when. I waited and waited, feeling his breath get closer. Finally, his lips ever so softly touched mine. His kiss was so gentle. The opposite of what I'd expected given the fiery way he danced and had scolded my dancing.

His lips brushed mine again and again. His tongue rolled over my bottom lip, then slowly began to seek entry into my mouth. The fact that I couldn't see his face and had no expectations about what might come next made his actions all the more exciting. Just as I began to part my lips, he released me, and I sensed his body heat receding a bit. He'd backed away.

*Why?* I didn't want that. Was he being a tease or having second thoughts? I felt myself automatically inching toward him, at least from the waist up. When my lips met only with air, I became self-conscious about what I was doing and didn't allow myself to take a step—that would have been too needy!

Then suddenly, thankfully, I felt his heat on me all at once. He grabbed me into a full embrace, both arms surrounding me, chest heaving against mine, heart beating into me. He'd inched his leg between mine, and I wrapped my left leg around his. His lips pressed harder and he tongued my lips open. His whole mouth tasted like cinnamon sugar. He tasted so good. I must have tasted like beet juice. *Ugh.* Well, if he didn't like it, he shouldn't have served it to me. I put my arms around his neck and brushed his shoulder, feeling his solid muscle. The skin of his neck was like silk. I wanted badly to rip off his shirt and feel the entirety of his bare chest. And to see the entirety of that tattoo I'd glimpsed on his shoulder.

He took his mouth off my lips and moved his head back. But his body remained entwined with mine. I cocked my head toward his face and waited, lips slightly parted. He was either taking a breath or teasing me. The way his body was wrapped around mine told me he wasn't going anywhere. Soon, I felt his lips brush softly against my cheekbone. They continued past my cheek to my ear, before moving down to trace the bones of my face, ending at my chin where they briefly stopped. I felt his breath as I caught my own. He was still for a moment. I could feel him thinking.

He whispered something in Russian. It sounded more loving than kinky.

"What?" I asked, leaning forward.

"Shhhh," he said, placing his silky finger to my lips. Then he slowly traced the other side of my face with his finger, ending on my chin. He caressed underneath my chin, then tipped my chin up, pulling it toward his lips, making me think he was going to kiss me deeply. But no, his lips landed in that same spot he'd just caressed with his finger. They traced the underside of my jawline, ending at my earlobe. My entire body clenched and bolted upward at least a couple millimeters as his lips brushed against the sensitive area behind my ear. I unintentionally let a brief moan escape.

He obviously realized this was a sensual zone; he began making small circles with his tongue right in that area. I clawed at his rock hard pec. He let up a bit and took a breath. I released his shoulder, which I was now clinging to, and took a breath as well. Then his lips were on me again, this time creating a trail of kisses from the back of my ear, down my neck, to the crevice between my neck and shoulder. He traced my clavicle with his tongue, ending at the hollow of my neck, another hyper-sensitive zone for me. I lifted my head, opened my mouth and drew in a long breath. He took a step back. He was no longer touching me but I knew he was right in front of me. I didn't need my sight to know exactly where his body was.

Suddenly, I felt his fingers on my abdomen. They were undoing the knot I'd tied in front of my sweater. As I felt the sweater open to reveal the top of my spaghetti-strapped leotard, panic surged through my spine—both because he was undressing me and I didn't know how far he'd go, and because I so wasn't Arabelle, with her perfect body. I'd just downed his glass of sugary beets, which, as usually happened shortly after I'd ingested something, made my stomach poof out. In other words, I felt fat.

But after he undid the tie and opened the sweater, he returned his focus to my neck, brushing his lips from my chin back down to that small, sensitive area. Suddenly, I felt both his hands on my chest. He ran his fingers along the opening of the sweater, up to the top, and gently pulled the sleeves over and off each shoulder. I felt his body heat fade and I heard footsteps. He was walking away. But he didn't go far. I wondered what he was doing but I knew he'd return. And now, I honestly didn't want to untie the blindfold. I wanted to be surprised. Sure enough, his body heat returned. But only with soft footsteps. He'd removed the Cuban heels.

He began kissing me again, softly on the lips. I felt his fingers trace my arms. I was wearing my favorite Mirabelle leotard. It was candy red, with a sexy velvet outer bra that was slightly low cut, showing a bit of cleavage. I was happy for the sweater to come off. It was getting quite hot, anyway. But the thought of anything else being shed both terrified and thrilled me.

He traced the bones of my face again, caressing his lips over my cheek, then jaw, then ear. At the same time, he began brushing his fingers down my sides, from my armpits to my waist, then down to my hips, then back up to my waist. It tickled and my entire body quivered. As he kissed the base of my neck, he took his hands from my sides and wrapped them around my back, massaging me. That felt very good. Suddenly I felt the back of my wrap-around ballet skirt being untied. Before I could think, it fell slowly down my legs, landing in a satin-y puddle around my feet. Initially, I couldn't help but worry about my now-exposed stomach. But it was just hard to remain so self-conscious around this man as his lips pressed farther into the hollow of my neck, only briefly leaving it to kneel down and whisk the skirt away.

I was now standing there in Latin high heels and a red leotard with nothing underneath but a pink thong. I could hear him whispering something in Russian. He was sitting at my feet and I could tell from the angle of his voice he was looking up at me. It sounded like he was saying something good, like that I was beautiful. He sounded genuine, passionate. I was now glad I was blindfolded. If I saw myself in the mirror I'd probably really freak out over every flaw and totally destroy this beyond-amazing moment.

He lightly ran his fingertips up my legs, from my ankles to my knees. They felt like a feather. A current of electricity shot up my spine. I sensed him stand up as he continued tracing his fingers, up to my hips. He placed one palm on each hip and kissed my earlobe, whispering more intoxicating Russian. He angled his hands in so they were resting on my pubic bone. His fingers slowly began tracing the leotard's elastic. With a finger on each leg, he pulled the elastic up and traced my skin underneath. As he brought his fingers closer and closer to the front of the leotard, I felt my sex clench and a downright spasm shoot from the front of my crotch straight up my insides, right to the hollow of my neck. I almost released a groan upon feeling the spasm, but held it in at the last minute and merely issued an open-mouthed breath.

Then he let go of me. The air was still and silent and I wondered what he'd do next. My heart was nearly pounding out of my chest. I raised my head to where I sensed his face was, angled my lips toward his. I could hear him breathing. His cinnamon breath seemed to be coming from several inches away. I waited. And waited.

"Sash—" I'd begun to call out when his lips landed on mine. He tongued my mouth open and kissed me deeply. I put my arms around his back, hugging his muscles. I wanted to drink in all of him.

Suddenly his hands were on my shoulders, his feathery fingers trickling down my chin to the hollow of my neck and outward to the edge of my shoulders, stopping at the spaghetti straps of my leotard. I knew what was coming and, scared as I was about what he would see, my sex was pulsing harder and harder. Screw it, I thought. I needed him to touch me. *There. Everywhere.*

He pulled down on the straps so blasted slowly, seemingly going one millimeter per minute. I shivered with anticipation. When the straps neared my elbows, my lower belly was on fire. So much so it almost hurt.

I sucked in a breath so fast I nearly choked on air as the top of the fabric rolled down past my nipples, which were now hard as pebbles. My breasts jiggled as the fabric slipped below them. Suddenly, a feeling of nervous embarrassment lodged in the pit of my stomach. My hands immediately went up to cover my breasts, which were too big for a ballerina, for a dancer. The straps were still wrapped around my wrists and I brought part of the fabric back up when I raised my hands.

Sasha whispered something in my ear—Russian again—and gently pulled my hands from my breasts. Before I could move them back and re-cover myself, he cupped my breasts in his hands, caressing my nipples with his fingers.

Between the sweet Russian whispers and the way he traced each nipple as if he were sculpting it, as if my body was a piece of art, I calmed. Soon he hooked his fingers back around the straps and pulled the material down, till it was at my belly button. Another sensitive spot—my abdomen. I must have flinched because he began whispering again, this time in English.

"You are so breathtaking, Rory. Exquisite. I don't know how you don't know. My angel. You are so worth the wait."

I gulped in astonishment at his words as the leotard rolled down, past my waist, past the thin wedge of pubic hair, then fell all the way down to my ankles, completely exposing me. The thong must have come with it since I could feel every millimeter of my skin connecting with raw air.

My emotions were a jumble of self-consciousness and excitement. My entire abdomen was pulsating, and I was shivering.

"I think you're going to have to take those nasty stilettos off now," I said, trying to joke, not knowing what else to do, my voice shaking so I could hardly get all the words out. "I mean, if you don't want me to trip and kill myself, that is!" I shifted my weight from one side to the other, feeling the material wrapped in a puddle around my heels.

"Shhhh," I heard him say from below. He was looking straight up at me.

I didn't let myself wonder what that view looked like. My stomach muscles were already automatically clenched as tight as they possibly could, as they'd been throughout the whole thing. This was actually good exercise.

I felt him unbuckling the strap of my right shoe. Yes, I'd won something!

"Oh, thank you, thank you, kind sir, for removing my footbinding!" I teased, giggling, voice becoming less shaky the sillier I acted.

He said nothing, but I heard a sigh and sensed him shaking his head at my babbling. He gently arched my foot out of my shoe and placed it on the floor. That was a bit tricky, since I was now totally off balance.

"Sash—" I called out.

"Just trust me," he said, wrapping one hand firmly around my thigh to steady me while he unbuckled the other strap. "Here," he said, removing his hand from around my thigh to hold my hand. He lifted my ankle out of the shoe and guided my foot to the floor. As soon as I was firmly on my own two feet, he released my hand and bent down again.

He wrapped his hands around my ankles and began massaging upward to my calves. It felt so good after being in those heels for so long.

"Mmmmm," I said, trying hard to focus on the sensation and not my stupid body insecurities. When his hands worked their way to my thighs, I suddenly felt his lips on my abdomen. Again, it was like he read my mind.

"You are superb," he whispered.

"So are you," I whispered back. "I mean, I think." He was obviously talking about my body and I hadn't seen his yet. So what was I saying? "I mean, I know. Well, I mean, your face, your face is." I sounded like a bumbling ass. I giggled nervously. "But seriously, am I going to see more of you? Am I going to see, period?"

He held a finger gently to my lips. When I took the hint and stopped talking, he caressed my cheek and, cupping my chin, kissed me slowly and deeply again.

"Plié," he then said, voice now taking on a commanding tone.

"What?"

"We will do the cradle lift."

*Seriously? Wow.*

He took my left arm and wrapped it around his neck. My left breast now lay firmly against his pec. Another bolt of electricity surged through my belly. He pulled me closer to him, till I could feel my bare hip align with his pelvic area. My belly filled with liquid heat.

"Rrrready?"

I nodded, unable to speak, and bent my knees then jumped into his arms. His arm lay underneath my thighs, oh so close to my now throbbing vulva. He carried me. I could hear his feet hit solid wood, then tile, then carpet. Then I felt his chest muscles tighten and his biceps flex as he raised his legs higher and higher. He was climbing. He was taking me upstairs.

The ride up was a bit wobbly but I trusted him, with his sturdy build and solid biceps. He'd never drop me. I felt his leg kick out and heard a door breeze open, and he held me more compactly—moving his arms closer together—as we walked through a doorway. He carried me a short distance, then lay me down on a super soft, plush blanket that felt like velvet. I gathered the soft cushiony material and pulled a bit of it over me. I didn't completely cover myself, just a little thigh. My heart was racing. I sensed his presence but couldn't feel his heat. He must have been standing at a distance and looking at me. Tingles shot up and down my legs and belly. I was so excited for what would happen next. For the surprise of it. But damn, was he making me wait!

"Sasha," I finally called out, unable to take it anymore.

"I'm right here," he said, and I could feel his breath off to my right side. His voice came from above. He was still standing.

"What's taking so long? Hurry up!"

"Maybe…I just want to look at you," he said slowly, after a long pause.

My whole torso prickled with goose bumps. I moved my right leg across my left to cover my sex and gathered more cloth at my sides, though I didn't do anything with it; it remained in my fists.

"Well, maybe I want to look at you…at some point." My voice was ridiculously shaky. I wanted that to stop. I longed to sound sexy and in command of my faculties, not ruled by my anxious reactions to things.

Finally I felt his weight settle on the bed next to me. He didn't touch me yet, though I felt his torso arched over mine. He smelled like musk and pine. We remained like this for what felt like an agonizing several minutes, though it was probably only seconds. He was killing me.

"Do you want me to remove the sash?" he whispered.

"No!" I said with a nervous giggle. "I mean, not yet."

And then I felt him. His tongue at first wetting my lips, parting them, then gently biting at my lower lip. He must have been doing an extended push-up because I still didn't feel any other part of his body.

*Yes, you are strong.* Very sexy strong, Sasha Zakharov, I thought. You've more than proven that. *Now go!*

As suddenly as it had arrived, his mouth was gone from mine. Another tantalizingly evil few seconds of nothingness, of me lying there, my sex swelling until it began to hurt, wondering what was going to happen and when. Finally his lips returned, this time to my earlobe, then my neck, then my clavicle, then the top of my rib cage.

His hand began moving up and down along my right leg, still raised over the left. He used his fingertips, and it tickled slightly, but was so incredibly sensual. He went higher and higher with each stroke up my thigh, until his fingertips reached up to my belly and began their feathery, ticklish descent downward. His tongue arrived at the space between my breasts and his hand right at the top of my pubic hair. Then he lifted both tongue and hand.

The air was still. Again I waited, my sex starting to throb, my heart making my entire chest pulse. I could kill him. Then his lips landed atop my right nipple. He circled the areola slowly with his tongue, then lightly sucked. His mouth grew bigger and he began to take my whole breast in. I felt his finger on my left nipple, circling that areola, then lightly squeezing the nipple and cupping the whole breast. Electric currents charged through my entire body, from that nipple straight through my belly, down my legs. Totally forgetting my breast-size issues, I breathed deeply and arched my back, trying to fill my lungs and enlarge my breasts as much as possible so as to better fill his mouth and hand. Then, as quickly as he began, he stopped, and was off me. I felt his heat to my side. I heard his breath. I heard something crinkle and tear. A condom package.

I gulped and covered myself with the plush material I still held in my hands. I felt his heat coming nearer. It was uncanny how I could feel how far his body was from mine now. Then I felt his hand, this time to my raised knee. He was suddenly much more aggressive, as he lifted my leg and pulled it outward. As he pulled, the covers fell completely off. He knew I was flexible and moved my legs quite far apart, leading me, effectively, into a straddle split. My quick breaths and heart palpitations made my face flush and eyes water.

He hovered over me, propping his taut, dancerly body up with one hand while the other rubbed aggressively along the inside of my thigh. His hand got higher and higher until he removed it from my leg and placed it gently but firmly on the crown of my clit, where it made tiny circles before plunging into my dripping wet opening.

"Sash—!" I cried, reaching my arms up to him.

That was all the encouragement he needed, because he immediately lowered himself onto me, kneeing my legs further apart. Excruciatingly slowly, he rubbed the tip of his rock-hard penis around my inner and outer folds. I bent my knees to open myself more and, turning out from my right hip, angled my right leg toward him, stroking his calf with my toe. He came inside me, gently but deeply. He wrapped his arms around me tightly and kissed me deeply as he moved. I put my arms around his back, caressing the soft, silky skin that tautly covered hard, sinewy muscle. I arched my neck as he moved his lips down my throat. He thrust deeper and deeper into me and I arched my back and pointed my toes around the backs of his thighs.

"Rory," he whispered. And nothing more but, "Oh, Rory, oh, Rory."

In the ballroom, I'd felt so exposed, but now his body covered every millimeter of my flesh. I felt so protected. I arched my back deeper and angled my hips so the top of his pelvis met my pulsating clit as he plunged into me. I pulled the pillow out from under my head so I could arch back even more. My back was as flexible as my thighs. I had never had such dancerly sex before! I turned my knees back to parallel position, and raised them higher, my toes now curling toward the ceiling as I felt an immense tingling in my sex that shot up through my abdomen with an almost violent intensity that made me flinch. He lifted his torso up a bit and propped his hands around me, then exploded as I felt myself open like a flower.

We breathed heavily, exhausted. He lowered his torso again, his head now on the right side of my neck, his arms still around me, now rubbing my shoulders. We remained in the same position, him still inside me, for a while, before he pulled out and lay to my left side. We continued to lie there, just breathing for a while. I wanted nothing more than to see him but also relished the last few moments of being naked in front of him, still blindfolded. My whole body was far too tingly for me to care about stupid self-image issues right now.

After a few more breaths I came to my senses and had to see him. I lifted myself onto my elbows. But I moved with too much haste. Knowing he was on my left, I turned toward him but, without thinking about his exact body position, did so with a bent knee. He jerked and I felt him jump off the bed.

"Rory!"

"What?"

"Nothing. You just…almost got me in a bad place."

At first I didn't get it then realized I'd nearly kneed him. "Yeah, well, maybe that's what happens when I, you know, CAN'T SEE," I teased.

"Okay, lie still," he said.

I felt his body weight on the bed next to me, and he reached around my neck. After some finagling, I was freed of the silky blindfold. When it first came off I had to squint. The lights were dimmed low but my eyes hadn't been exposed to light in I didn't know how long now. I tried hard to open them fully so I could see him. In my periphery I saw his shadowy figure approaching the door.

"No, stay," I said—more like shouted, reaching toward him.

"Rory, I was only going to go downstairs and get us something to drink. It will give you some time to adjust your eyes. And I'm thirsty. Aren't you?"

"Fine, but don't put anything on. It's totally not fair that you've seen me naked for hours and I haven't seen a millimeter of you."

"Hours?" he laughed and shook his head. "And you wanted to be blindfolded."

"What, no! Not at—" I began as he fled the room. Through the slits in my eyes I was able to glimpse a gloriously muscled ass receding from my view. His entire backside was a splendid shade of light brown. No tan lines. At least not that I could make out in my still cloudy vision. And I could make out some intriguingly huge body art spanning across his entire back and up and around his shoulders. I would definitely need to explore that on his return. "Promise!" I called out as I heard him running down the winding staircase.

While he was gone, I put my head down and blinked many times, trying to open my eyes a little wider with each blink. The plush covers were cinnamon red. Funny because that's how I'd seen them in my mind, how I'd sensed them. I pulled the top one back and climbed inside. Mmmm, I was ensconced in warm, velvety fuzz. I looked around the room. It was simply huge. The bed itself was enormous. It was like a double king or a king plus, if there were such things. And his entire double-long closet was mirrored. I looked at myself. My vision had adjusted and I could see myself clearly in the dim, hazy light. My hair was all mussed up in back and on the sides from the blindfold being there for so long. *Ugh.* I fluffed it out as much as I could. My eyeliner and mascara were a bit smudged from being under the blindfold. I wiped the area underneath my eyes. Other than that, I was okay. Of course all I could see of my body at this point was the tips of my shoulders.

The floors were dark polished wood with a long cinnamon rug snaking about that matched the bedspread. The room was painted an eggshell white. Big as it was, it was fairly sparse. There were identical nightstands that seemed to be made of the same dark wood as the floor on each side of the bed. Each looked like a piece of polished driftwood and held a reading lamp. Very cool. But besides those, there wasn't much on either stand. Nothing on the one to my right but my blindfold and a condom wrapper, and on the other, only a fancy, complicated-looking alarm clock. There were large speakers hanging from each corner of the ceiling. He had track lights running diagonally along the ceiling that emitted a magical-looking, almost fuchsia glow. And down to the side, I could see a door slightly ajar which led into a room floored with sparkling white tiles, which I imagined was a bathroom. I couldn't see very far inside. The room was so clean. I didn't even see his clothes. He must have hung them up or put them in the bathroom.

Suddenly, I felt his presence. I looked at the doorway. There he stood, perfectly centered in the frame of the door like a piece of art, a glass of sparkling wine in each hand. Completely naked. His form was slightly shadowed from the light behind. But not too much to prevent me from seeing everything in its splendid perfection. Oh my, the man was simply stunning. His black hair hung long and wavy, falling almost to his shoulders. His beautiful face glimmered with sweat. His chest and shoulders were solid, taut muscle. He had very little chest hair. His nipples were dark red and there was some kind of tattoo right above his left nipple that I would have to examine. Ditto for a colorful, snaky-looking tattoo down his bicep. He held his hands to each side as if to perfectly frame his spectacular center. He had closely trimmed, jet black pubic hair, which wasn't a surprise. Dancers, I knew from my ballet days, were always coiffed. Everywhere. His substantial penis, larger than usual, was simple perfection. Well, I thought larger than usual; larger than James. I hadn't been with very many men, to be honest. He was lightly bronzed everywhere; the color of caramel. No tan lines. But he only gave me half a second to absorb and ponder all this. He strutted right in after standing still for only a flash.

"Why are you covered?" he said with an admonishing tone, handing me a glass.

"Just shifting the tables," I said, trying hard not to fixate on his penis, now rubbing into my side.

He squinted at me and his wily smile returned. I felt my sex flood with liquid heat again.

I cleared my throat as if that would somehow help and lifted my hand to take a glass. He took advantage of my raised hand and pulled the cover down to reveal my right breast. I would have protested but I was mid-sip.

"Whoa, what is this?" I said, taking a hard swallow. The liquid was thick and syrupy, and extremely strong. A little sweet and nutty as well. I looked at the glass. It was kind of a golden liquid, not at all the light champagne I'd thought it was. I guess I hadn't really been focused on what was in the glasses when he was standing in the doorway.

"It's just a little Frangelico, my angel," he said, trickling a finger from my bottom lip down my neck, then my chest, then to the tip of my pointed, exposed nipple. "Do you like it?"

"Mmm hmm." I nodded, unsure whether he was talking about his hand fondling my breast or the drink. The answer to both was yes, though. But the liqueur was strong and I hadn't eaten much. Two sips in and I was already tipsy.

"I'd say. You're drinking it better than the juice."

That was true. What was up with me being so careless with calories? But I was getting too woozy to care. Albeit not too woozy to forget about that hot tattoo on his back.

"Turn over," I commanded.

"What?" he said, confused and taken aback by my forceful tone.

"I mean lie on your stomach. I want to check out that tattoo."

"Ah, the winged thinker," he said, rolling onto his stomach.

At first it was hard to concentrate on the design in light of his perfectly sculpted glutes. But once I took my eyes off his gorgeous behind and focused on his upper body, I saw how absolutely beautiful the artwork was—the drawing as well as his amazing musculature, his taut silky skin, the svelte bones of his shoulder blades, wide apart, jutting out just enough to give the wings of the drawn creature shaping.

And the drawing was truly extraordinary. It was partly a copy of Rodin's "The Thinker," a man sitting, resting his chin on his hand, obviously deep in thought. The man was outlined in black, but spreading out from each shoulder was an enormous wing. The wings were magnificent, each spanning the entirety of Sasha's back and reaching out and up over his shoulders, to encompass the front of each shoulder as well. That's what I'd seen peeking out of the arms of his shirt in class. The wings were colored a gorgeous golden hue, with some hints of silver, and these brilliant strokes of crimson were strewn throughout like flames.

"Wow. Just, wow. Did you get it here or in Russia?" I asked, tracing the outline of the man's figure with my fingertips.

"Here," he said with a slight laugh I didn't quite understand.

Did they not have tattoo parlors in Russia? Or were they dirty and dangerous? For some reason, I didn't want to ask.

"At a salon in West Hollywood," he added.

"Oh. How did you come up with the idea? I've never seen one like it."

"The artist had the idea. He's a friend of mine, actually, and he showed me a drawing. It just, I don't know, spoke to me I guess is the way you say. The mind and body combination, brains and beauty, which you need both of to make art, to make dance. And it's like escaping, maybe. Like his thoughts allow him to soar."

"That's brilliant," I said, wowed, wondering if Sasha had something to escape from but not daring to ask right now.

"How do you know him?"

"What?" He seemed like his thoughts had momentarily taken him away.

"You said you were friends with the artist. How do you know him?"

"Oh." He paused. "Just, he's just a friend I met through a friend."

I traced the outlines of the wings. Sasha's skin was so soft yet it covered such hard muscle. "A friend from Russia?" I asked.

"No," he snapped.

*Okay, then.*

He breathed deeply and his back muscles noticeably tensed. I could literally feel them tighten. I massaged his shoulders to release the tension, then touched the top of his spine, and lightly traced it down as far as it went, until it dipped into the small of his back. I couldn't help myself. I rubbed my palms over his brawny ass cheeks, becoming too absorbed in his body to worry about why he'd snapped and tensed at the mention of his homeland. I swung my leg around him and climbed on top, then began kissing his shoulders, running my tongue down his spine, making the same line with my tongue I'd just traced with my finger. But before I got all the way down to the small of his back, he began turning over underneath me. I lifted my hips to let him turn. He was now partially erect. I rested my hips on his lower abdomen.

Now that I had his body in front of me, I just wanted to drink it all in. I kissed one side of his chest, tonguing his nipple, then kissed my way to the other. I returned to the middle of his chest and, lifting my hips, began tonguing my way down his torso. But he lifted me up, holding me above him with his arms. I looked down at him through heavily hooded eyes. His devilishly sexy smile was back. He released his hands and stroked my neck, then snaked his fingertips down my front side to my breasts, where they rested, caressing my nipples. I sat up straight, arched my back and pushed my chest out. I was getting wet, as was his stomach where I sat.

"You're even more than I expected, Rory," he said, eyelids lowering.

"More? More what!?" I asked, wondering what he meant. Did he mean bigger, fatter? "More body, as in more fat, bigger boobs?"

"Rory," he said, rolling his eyes, which now held a wistful look. "More everything. Everything good, all the good words I can think of. More beautiful, more exquisite, more…shapely, yes, which is good. Which is very, very good. Absolutely not fat. Definitely not. Don't ever say that again." He sighed and shook his head. "And, ah, more…blonde." He looked down at my pubic hair.

I giggled. "You didn't think I was a natural," I said, play-smacking him in the bicep.

"Stop," he laughed. "Of course I did, I just…it's just that you're so blonde you look bare. Beautifully so, blissfully so."

He really did have a good vocabulary.

With this, he took his hand from my left nipple and lightly ran his finger along my clit from my opening to the crown, where it stayed and circled.

"Sasha!" I lifted my hips.

He took both arms to my waist and flipped me in one fell swoop onto my back. He opened my legs wide and slid down on the bed, his face right between my legs. I breathed hard, initially fixating on my thick thighs and butt flab. But as he used his tongue, stroking up and down my clit, licking my folds, darting in and out of my increasingly wet depths, it became impossible to obsess over such stupid issues. I arched my spine and threw back my head when he returned to the crown of my clitoris. My orgasm was coming too quickly. I wanted this to last longer. I tried to restrain myself but couldn't help it. I grabbed the pillow and tugged both sides, as if that were going to help. The sensation between my legs felt like a pin pricking me, more and more intensely, almost painfully. I finally exploded with ecstasy, the thrill riding up and down my spine.

I released the pillow, then moved my hands down and ran my fingers through his thick, wavy mane. I wanted his whole body on top of me again, inside me. I looked down at him and held my arms out, indicating I wanted to wrap them around him. He got the hint and climbed back over me.

I felt his fingers spreading me open and I moved my legs farther apart, in the best straddle split I could manage.

I felt the tip of his penis. "Oh," he said just as he was about to enter. He stopped. I looked at him. His eyes were wide. "I need to get something. I mean, you want, right?"

I was so in the thrall of passion—as was he, indicated by his abbreviated English—that at first I was confused. Then I realized he meant a condom. "Do you have anything?" I said.

"Yes, of course. They're in the bathroom." He began lifting himself up.

"No, I mean, do you have anything bad? Like a disease? I don't."

"Oh. Me neither," he said, smiling. "But what about—"

"I take the pill every day," I said, pulling him back on top of me. "Now don't leave me."

"Don't worry. I won't," he said with a sincerity that made my heart skip several beats, before enveloping my body.

# CHAPTER 4

I woke up to the sound of birds. They were chirping very loudly. Very loudly, as if they were inside my room rather than outside my window. As if they were in my bed.

*What in the world?*

I opened my eyes widely and turned to the direction from which they were coming. There sat a very expensive-looking oak nightstand bearing an intricate-looking alarm clock. Holy crap, I was at Sasha's! Right as I felt the plush, velvety, cozy bedding, and my nakedness, the whole night came back to me. It wasn't a dream! Sasha didn't seem to be in bed, though.

I had to stop those birds from chirping. I grabbed the alarm and fumbled with it, finally finding the "off" button. The numbers read 7:01. On my gosh, it was Tuesday morning. I had to go to work. He'd remembered I'd told him I had to get up at seven a.m. for work and he'd set the alarm.

There was sunlight coming from above. I looked up to see blue sky and sun shining through a skylight. Morning at Sasha's was simply beautiful.

About the last place I wanted to be right now was work. Where was he?

I sat up to look across the bed but first got a glimpse of myself in the mirrored closet across from me. Mussed up hair, black eyeliner running down my face. *Ugh*. I peeked over at the space beside me, now relieved when I didn't see him sleeping next to me. I looked at the other bedside table. Two empty cocktail glasses were sitting on it, along with a white silk sash. Oh yes, that's how this happened!

I jumped up and tiptoed to the door I assumed opened to the bathroom.

*Holy crap*. The room was gigantic. There was a long multi-colored marbled countertop bearing three sinks made of the same glassy marble. Across from the line of sinks was a sheer wall. A door at the back corner of that wall opened into the most titanic shower I'd ever seen. There was a large flat-floored tiled area with a showerhead—no, make that four showerheads, one on each side of the wall—and beside it was a counter containing shampoos and soaps and moisturizers. Then, if you walked several feet, the tile became clear porcelain and that sank down into a tub. There was a waterspout at the end of its length and another counter containing more shampoos, as well as bubble bath and a ginormous bottle of Epsom salts. Yes, a dancer lived here. There were several different levels, but at its deepest the tub appeared to be about three feet deep, and about five feet wide. It was like a hot tub within a bathtub. There were a few steps toward the front with webbed matting whose purpose seemed to be so you could go down the different levels without slipping. I had never seen anything like this in my life.

As mesmerized as I was, I had to wonder what all had gone on in here. This was a sex god's bathroom. The thought simultaneously thrilled and panicked me. I was so inexperienced. How many women had he had?

A long mirror faced the shower, above the sinks. I grabbed some cotton, wetted it, and dabbed under my eyes, trying to get rid of as much of that raccoon look as I could. Not knowing if I should use one of his brushes, I ran my fingers through my hair until it looked not entirely unpresentable. Then I quickly used the toilet, whose lid was covered in similar plush velvet crimson as the bed, washed my hands with some very fancy-looking soap whose bottle bore writing in French, and returned to the bedroom. I guess Sasha was downstairs. Where my clothes were as well. Crap. I wasn't about to walk down there completely naked. I threw off the top cover of the bed and grabbed the second, slightly less plush but still furry one, and wrapped it around myself. Of course it was huge, the bed being a king-size-plus-plus-plus or whatever. I had to wrap it around myself several times, and hold it firmly around me as I opened the door to the hallway.

"Sasha?" I called out.

"Yes, good morning. Downstairs," he answered, the sound of his voice momentarily making my lower abdomen pool with liquid heat again.

I tiptoed down the long, winding stairway, remembering how he'd carried me up it last night. Naked and blindfolded. My cheeks must have been the same crimson as the bedsheet by the time I arrived in the dining room, where he sat with a cup of coffee, the table covered with a newspaper.

"Good morning, beautiful," he said, before eyeing me up and down and frowning. "What are you wearing?"

"Your blanket. My clothes are down here."

"Well, why would you need clothes?" he said with a sharply raised eyebrow.

"I can't walk around naked in front of you, in this foreign house!"

He frowned in mock contemplation. "Well, it's my house and I know very well what you look like naked now, so..." He made a motion with his hand, indicating I should lose the blanket.

I felt my face getting even redder, if that was possible. "No! I can't!" I said, somewhat teasing, but somewhat serious. I simply couldn't sit comfortably with him at the breakfast table stark naked the morning after.

"Fine, sit down and I'll make some breakfast. If you have the time, that is. I set the alarm but I don't know how long it takes you to get ready for work."

*Ugh, work.* I thought about it for a few moments. I'd had absolutely nothing to do yesterday. It'd actually been stressful trying to figure out how to appear busy so as not to make clear they didn't have a whole lot of work for an associate. The partner with the case that would eventually require the document coding said she didn't expect to have the documents until sometime next week. Maybe I should just call in sick. Guilt washed over me. But really, it was just one day.

He stood and walked to the kitchen counter. He was wearing form-fitting white briefs.

"You're not naked!" I hollered.

He smiled cockily. "I've been up for quite a while, Rory. That would have been strange to be walking around naked alone."

I tried to think of a comeback but couldn't stop fixating on the bulge in his front and his muscular backside. I felt like I had to pinch myself. Had I really had this man all to myself all night? Yes! He was mine!

"So, how did you sleep?" he asked as he peered into the fridge.

"Mmmm, never better since I've been in L.A.," I said, rolling my eyes.

"Really?" He raised one eyebrow.

Ugh, he needed to stop making little gestures that shot bolts of electricity down my spine and straight to my groin. "Really. That was the coziest, plumpest, plushest bed I've ever slept in. In my life!"

Now he raised both brows. "Well, I am glad you enjoyed my bed so."

*Cocky.* But so sexily so. Okay I was pumping him up maybe a little too much. He knew he lived in a veritable mansion.

"So. What shall I make? Eggs, Canadian bacon, sourdough toast? You haven't told me how much time you have before you need to go get ready for work."

And he cooked!

"It was really slow yesterday in the office. I was thinking of just taking a day off, maybe getting some good practice in." I immediately felt guilty. "I mean, things will probably pick up later. So maybe it's good to take a little breather to kind of calm myself before the storm." I don't know why I added that. I had no idea if things would pick up. I'd always felt guilty about missing classes, and work was the same. Even if there was no work to do.

But his eyes lit up. "Greta is coming over in a couple of hours for a private session. It would be perfect if you could stay and train."

Immediately I felt better. There was a reason for me to take a day off from work. I'd be doing a different kind of work. And I'd be working way harder than I would at the office twiddling my thumbs, or, at the most, drafting fill-in-the-blank wills. This was a kind of job, after all, training for a dance competition for which we'd be paid by sponsors and by winning money. Hopefully.

"Okay!" I said.

"Excellent." Boyish dimples lit up his face, while he removed a skillet and a saucepot from inside a kitchen drawer. "So, the works?" he asked.

Oh, right. He'd listed a lot of food. "Hold the bacon for me, please. I don't like meat," I added when he shot me a dubious look. "I'll have an egg and one piece of toast. Plain."

"Fine," he said, taking a breath, giving in. "Here, have some fruit in place of the meat." He set in front of me a large sapphire blue ceramic bowl that held a colorful cornucopia of bananas, apples, mangoes, oranges, plums and grapes.

"Thank you," I said, plucking a red grape from its stem and popping it into my mouth. *Mmmm, juicy.* "So when exactly is Greta coming?" I asked as he poured some oil onto a skillet.

"Nine."

I eyed the clock. If I lounged about much longer, I wouldn't be able to go home and change clothes beforehand. "I guess I don't have time to run home for a change of clothes, but I'll definitely need to take a shower. I don't want her to…you know…"

"What?" he asked, looking up from the frying pan at me, wide-eyed, completely deadpan.

But I knew he knew what I meant. I think he enjoyed watching my face turn all shades of tomato. It had been a long time since I'd had a morning after, which I think he knew as well.

"You know what I mean!" I squealed.

He returned his attention to the heating pan, but continued to frown.

"Stop acting like you don't. What will she think?"

He expertly cracked an egg on the edge of the pan and emptied its contents into the heated oil. Wow, I was impressed. I usually spilled yolk everywhere when I tried to do that.

"You can definitely use the shower," he said, shooting me a wicked eye that sent my heart plummeting to my stomach again. "And, please," he continued after a pause, "don't worry about Greta. She knows me."

*Hmmm, what?* "Um, what do you mean?" I tried to sound casual, though my thoughts were racing a bit. She knew he'd seduce me? He had it all planned? He always seduced his dance partners? I was no different than everyone else? Or maybe he meant this is how he taught female partners to follow him—with a blindfold? It was effective. But had last night been a teaching technique?

"Hmmm?" he said, reaching into the cabinet for a plate.

"I mean, she knows what about you? That you sleep with all your partners?"

He cocked his head over his shoulder, squinting at me. He eyed my lower half, seeming to notice that I was squirming uncomfortably in my seat. He turned back to the cupboard briefly, then back to me. "I, I probably misspoke."

*Probably?*

"I just meant, she's not going to care that we're lovers. Don't worry about her at all."

Lovers? It sounded so European. So grown-up. The word made me squirm, but definitely not in a bad way. Still, I had questions. "But do you sleep with all your dance partners?"

"All of them?" He laughed. "As if there have been so many, Rory. Just three." He placed the plate in front of me.

"Well, Micaela, Xenia, Arabelle…" I began.

"Not Arabelle," he said quickly.

"Okay. But the other two?"

"Yessss," he said slowly as if he wondered where this was going. "Is that a lot? Does that make me a man slut, as they say here?"

"Of course not." I laughed.

"Good. I am very glad to hear that." He returned to the pan, cracked some more eggs.

"Wait, if Arabelle wasn't one of them, who was the third?"

"What third? I don't know what you mean?" He answered too quickly, and he failed to hold my gaze. He was hiding something. Or someone, rather.

"Who was the third? Tell me!" I shouted.

"Okay, okay. I thought you knew," he said, turning toward me. "I was broken up with Xenia briefly and so tried Bronislava."

"Bronislava!"

"Yes, I mean, we tried to be partners. And it didn't work. At all. I mean...it was just crazy." He fluttered his hand about and shook his head.

I couldn't believe he and Bronislava had...I guess that explained some of her annoyances with him at the studio.

"And..."

"And what, Rory?"

"Just pro partners? Not any, like, pro/am partners, right?" I said.

"No!" He widened his eyes. "I would never...do that with a student."

I couldn't help but giggle.

"Rory." He was all seriousness. "You are not my student."

"True." I nodded. I still needed to know if he'd used the blindfold before on anyone. "But..."

"But what?" He looked a little distressed. Like he thought I was going to push the student/teacher thing.

It was so clear to me now he wasn't one to break rules. Sam was wrong about him. Whatever had happened in Tokyo must have been really urgent for him to leave like that. "I was just wondering if you've ever used that trick before?"

"Trick?" he asked. He was too busy scrambling his eggs to face me fully, but I could tell he was getting anxious with my line of questioning.

"Not trick. I just mean, have you ever blindfolded anyone else before?"

He turned off the heat and looked me straight on. "Of course not, Rory. That was necessary for you alone."

"Necessary for me alone! I'm not that bad of a follower!" I said, play-smacking him as he sat.

He simply raised his brows in response. The light shined through the window behind him, creating a kind of halo around his gloriously naked torso, highlighting the tattoos on his chest and the front of his arm. I hadn't examined those as much as the large one on his back. The smaller one on his bicep appeared to be some sort of clawed spider. It was black with a blue shell. The one below was a twisting, turning snake colored a fiery red with orange and yellow undertones. The tongue was on the bottom, so it was like the snake was making its way down his arm. I had to concentrate on the one above his left nipple for a moment to realize it was an abstract rendering of a lizard. The body was all black, but had snazzy, triangular cutouts in the middle, and serrated edges. The lizard had a long tail that wrapped all the way around Sasha's pec, though you'd have to be very close to notice that, as the tail was just a thin, curling line.

"More cool tats," I said, pointing to his arm.

"Thank you."

"What is the top one? Some kind of spider?"

"That's a scorpion. Scorpion and snake. Animals of the desert."

"And a small lizard here," I said, tracing the tip of my finger atop its delicate tail.

"Yes, the lizard. That's the first one I got."

"Did you get them here too?"

"Yes."

"Same artist?"

"Yes, same guy."

"He's very good. Did you meet him here or back home?" I ventured, hoping he'd give me some details about his past, where he was from. It was weird that as much as I knew about his professional life, I knew nothing about the personal life of the man I'd just spent the night with.

He paused thoughtfully, then said, "Home is here." He gave a conclusory nod.

*Ugh.* Would I ever get anything out of this man?

"That's great that you feel that way, like you belong. I'm not so sure for myself."

"You're not comfortable here?" Now he regarded me with sweet concern. "Why?"

"I dunno. I guess the traffic makes me nervous. And there's never any place to park. And, I don't know. I'm from a small town but I really liked San Francisco."

"Yes, you don't really have to drive in San Francisco," he said, smiling.

"Yeah, but it's more than that. There was the ballet and the bookstores and cafes."

"We have bookstores and cafes here, and a small ballet company, and many more touring companies who appear at the Walt Disney Music Hall downtown. Breathtaking building." He grinned widely, his dimples taking over his whole face, like a little boy who'd just glimpsed a tiger at the zoo for the very first time. It was clear he genuinely loved his new city.

"Yes, that building is absolutely gorgeous," I agreed. "Well, I'm starting to feel more at peace here," I said, looking around. Sasha's house sure felt homey. "I definitely feel like Hollywood suits me better than the westside, than James's place."

"Yes, well it wasn't your own. It was someone else's idea of where home should be for you, of who you should be."

I thought about that. So true. It was always a given I'd move in with James. Maybe my whole life here thus far was someone else's idea of who I was. I certainly didn't feel very content with my law career.

"Did you feel at home when you first arrived? I'll bet you did."

He nodded. "The second we stepped off the plane."

*We?* "Oh, so your family is here too?"

"What, my family? No," he snapped, his voice raised and his tone now sharp. I saw panic in his eyes. "My family has never been here."

"Oh, I'm sorry. You said 'we' and I just thought…"

"Xenia and I," he said, still snappish. But the panic in his eyes had abated, thankfully.

Okay, rule number one with Sasha: tread very, very carefully when mentioning his family.

"Xenia and I were working in New York and we came out for a visit. When we got here we knew we had to stay and work here."

"That's funny. What made you feel that way?"

"It's just so…American," he said, a glow in his voice. "So sunny, so warm, so much space, so many big houses." He waved his arms about. "Everyone has a car. A new car. Everything's so new. It's the land of movies, and it's like that—a movie. But it's not a movie. It's real life." His dimpled smile oozed boyish charm.

"I bet it's so different from Russia. I mean, especially the sun and heat," I said. His radiance almost immediately dissipated at my mention of that word, Russia. *Jeez.* "I mean, it's certainly different from North Carolina," I quickly added. "The year-round warmth especially, I mean."

But the conversation was over. He got up, pushed his chair in, the legs scraping the floor. "Greta will be here soon. You should finish and then take your shower." He eyed my plate and pushed it toward me.

"Yes, the shower," I said, beginning to rise.

"Rory, energy." He stood right behind me, preventing me from moving my chair.

"Oh. Your cooking was awesome. I promise. I'm just not very hungry. I'm never hungry in the morn—"

"I am serious about the energy," he said, not budging. "Just two more bites, okay? Compromise?"

I pondered telling him I'd compromise by finishing my entire plate if he answered my questions about Russia, but I was honestly scared of how he'd react. I harrumphed and placed another forkful of egg in my mouth. Two more bites wouldn't hurt. He'd seen me very naked, and hadn't had a problem with it. Quite the contrary!

\*\*\*

The shower was a dream. I could lose all my troubles in there. So much endless space. And multiple spigots meant I had warm, soft water enveloping me. It was like a standing bath. Of course I badly wanted to try that bath but that would have to wait. I was in too much of a hurry. He had a stash of beautiful-smelling shampoos, conditioners, soaps, and lotions. The entire bathroom was like a perfumery. He told me to use anything I wanted—there were extra loofah sponges in the cabinet. It was absolute bliss. I really had to force myself to get out.

I had minimal makeup with me—just lipstick and powder. So I wouldn't be as made-up as usual. Well, like Sasha said, Greta wouldn't care, if she even noticed. I sniffed my leotard and skirt. They seemed fine. After all, nothing really happened until they were off! Although the crotch may have been quite damp for more than a few minutes at the start… Well, couldn't worry about it now. I put the thought out of my mind as I stepped through the legs.

I was embarrassed at first in front of Greta, but that went away very quickly thanks to Sasha and his immediate uber-intensity. He and she were both correcting every miniscule detail from the first step of the first syllabus.

"Sasha," she said, her voice admonishing.

"Yes, yes, I know," he said, releasing me and taking a step back.

"What?" I said.

Greta raised her eyebrows and lowered her chin at him. "Sasha has agreed to let only me correct you. Now that you are not his student, you are equal partners. I am the coach. I and I alone am the teacher. I and I alone make the corrections."

Oh my gosh, that sounded so wonderful. It didn't mean he'd never get frustrated, or that her constant corrections wouldn't drive me nuts, but at least he couldn't yell at me for things, like he clearly had with Xenia and Arabelle. I wondered whether it was his or her idea.

"Rory, I want to speak with you alone, if that is okay?" Greta asked at the end of practice. Sasha nodded. The way she said it made me nervous. "Good, walk me to the door." I followed meekly behind her, my stomach filling with butterflies. Once we were outside, she said, "You are following much, much better."

"Seriously?"

"Yes, very seriously," she said. "It doesn't seem like you are overthinking things. You're sensing better what your leader wants. Overthinking and back-leading often go hand in hand." There didn't seem to be any indication she had any inkling of what had happened, so I assumed she didn't. "It also seems to me that you have grown in confidence."

"Really?" I said, even more astounded.

"Yes." She laughed, a bemused look on her face. "It's good because you will need it. That's why I wanted to talk to you alone. He will get more panicked as Blackpool nears, and this will make him harder on you. You will need that confidence to assert yourself, so that you can shine, and not be beaten down by his harshness. As, you know, others have."

I swallowed, and nodded. I didn't know if I had that much self-confidence. Or if I ever would.

# CHAPTER 5

"Feeling better?" Gunther said, eyeing me up and down as he passed my office. His look indicated he knew I hadn't been sick.

"Oh, yes, thank you," I said. "It seems I had a twenty-four-hour flu or something. Feeling so much better today," I babbled as he continued eyeing me over his shoulder.

As I'd foreseen, I hadn't received any serious assignments yesterday. There were only two wills in my inbox. It wasn't like I'd missed a deadline or had anything urgent to do. His dubiousness confused me.

*\*\**

Bronislava's silver-level cha-cha class was an emotional roller coaster for me. All I could think about when I looked at her was that she'd been with my man. She'd seen him as I had and he'd done to her the same things he'd done to me. Well, some of the same things. Obviously not the blindfold. I felt like she could read my thoughts, and could tell I'd been with him too.

When I rotated to her I honestly thought she was going to say something.

"You are so improved, Swan Lake Girl," she said instead. "You've come very far so fast. You should be proud." There was sincerity in her eyes.

I almost wanted to cry. Now I couldn't have any more jealous thoughts toward her.

\*\*\*

It was weird running into Sasha in the studio. I stayed out of his group class, as instructed. Every time I ran into him, he merely gave me a polite nod. It stung a bit, but I understood he wasn't into PDA and didn't need all of his students and colleagues knowing our business. We were professionals, after all.

Sasha had booked me a private coaching with Greta for the same time I'd formerly had my private with him. I arrived a little early and began practicing myself while waiting for Greta. Sasha was with Cheryl in the back room. I noticed her eyes on me. Our gazes connected in the mirror. She smiled smugly and lifted her chin to me, glaring down at me through the slant of space just under her eyelids as if she thought she'd won something. I guess in a way she did: she'd won back her private with Sasha that I'd so unjustly snatched away from her.

But her attitude did a one-eighty after Greta showed up. I concentrated hard the entire time I was with Greta, and didn't have time to take much notice of Cheryl until after our respective sessions had ended.

"How's it going?" Sasha asked Greta after he left the back room and was on his way out of the studio.

Greta raised her brows and nodded, as if I was doing decent. She glanced at Cheryl, then back at Sasha. Cheryl looked confused, and waited, seeming to expect Sasha to leave with her.

"Oh. I'll see you next week," he said to Cheryl, placing his arm gently on her back. "Same time, same place." He flashed her his dimpled smile which, for a fleeting second, made me a bit jealous.

Until I did a reality check.

She softened and smiled back. "Of course," she said then gave me an evil up-and-down look before blinking dramatically and sashaying off.

"I think we made a lot of pro—" Greta began, just as the door opened and in marched Luna, Sadie, Sveta, and about four of Sasha's other Russian students.

They all took positions on the practice floor but their eyes were clearly on us. I wondered if Cheryl had said something to Luna on her way out.

"We'll talk later this week. At my place," Sasha said under his breath, looking between Greta and me. "I'm off for the night," he said, now more loudly, to Greta. He patted her shoulder and walked out.

"I'm behind you," Greta said, following him. "You did well, sweet," she said to me as she dashed away.

I smiled and nodded. But the second the door shut behind her, the atmosphere in the room immediately darkened. I felt several pairs of hostile eyes on me. I grabbed my things and practically ran to the door.

"Ooooh la la, look at you! Taking coaching with the queen!" I heard Paulina's singsong voice on my way out. She'd been practicing cha-cha in the far corner. I'd been so immersed in my lesson and then the ensuing drama involving Sasha and his groupies, I hadn't even noticed her.

Still feeling the weight of stares behind me, I walked toward her, shrugging as if taking lessons with Greta was nothing. I didn't really know what to say. I didn't want to violate any loyalty to Sasha by telling someone in the studio about us, even if it was a friend.

"Girlfriend!" she squealed, cutting me off before I could even say anything. She shook her head in awe and gave me a high five. Her high five was delightfully gentle, given her size.

I didn't know exactly what she was commending me for, but I couldn't help but giggle.

"You are glowing, girl! I've been around the block a few times. Don't try to hide it. You own it! He chose you! And they," she said motioning toward Cheryl, Luna, and the Russians, "they can just…" And with this she raised her fist and crossed it over her other arm in an eff-off motion.

I couldn't help but crack up. We were out of earshot of the others, but they definitely saw her gesture. What would I do without Paulina? Sasha was trying in vain to be so secretive. But could I help it if my passion was written all over my face?

*** 

"Okay, guys, we finally have our first competition date," Ron told the mambo team at practice. The first one was local—in Irvine, on the U.C. campus. It was only a month away. We collectively gasped. We'd now choreographed almost all of the routine but were still getting stuck on the early tricks. All the women were pretty much getting through their guys' legs without teabagging now, though it was still a running joke and hard not to snicker every time we passed through.

But many of us—myself included—were still having problems with this seated spin called a pot stir where you sat in front of the guy holding his hand, balanced on one foot, while he spun you around and you had to spiral upward from sitting to standing position. It was really cool and looked, as its name implied, like the guy was bending over, stirring a pot. But it was blasted hard. It took a lot more upper thigh and core strength than it appeared. If the guy pulled you up with too much haste or power, he could bring you up too early, and he could also hurt your wrist or arm. You had to kind of rise on your own, while lightly holding his hand, and while still spinning like a mad whirling dervish. Judy was the only one getting it perfectly.

"You gotta hold your core really tight on the way from the snake, lifting into the spin and then up. You're leaning over too much, like you're tired," Pepe said. "Are you tired? Are you doing too much?"

"Nope," I insisted. "Let's try it again."

This time, I was so focused on keeping my stomach and core muscles pulled in and tight and upright so I'd be light, that when I snaked through Pepe's legs, I'd made myself too tall and, far from a light teabagging, I smashed my head straight into his groin.

"Sorry, sorry, sorry," I murmured.

"Keep going, keep going," he squeaked, clearly in pain.

I kept hold of his hand, continued passing through his legs, then fell straight onto my butt in front of him. Youch, that hurt my tailbone. I ignored the pain, quickly turned and righted myself and, still in a low, seated position, extended one leg out, balancing on my other, as far forward-weighted on my toes as possible. I tucked my stomach muscles, trying to keep myself as light as possible so he could spin me. But in focusing on keeping my stomach muscles tight, I forgot to curve my outstretched leg, which resulted in me tripping him as my leg helicoptered smack into his ankle.

"Ow," he yowled, this time letting go of me and falling backward. I fell flat on my butt, twisting my knee on the way down. It was just a slight twist but I definitely felt it.

Of course the room broke into hysterical laughter, Ron included.

"*Chica,* f—!" yelled Pepe, trying hard not to curse.

"I'm sorry. I was concentrating so much on my stomach I forgot my foot," I said, out of breath, now collapsed on my back, realizing my knee did kind of hurt a bit.

"Let's try it again," he said, still lying flat on his back.

He finally got up and pulled me up. I felt a bit faint when I was standing. I tried to ignore it. We were definitely having the biggest problem and the rest of the team was depending on us to get it.

When we tried again, I pulled all my muscles in, kept my head down on the way through his legs, and managed to get myself to my toe for spinning, all without incident, though we went through it a bit more slowly than we should have, making us off the beat of the music. As I was spinning and trying to rise, I felt some more knee pain. I tried to ignore it. Once I was straight up and, amazingly, still spinning, the whole room applauded wildly.

"See, you can do it. We all knew you could," Ron said. "Should we try it one more time or move on?"

I grabbed my knee. It didn't hurt when I straightened my leg and put my weight on it, but when I bent my knee I felt the pain. Ron and Pepe both saw me wince.

"Uh-oh," Ron said. "You okay?"

"It's just hurting a little when I bend it. Mind if we move on and leave the pot stir for later when it's had a little rest?" I remembered injuries from ballet. If the pain wasn't really sharp—and this one wasn't—you usually just needed rest and maybe some ice and elevation.

"RICE, *munequita*," Pepe said, reminding me of the acronym instructing what to do in case of a sports injury. "Rest, ice, compression, elevation. It's probably just sore. But do the ice and elevation tonight, anyway. You never know."

"Wear a bandage for the next few days, anyway. To be a dancer is to be permanently sore. But if you start to feel a sharp, shooting pain, they can recommend a doctor at the front desk," Ron said.

Ugh, it had better not be that bad, I thought. I had no time for an injury. Not with Blackpool on the horizon.

After the trick with the snake leading into the pot stir leading into the crazy standing spins, the choreography had a section of basics whose main purpose was to give us the chance to rest before the next set of tricks. My knee didn't hurt the rest of practice, which made me hope I wasn't injured and it was only sore. But I did continue to feel weaker and even a bit lightheaded. I had no idea what that was about. After practice ended, I made it down to the lobby with my things and then had to crash on the sofa before walking home. I was a little embarrassed when the receptionist told me they were closing and asked me if I'd be okay getting home.

"Of course," I said with a laugh. I took a huge slug of water, and picked myself up off the comfy sofa. Fortunately, there were some benches on the sidewalks and I was able to take a couple of little rests on my way home. I'd downed three-quarters of my water bottle before I arrived at my building's outer gate. As soon as I got myself up my steps and through my door, I crashed on my living room sofa. My heartbeat was faster than usual. I took several breaths and finished my water. Soon, it went back to normal. That was scary.

When I felt up to it, I got up and poured myself a large glass of fresh-squeezed orange juice—the only type of juice I'd heard had no added sugars. I also wrapped some ice cubes in a towel and held them over my knee, though it was no longer hurting. Or maybe I was just focused on something other than that pain.

I got up a little later to turn on the TV, and then a little later to make myself a mini quesadilla. The nausea continued but every time I got up I felt it a little less. I knew I was watching what I ate but I was still ingesting nutrients and calories. I went to bed early, with my knee propped up under a pillow, hoping the nausea would be completely gone by morning.

When I woke up the next morning, I had no knee pain. But then I tried several times to do a deep knee bend, putting myself in the position of the pot stir. Then it would sting. I guess I'd have to take it easy on the pot stirs for a little while. But if I'd really damaged a ligament or tendon, it should always be painful, I thought.

The nausea was all gone—at least while I took a shower and dressed, and ate my handful of strawberries for breakfast. But once I was on the subway, standing, I suddenly felt like I had to sit. I didn't want to bother anyone; I was far too young—and non-pregnant!—to be asking anyone for their seat. So I just held on to the bar above the seats. When I got to work, I practically fell into my chair. I could feel that my forehead was covered in sweat.

I called my doctor to make an appointment, mainly to make sure my knee was just sore and not injured. Once I tacked on my feelings of nausea and lightheadedness, she told me to come in right away. Fortunately, my doctor's office was on the Red Line as well, so I wasn't screwed by not having my car.

\*\*\*

"You've lost fifteen pounds since I last saw you and that was only…four months ago," the doctor said, checking my chart. "You only weighed a hundred and twenty to begin with, so your BMI is now a little below normal. Not much, but a little." She looked concerned.

"Really? You're kidding." It certainly didn't feel like I'd lost any weight.

"You haven't noticed it? Haven't your clothes been feeling different?"

I shook my head.

"What did you eat yesterday?" she asked.

I told her about the quesadilla, the orange juice, the apple half and cup of low-fat cottage cheese I had before team practice.

"Okay, and today?"

"Um, five strawberries."

"That's all?" She frowned.

"Um, a bottle of Evian?" I added more as a question than statement.

"That's all?" She sounded a bit shocked. I didn't say anything. "That's not enough, Rory. You realize that, right?"

I didn't like the way she was looking at me—her deepening frown. It reminded me of the doctor my mom took me to right before she permanently pulled me out of the dance program at North Carolina School of the Arts. She was so judgmental. She had this way of looking me up and down like my body was diseased, like I was a leper. The doctor picked up my file and began flipping through it.

"Okay, I'll eat more," I finally said. "Can you look at my knee, too. That's what I'm more worried about."

She continued reading my file for a few more minutes, then looked up at me. "Of course I'll look at your knee. The thing is, if you're dancing a lot and your body isn't getting adequate nutrition, you're making yourself more susceptible to injury."

I knew that. I'd forgotten. But should have remembered.

She rose and walked toward me. She asked me to straighten my leg, then bend it, and show her where it hurt.

"It's actually easier if I just do the pot stir," I said. "It's harder to feel it when I'm just sitting."

"I'm sorry? You feel it when you're stirring a pot of stew?"

"No!" I laughed. "It's a dance move." I stood, squatted into a deep-seated position, then lifted one foot off the floor and rose on my grounded foot as close to my toe as possible. "It hurts right here," I said, pointing to the spot of the pain.

"Oh, goodness," she said, now with a bemused look. "Well, yes, I see where you're pointing. That's a really unnatural position. That's not good for your knees. It wouldn't be good for anyone's knees. I recommend not doing it." She said this with a firm, curt nod, as if this solution would easily solve my problem.

"But I have to do it. It's a step in the choreography. For our team competition. I can't be the only one not doing it."

She continued to look at me like I was speaking in another language. Like I was being completely illogical.

"I need to know how I can best prevent injury, given that I must do this step," I said, trying to sound as sensible as possible.

"Stand up," she said. When I did so, she felt around my knee.

There was no sharp, shooting pain but there was definitely a dull ache. "Ow, it's a little sore there."

"Well," she said, shaking her head. "I think you just have some stress there, for right now. But you could tear your meniscus. In which case, you wouldn't even be able to straighten your knee completely. And you'd be in a lot of pain."

"Is there a way to protect myself?" I asked, feeling like I was repeating myself.

"Well, not really. Honestly, I would do that step as little as possible, and when you do practice it, wrap your knee tightly in an Ace bandage. Tell your teacher I told you this—you're not to do that step any more often than is absolutely necessary. If it gets worse, I'll have to send you to an orthopedist. And he's going to demand you stop. Let's try not to get to that point."

"Okay, thanks," I said, getting up and reaching for my bag on the side chair.

"Hold on a second," she said. "I just want to ask you some more questions."

I knew she wanted to talk about my prior eating disorder. I so didn't want to go there. I sat back down on the examination table, but clutching my bag. "I should get back to work soon," I said.

"How long have you been ballroom dancing?" she said, ignoring me.

"A few months." I shrugged.

"And when did you stop your healthy eating habits? Around the same time?"

She looked up at me when I didn't answer. I didn't believe I wasn't eating healthy. Low-fat foods, fresh fruits and vegetable were not unhealthy.

"Rory, when you first filled out your questionnaire, you admitted you'd had an eating disorder in childhood. When I questioned you about it then, you said it was related to ballet. Do you think it's returned now that you've picked up dance again?"

I looked down at the floor. It was squeaky clean. I could see the reflection of the light above me.

"No, it's under control. I'm eating healthy food," I said, still looking at the reflection of the light on the floor.

I heard her typing something on the computer. Then there was silence. I could feel her looking at me.

"I think I just lost weight because I suddenly started exercising so much again. It's the most I've moved since starting law school."

She shook her head. "But your diet is way too slight."

"Okay. I'll eat more," I finally conceded, after what seemed like several minutes. "Of the same healthy foods."

She looked very serious, and somewhat dubious. "I'd like to see you back in a month."

This exchange was feeling a little too déjà vu. Was my problem really back? Was I really not eating adequately?

"On your way out, stop by the nurse's station. She'll give you a nutritional guideline. And yes, you are eating healthy foods. And that's good. You just need to eat more of them," she said with a firm nod.

\*\*\*

"Uh-oh," Pepe said upon seeing me in mambo class that night with the Ace bandage wrapped tightly around my right knee. "How bad is it, *dulzura?*"

I laughed to myself. *This one and his names!* Someday I'd have to ask him what they all meant.

"Not very," I said. "Doctor wants me to be careful when I do the pot stir; she actually said not to do it too often. There's no damage yet but it's weak, so I really have to be careful. There won't be too many other pot stirs in the routine, right?"

"That's the only one." He laughed.

I laughed along with him, but I couldn't stop thinking of how pissed Sasha would be if I really did injure myself right now. I had to be careful.

# CHAPTER 6

On my way home from the studio, I received a somewhat cryptic voicemail from Sasha.

"Hi, Rory," he said. The man's deep voice still made me quiver. "I'm between private lessons now and have to be brief, but I don't want you to have your coachings with Greta in the studio anymore. So we're going to do them all at my house. Even the ones you have with her alone when I'm unavailable. You have one scheduled with her tomorrow at seven. I'm hoping you can drive up to my house by then. I'll give you your own key when I see you tonight."

My heart skipped several beats. *My own key to that mansion!*

I wasn't sure how it was all going to work because I was going to go to Bronislava's class at the studio from six to seven, and then Mitsi's social salsa from eight to nine, before coming home and waiting for Sasha to pick me up for our practice. Now it seemed silly to be going back and forth between his house and the studio all night. Hmmm, maybe I'd just stay there and rest my knee in that hot tub!

I knew he had a lesson so I texted him back a simple message.

*Perfect. I'll see Greta at 7 tomorrow at your place.*

We could talk about studio logistics when I saw him. My lower belly began aching just thinking about being in his arms again. But we were not going to get carried away any more this week. I didn't want to miss any more work. The weekend was almost here anyway!

\*\*\*

It was a roller coaster of a day at work, to put it mildly. I spent the first three-quarters with absolutely nothing to do. I asked all the partners if they needed any research, any deposition summaries, any wills drafted. But no one had anything and each told me to ask the others, as they were sure the others had something. I sat at my desk staring at my computer, worried about how I was going to account on my hours sheet for the day, and possibly for the next if the work drought continued.

It turned out I had nothing to worry about. At least hours-wise. At about four o'clock, Gunther crashed into my office and dropped a box on my desk.

"The next pro bono criminal case assigned to me. And I need your help. We just got reassigned because the public defender's office is representing his co-defendant. So it's a conflict of interest. This one's serious, Rory. Guy's accused of standing lookout while two of his friends robbed a check-cashing place. They ended up killing all of the people inside—the store owner and a security guard, who was an off-duty police officer. D.A.'s seeking the death penalty for the two who went inside and shot up the place. They haven't decided on our guy yet. They believed him to be the ringleader, a person with the ability to get others to do his dirty work for him. Anyway, I need you to stay and read over his entire file tonight. I'll let you know what I need tomorrow."

My heart momentarily stopped at the possibility of a death penalty case. This job was downright bipolar. Weeks upon weeks of boring, trivial assignments—besides that insanely stressful Warren case. And now the most serious it could possibly get. I caught my breath and began flipping through the file papers. Most of the records were of the co-defendants. Our client had no criminal record. No convictions, no arrests, nothing. There was hardly any casework on our guy at all. There were three videotapes, each marked "Statement to D.A." followed by a different co-defendant's name.

*Crap.* I looked at my phone. It was already past six. For once I'd been so engrossed in work I'd actually lost track of the time. I'd never be able to subway to Hollywood, walk home, and drive up to Sasha's by seven. Plus, I was nowhere near finished going through all the paperwork in the file. And it looked like each videotaped statement was over an hour long. Gunther had made it clear I needed to go through everything—or most of it, anyway—before I left tonight. Maybe I should just clarify.

I walked down to his office. He had his head down on his desk, every square inch of which was covered in paperwork. I'd simply lifted my fist to knock on his door when he blurted out, "Rory, I really need you to stay tonight until you've gone through it all. We need to see him tomorrow and I need you to prep me on what's in the file. I need you to know everything."

Okay, I thought, wondering how he always knew I was hovering at his door without actually seeing me. Uncanny, bordering on the creepy.

"Okay, I will," I said and walked briskly back to my office, unnerved.

Well, that would have to be that. No group classes, no seeing my friends at the studio. No seeing Sasha at the end of the night. I felt deflated. At least it was almost the weekend.

I decided my late cancellation required both a voicemail and text message to Sasha. I apologized profusely in both, promising, in my sexiest, most vixenish voice possible that I'd more than make it up to him over the weekend. I wasn't kidding myself, though. I knew how upset he'd be.

I read through the entire case file. Gunther's new client's name was Jamar Jackson and he was sixteen, just old enough to be tried as an adult. Police found him outside a check-cashing store in Watts at four in the morning. The store had just been burglarized and two men were found shot to death inside. When police tried to stop Jamar and question him, he took off running. They gave chase, caught him, and brought him to the precinct where he was identified in a lineup by a woman who owned a restaurant across the street. She told police she'd seen him walking by and checking inside the store on numerous occasions. Two of his friends, one of whom confessed to the shooting, were arrested that night as well. They claimed Jamar was the ringleader, having planned the whole thing and convincing them to do his dirty work while he merely stood lookout outside. He told them to take all the money, and they'd evenly divide it. He'd promised them there would be about twenty thousand apiece. He warned them to leave no witnesses. After eleven hours of interrogation, Jamar confessed.

I opened the box containing all of the defendants' videotaped confessions. None of their interrogations had been videotaped, unfortunately, so I couldn't see the police questioning, only the ultimate statements they made.

I watched the videos, starting with the co-defendants.

Wilton Simms, aka Bullet, was twenty-two, the oldest of the three. My first thought was, what was he doing hanging out with a sixteen-year-old? Simms was tall and thin and wore his hair in long cornrows. He seemed smug and self-righteous. He held his chin up and looked down at the assistant district attorney as she questioned him. He kept yawning every time she asked a question, but not as if he was tired; more like he was bored with her and her silly questions. She practically had to plead with him to get him to answer, asking him throughout if he'd like the officers to get him anything from McDonald's, or candy from the CVS down the street. Three cheeseburgers, four Cokes, and two packs of Twizzlers later, he confessed to pulling the trigger of his semi-automatic Sig Sauer straight into the foreheads of first the store's owner, then the security guard, but not before making them beg for their lives. It made me so sick to my stomach I thought I might actually throw up when he described, in smug detail, how the security guard cried and asked him to consider his two young children and wife. I had to turn off the video and gather my emotions. Without knocking, Gunther opened my office door, startling me. I jumped. I hated it when he did that.

"Damn, calm down, Rory. I just came to ask you for a description of the confessions."

I shook my head. "I'm watching them now. Should be done soon," I managed to say, hoping my voice wasn't too shaky. I certainly didn't want to appear like I couldn't handle a disturbing case.

He sighed and shook his head. "By eleven?"

I looked at the clock. Crap, it was getting late. We really were going to be here all night. I nodded, a little worried about how I'd get home since the subway stopped running at eleven p.m. on weeknights. I could call Sasha, or Rajiv, if Sasha was too mad. I guess I could always stay over at the office if Gunther wanted more work.

Like clockwork, my phone dinged that I had a message. It was from Sasha.

*I'm very sorry you couldn't make it. We will have to make it up. Don't work there too late. Downtown isn't safe late at night. Call me when you are finished.*

Ugh, I couldn't really read his tone. Yes, I'd make it up with him, of course. He had to understand though, this was my job. I texted him back.

*Thank you for understanding :) I will let you know when I'm leaving.*

*Before you are ready to leave. I am coming to pick you up,* he wrote back.

*Ok. That's nice :)*

Ugh, could I stop it with the smiley faces? Childish, I knew. I was just trying to be as sweet as possible. I was a little worried this case would mean I'd have to miss more practices. Why did work have to get crazy right now?

The other co-defendant, Roberto Jimenez, was a small, thin man, also twenty-two. These two were in their twenties and their sixteen-year-old friend was the ringleader? His manner was very straightforward. He spoke quickly and his voice was strong. It was almost as if his story was rehearsed. He said their friend's younger brother, Jamar, often passed the check-cashing store on his way home from the McDonald's where he went every day for his meals. Jamar had told them security in the store was often lax, especially at night, and it would be an easy target with high monetary yield. Jamar's older brother was currently serving a long prison term for murder. Jamar supplied Simms with the gun, which had belonged to his brother. Jamar ordered him to kill the store owner. They hadn't expected to have to kill the security guard as well. Jimenez showed no emotion whatsoever as he described in detail Simms pulling the trigger two times. It made me feel sick all over again, both the act of murder and how someone could be completely apathetic toward two deaths.

I popped in the third video. The first thing that surprised me was Jamar's physicality. Though the youngest of the three, he was by far the biggest, and he looked a good five years older than he was, easily. He was tall and at least thirty pounds overweight, with a heavy brow that made him mean-looking, like he had a permanent deep frown. He had wide-set eyes, and close-cropped hair. He, like Simms, was black; Jimenez was black/Hispanic. He spoke very slowly and hesitantly, as if he had to think hard after every question the assistant district attorney asked. He seemed continually confused, which could have been a function of the look of that heavy brow. But he really did seem to keep forgetting details. Despite his size and initially fearful demeanor, the female D.A. had a stronger personality than he. Unlike with the other two—particularly Simms—she clearly had the upper hand here. She spoke in a loud voice that intimidated even me, and had an impatient, demanding, often condescending tone. Jamar sat slumped over, his gaze concentrated on the floor.

"You told me you cased the store on Monday, Tuesday, Friday, Saturday and Sunday of the prior week, right?"

"Case?" he said slowly.

"You've been over this with the two detectives many, many times and me once, Mr. Jackson. You agreed to tell me on video what you just told me, did you not?"

"Y-yes?" he answered more as a question than a statement.

"So why are you withholding from me now? Huh?"

He shook his head and continued frowning. "Withholding? ...I..."

"Come on, snap out of it, Jamar," she said snapping her fingers in his face. "How much longer are we going to have to be here?"

He shook his head slowly, looking both confused and defeated.

"Were you casing the place on all of those days I just mentioned?" She harrumphed loudly and threw her hand up. "Did you pass by the check-cashing store and look inside on those occasions?"

He appeared to be thinking. "Ye-yes, I passed the store and looked at it," he then said very slowly. He talked slowly and loudly, trying to enunciate words even though his diction was slurred. It sounded as if he was talking with cotton in his mouth.

"Okay, and you were looking inside in anticipation of robbing the store later in the week, right? Isn't that what you told the detectives and me earlier?"

He looked confused and his eyes began darting back and forth between her and someone off camera.

"Mr. Jackson, please. I have your signed statement in writing right here." She waved a piece of paper around in the air. She was nearly shouting.

"Wha…yeah, yes, that's what, I did," he said, now stuttering. "Yes, casing," he continued as if he'd just remembered the word. His eyes began to look a little glassy.

His entire confession was like this, with him either giving her a hard time on purpose or genuinely not really understanding what was going on. It was difficult to tell if he was pretending to be daft, as she apparently thought, or if he really wasn't all there. His speech was slurred. I wondered if he had some kind of mental impediment. Or maybe his hearing was weak. He spoke the same way as a cousin of mine who'd been hard of hearing since birth.

Instead of being sick as I'd been with the first two defendants, I became curious and intrigued with Jamar. I played the video a second time, filling a notebook with potential questions for Gunther to ask the police who'd interrogated Jamar at the hearing.

He seemed particularly confused when the assistant D.A. read him his Miranda rights, about his right to remain silent and have an attorney and all. He even got stuck on the word "waive."

"I wave…at rights?"

She nearly threw the paperwork at him. "You've already waived all your rights to officers Donnelly and

Braggs. I have your signature right here. Stop playing stupid!"

But was he playing? And who did he keep looking at off camera, I wondered? I flipped through his file to see if there was any history of his IQ or mention of him being in any way mentally handicapped. Nothing. He had no prior arrests or convictions so there was very little paperwork on him. Perhaps no one had ever bothered to check him for that. He'd never gone to high school. There were no grade school records in his file.

I looked through the case file for a parent or relative's phone number. There was one listed, for his mother. Excitedly, I went to dial it and then realized the time. I put a note in the file to call tomorrow. As Jimenez had said, Jamar had an older brother who was serving a ten- to twenty-year prison sentence for homicide.

Unlike Jamar, Jimenez and Simms had priors up the wazoo. Jimenez had a string of drug sale convictions, two for weapon possession, and one for a first degree assault in which the victim almost died. Simms had one conviction for aggravated assault, one for manslaughter, and pages of priors for weapon possession. That alone made it unlikely, to me anyway, that Jamar supplied him with the gun.

Again, Gunther burst into my room and made me jump in my chair.

"I finished and I have some—" I began, waving my notebook full of questions in the air.

"Yeah, I just stopped in to tell you I'm leaving for the night. You took too long. We'll do it in the morning. See you bright and early, Rory." With that he slammed the door shut. I looked at the clock. It was only ten forty-five. I thought he'd told me to be done by eleven.

\*\*\*

Sasha texted me when he was downstairs, as we'd agreed he would. I elevatored down. He was the only one in the lobby, save the security guard. I was glad to see him. I would have been nervous going home alone this late. He looked tantalizing. He wore jeans, black boots and a black leather jacket. I realized I'd hardly ever seen him in street clothes before. His hair was mussed about, his waves flying wildly around his face.

He didn't smile upon seeing me and I was worried he was still mad about the missed practice. But when he held his arms out and embraced me when I reached him, I knew it would all be okay. He kissed my forehead.

"Thanks for picking me up."

He harrumphed. "I don't ever want you leaving here alone this late at night, Rory."

I giggled at the commanding sound of his voice.

We walked, his arm around me, out to the lot. As he opened the car door to let me in, I suddenly had an eerie feeling we were being watched. I looked around. There were cars sparsely parked in that lot, and the one across the street, but I couldn't see if there were any people inside. I didn't see anyone standing around.

"What's wrong?" he asked.

"Nothing," I said, feeling stupid. I was sure it was nothing.

I told him about my case on the way home, about how I felt like my client might be mentally handicapped, and quite possibly have been set up by those boys and be totally innocent.

Sasha nodded throughout. "This is a big case," he said. "Very important. Like John Grisham."

I laughed. "Yeah, it's true. I've had mostly crap, until now."

"It's good that you like...no, that you..." He seemed to struggle for a word, for once. "That you see the humanity in your clients, Rory. You don't judge. You look deeply. You trust."

Hmmm, no one had ever said anything like that to me before.

As much as I wanted to ask him in, I knew I needed to get to sleep and get up early. He made it clear he thought the same.

"It's late. Let me give you the code to turn off the alarm tomorrow night. For now I will deactivate it. Here is a remote for the security gate, and the keys." Ooh that's right, he was giving me the keys to his kingdom! "You get a good night's sleep," he continued. I will see you tomorrow night after your private with Greta, and we will prrrractice very, very hard," he said, giving my cheek a deliciously delicate little peck.

*** 

I got to work extra early and gathered my notes so they'd be ready for Gunther. As soon as he walked in, I followed him down to his office.

"Let me just get in and settled, Rory," he said to me, clearly annoyed.

I just couldn't figure out how to please this man.

"Okay, um, do you want me to come back? I just wanted to give you my notes on the videotaped statements."

He sat and turned on his computer, frowning. Without answering, he looked around his desk. He shook his head as if shaking off some frustration, then looked at me. "Forget about that case for today. I need you to research something else for me."

Excuse me? I felt like saying. "Oh. Sure," I said instead.

"I'll come down in a few. Go work on some wills or whatever."

"Um, okay. Here are my notes, anyway," I said, a bit stunned. I handed him the notebook filled with questions for the police to be asked at Jamar's hearing. He didn't take it. "I think Jamar may have been taken advantage of by his older co-defendants and I think he may even be mentally slow."

"Rory, a lot of these people are mentally slow. That's not going to go anywhere." He rolled his eyes.

*A lot of these people?* I wondered what he meant by that.

"But never mind that right now. Keep that," he said, eyeing the notebook. "This is more important." He waved his hand at me as if to shoo me out, along with my silly notes.

I slowly got up and walked out. His gaze remained focused on his computer. I began to wonder if he was testing me. Or if he was bipolar.

So, after working until eleven last night, getting what I thought was urgent work done, I now sat still, with that urgent work on my desk, with nothing to do. Two hours went by and still nothing. I asked the other partners, but Wills Guy didn't even have anything for me.

Finally, Gunter called my name from his office down the hall.

"Yes, I'm coming," I answered, grabbing my notebook.

My mind was aflutter, having been so totally absorbed in Jamar's case and having to suddenly switch gears. He rattled off my new research assignment, for a totally different case, at lightning speed. I wrote as fast as I could, hoping I could read my scribbles.

"Good. End of day?" he said when I got up.

I glanced at the clock. I didn't know how long this would take me.

"Ahhh…"

"Great," he said, shooing me out again.

I tried to work as fast as I could on the research assignment he'd given me, skipping lunch. But it was hopeless. As boring as this assignment was, compared to Jamar's case, the case law was ridiculously complicated, as decisions even within the same court seemed to go back and forth, sometimes completely contradicting each other. I'd easily be here till nine, which was when I was supposed to meet Sasha, and two hours after I was supposed to have my lesson with Greta. Ugh. I texted Sasha that I was humongously sorry but had to miss my seven p.m. with Greta and may be a little late meeting him.

At seven I could see Gunther's light still on down the hall. I sauntered down. I tapped on the door and he lifted his head.

"Done?" he asked hopefully.

"Um, no. The case law is pretty complicated. Could I take the assignment home with me over the weekend, give it to you first thing Monday morning?"

"Rory, no. I need it tonight. I thought I made that clear." Panic inundated his words. I wasn't sure why he needed it before a Saturday morning, but I didn't ask.

"Okay, okay, I'll have it to you ASAP," I said, hotfooting it back out of his room and down the hall. I texted Sasha that I was still working and would probably have to be a bit late for him, then read and typed as fast as I possibly could.

A bit late turned into way late, as in too late to practice at all. It ended up taking me until eleven to finish the assignment. Gunther stayed and waited, insisting he needed it before either of us left. I could have just flubbed it and not included all the cases, but I could never do such a thing. I could never hand in something that wasn't my best work product.

I'm sure Sasha understood that, silent as he was on the drive home. Of course he insisted on picking me up again, even though the subway ran late on Friday nights. He nodded throughout my defensive explanation, and at one point even said, "Don't worry, Rory. It's work. I understand."

But his disappointment was palpable. And I felt doubly bad because we wouldn't be able to practice Saturday either, since he had privates all day and at night had already committed to doing a show dance with Xenia at a chi-chi Beverly Hills function. He'd tried to book another private for me with Greta over the weekend but she had a rare booking in San Diego.

"Rest up tomorrow," he said, giving me a light peck on the lips in front of my apartment door. Again, I wanted badly to invite him in, and again I was so tired it took all of my mental faculties just to get the key in the lock. "I will need you to be in top form mentally and physically for Sunday."

I nodded.

"And Rory," he called out right before I shut the door.

I opened it again and peeked out.

"Please eat well," he said.

I hadn't told him about what the doctor had said about my eating disorder returning, or about the mishap with my knee, particularly since both seemed under control. I didn't want to worry him. But it was like he knew.

# CHAPTER 7

Team practice Sunday was getting high-charged. We'd finally finished our routine. Now it was a matter of memorizing it and all of us getting the footwork perfectly in sync, Rockettes-like, the formations in proper order, the technique as perfect as could be. And yes, ironing out those tricky tricks that led to embarrassing accidents like teabagging.

Our first competition was right around the corner now and people were getting nervous—particularly Roxy, who was now complaining ad nauseam that her partner was constantly off, and Lilly, who I was coming to realize was high-strung, driven, and therefore always hysterically worried she wouldn't be good enough. But of course that seemed to pay off. She placed well in her own pro/am comps.

Making everything all the more fun, Ron announced that Mitsi was joining as co-coach! She watched as we made our rather sorry attempt to go through the entire choreography at once. There were several places where the majority of the couples totally forgot the routine. I was lucky since I was mainly partnered with Pepe, who obviously knew everything well. But there was one point where the ladies switched partners and rotated down a line, dancing with each man. At that point, I realized why I'd constantly heard screams of "crap" "shit" "what the f—" "ouch, other direction, other direction" "that was my little toe, now I'm crippled" "ow, my wrist, wrong turn" etc., etc., etc. throughout the routine thus far. None of the men, besides Pepe, remembered the entire choreography, which meant if the women didn't put up a fight and back-lead, we'd be totally out of sync and off our marks when we went to do the formation.

Which was exactly what happened. When Larry released me and I was supposed to rotate back to Pepe, he was nowhere near me. Larry had me too far away.

"What the...Rory?" he called out, holding his arm toward me.

I had to jet across the room to reach him. Roxy had to do the same to Enrique. We were each trying hard to get to our men so we could be on time for the formation, and didn't see each other. Of course we ran smack into each other in the center of the floor, both of us falling down. The group was to end in a long diagonal with men lifting the ladies waist-high, the ladies in a split. Paulo and Judy were the only couple who actually ended as such and they were at the very front of the room, not at all where they were supposed to be in formation. I ended the routine flat on my behind to their left. Roxy ended up likewise but off to the right, as if we, the two fallen ladies, were framing them. Lilly and Larry were diagonally behind them— Lilly with one leg on the ground, one leg in Larry's hand, wobbling on her standing toe, on the verge of falling. Pepe and Enrique were on opposite corners of the room, staring at their fallen partners in disbelief.

"Oh my gosh, are you two okay?" Mitsi asked.

You could tell she was trying to sound as concerned as possible but the extreme shakiness of her voice revealed she was having a damn hard time not bursting out in laughter. Ron didn't even bother trying to hide his. Mitsi covered her mouth as he fell to the floor guffawing.

"Wait a minute, wait, wait," Ron yelled, now bolting up and running toward his bag. "I've got to get a picture of this. This is too good! Everyone stay right where you are!"

He returned, commanding Pepe to look at me again in disbelief as he was when the music ended, then snapped several pictures. Mitsi was now propping herself against the back wall, cracking up.

Glad we could be of amusement, I thought as I eyed Roxy next to me. She looked as flummoxed as I felt.

"Okay," Ron said, recovering. "Let's do it again. And I think this time, maybe I should call out the steps."

When I got up, I realized that when I'd landed, it was on the side of my bad knee, which was now more than a little sore again, after doing the pot stir then crashing.

"Just a sec," I said, jogging over to my bag where I grabbed the Ace bandage and wrapped it up tightly. I should have had the bandage on to begin with but...my bad.

This go-around began better—Ron calling out the steps definitely helped. Still, poor Enrique tried to turn Roxy the wrong way, causing her to erupt.

"I swear, he's going to rip my wrist right off!"

"No he's not. I have faith in the strength of your wrist, Rox. Just keep going," Ron boomed over the music.

But then it was my turn to screw things up. On the pot stir I got nervous and held my knee in an attempt to further stabilize it—just to make sure I didn't hurt it more. That put me a slight bit off balance, but it was enough to worry me and make me change shape, again ever so slightly, but enough to majorly teabag Pepe big time on my way through his legs.

"Ah, f—" he howled.

As loudly as the music was playing I could hear Mitsi and Ron screaming with laughter.

"I'm sorry, I'm so sorry," I said, trying to still slither sexily around his leg and wind up in front of him on the right beat.

"It's okay," he said under his breath. "Come on."

He reached out for me, pulling me up in time with the music. But Ron was laughing so hard he forgot to call out the next few steps and our first formation got screwed up.

So, we stopped and started over again.

We went through the routine a couple more times, each time getting ever-so-slightly better, though the improvements we needed to make were nothing short of gargantuan, especially since Ron couldn't be calling out our steps during the actual competition.

"Before you all leave, Mitsi's got something for ya," Ron said.

"You guys, the competition is only weeks away, so next week we wanted to take you all to the designer for the costumes. Start thinking about what you want to wear so we can give the designer the details. We're thinking red or black or a combination. And I was thinking halter tops and either skirts or pants for the ladies, at least part of it fringed, so it shimmies when you move! Problem with that kind of costume, though, is, everyone's got to move at exactly the same speed in the exact same direction at the exact same time."

"Ha, like that's going to happen," Roxy said under her breath.

"Also, we want you to perform at the next end-of-month party. That'll give us about three weeks to iron out all the kinks before we perform this in competition. We're busing everyone down to Irvine. So make sure you tell everyone you know at the studio and every other studio, all of your friends and family, so they can go down there with us and cheer us on. We're going to need it!"

I'd never had anything custom-made for me before. That would be exciting! But I was not so keen on performing in front of our studio. If I made any mistakes, ugh, how Cheryl and Luna would gloat. And how stupid would I feel if I smashed into Pepe's crotch?

*** 

My heart nearly bounded out of my chest that night as I heard Sasha's footsteps approaching my door. I'd waited far too long for a whole evening with him! I opened the door to that same playfully sexy smile that immediately flooded my nether regions with liquid heat. But his eyes went directly to the bandage on my knee.

"What happened?" he said, voice falling.

"It just gets sore when I do a pot stir—a move we do on the team. I guess I'm kind of at a weird angle when I sit and spin so I get some pain there sometimes. I went to a doctor and she said it was okay, the meniscus wasn't torn or anything, but I have to be careful on that move so that I won't hurt it further. Oh, and then I smacked into another girl in practice today and fell on it, which made it worse." I couldn't help but laugh, remembering how ridiculous we all looked in the photo Ron took of us. "It was actually pretty funny. You should have seen us," I said.

But he didn't laugh with me.

"The doctor just told me to wrap it up and it should be fine," I added, nodding assuredly.

He raised his eyebrows and looked out the window. I could see the worry in his eyes. "Rory, please be careful. Please take care of yourself. As dancer, you must take pains to keep yourself healthy. One little thing can damage entire career."

He wasn't playing around. His broken English and his demeanor clearly indicated that. I knew he was right, and it kind of shamed me.

*I should take better care of myself.*

Still, I'd had fun laughing at myself and even being laughed at on the team. It was important to let loose and have a good time with this. Pepe was so happy and carefree and Sasha was sheer seriousness. They were night and day.

He remained annoyingly sober all the way up to his house. I desperately wanted his wily smile to return.

"Is something wrong?" I asked.

He breathed hard. "No, nothing wrong. You just have to take injuries and potential injuries more seriously. They're no laughing matter. They can destroy a dance career."

"I know, I know. Message received," I said, play-slapping him. His lips curled up ever so slightly at the edges. Finally, he was coming out of it. I couldn't believe how much my "pot stir knee" had spoiled his mood. "And 'no laughing matter'—your Americanisms crack me up!" I giggled, trying to get us off the topic of my blasted knee.

At this, he breathed hard and turned his head slightly away from me. He wasn't smiling.

"I find it very sexy," I added, stroking his bare, iron-hard bicep lightly with my fingernails. "I mean, not so much the words themselves but that you learned them and made them part of your vocabulary. You're a fast learner."

He said nothing but his eyes softened and his mouth turned up ever so slightly more at the edges.

*** 

"Rory, you're back-leading again," Sasha said, a clear note of annoyance in his tone.

We were back on his studio floor, and he'd stopped me mid-turn. We'd been doing the same set of steps for a while, so I guess I'd gotten used to this pattern. I began to explain that to him but he immediately shook his head, eyes pouncing on mine.

"That's a non-sequitur, no excuse."

I almost fell over. I barely knew that word. "How long have you been here?"

"What?" His eyes fluttered in confusion. "I bought this house about three years ago. Why?"

"No, I mean in the country. How do you have a better vocabulary than mine?"

He rolled his eyes at the suggestion, then exhaled in frustration. "Five years. Look, Rory, it doesn't matter if we are doing the same steps. You are anticipating and moving my arms and stepping without me guiding you. You are basically dancing on your own, not with me."

"Okay, I'll try not to anticipate," I said, abandoning my attempt to alter the focus of the conversation and find out more about my mystery man. "I'll try to read your mind again." I closed my eyes. "I mean your body," I said when he made no movement toward me. "Do we need to get the blindfold again?" I opened my eyes and squinted at him.

He twisted his mouth and that wicked grin flashed in his eyes. But unfortunately it was only a flash. "Rory, we need to be serious right now. You need stronger frame. That is part of the problem of why you can't read my signals. I'm seeing that now. You're all loose arms. Look." He flailed about like a bird. "See, loosey goosey."

"I wasn't doing that," I countered.

"Try again."

I took a breath. "Fine."

"Now you're too tight." He sighed and let go. "You have to resist but not too much."

He sounded exasperated, and he was making me nervous. We tried again, but almost immediately he stopped and released my hand.

"I'm trying, Sasha," I wailed. I couldn't believe this was the same man I'd slept with only a few days ago. He really did have two personalities. "Hey, didn't you and Greta agree that only she could criticize me?"

"Yes, but now we are too far behind. We have too much catch-up to do and she isn't here. We can't always wait for her. You have to learn."

He walked away from me to the patio door, where he opened the curtain a few inches and looked out. He shook his head and took several deep breaths before turning back around to me. When he did so, he blinked hard, then ran his fingers slowly through his hair.

"I'm trying," I said again, my voice cracking.

He nodded. "I know." Although he didn't smile, it made me feel better that he recognized my attempts. He walked to the iPod and changed the music. "Maybe we will wait for Greta to help with the connection," he said, turning back to me.

Whoa, was he actually conceding?

"Let's work on jive. We'll do side-by-sides that don't involve a connection. We need to get you up to speed on that dance. You are not fast enough. Yet," he added, walking back to me, while the iPod began blasting "Rock This Town" by the Brian Setzer Orchestra.

*Ugh.* He loved this song. And I did too. I loved listening to it, that is. But the live version was crazy-fast to dance to. "Can you slow it down to like three-quarters speed? At least?" I pleaded.

He sighed right before reaching me. "Rory, we need to get your speed up on this. They are not going to be slowing down the music to three-quarters time or anything else at Blackpool. It's not hard. You can do it."

It's hard like hell for someone who hasn't been at it for all that long and is dancing in three-inch heels, I felt like saying but didn't. I was tired of making excuses for myself. I could keep up with him. I'd make myself.

The music began, and the bass player was on Speed, I swear.

"Come on," Sasha yelled over the music. "Triple step, triple step, rock step," he said before taking off.

He was beyond amazing. The sheer speed with which he could move, the razor-sharp precision he maintained while doing so, and just the crazy sexy way he moved his hips, his pelvis, his entire body from side to side while kicking, flicking, jumping, and just doing the basic step. I couldn't help just losing myself watching him, which brought a serious spasm to the space between my legs. Then his eyes caught mine in the mirror. He stopped, realizing I wasn't dancing alongside him. He walked quickly to the stereo and turned the music off.

"What are you doing?" He turned to me, hands on hips.

I guess the look in my eyes made the answer to that question crystal clear because his sly smile returned. But only for a millisecond. He rolled his eyes and shook his head before letting a little laugh escape. He looked around the room then returned his gaze to me. He tried to remain pissy but I could see the mischievously sexy smile threatening to return.

"Rory, I desperately need you to concentrate at this point," he said, now forcing his smile into a frown and stomping his foot to the ground for effect. "Come on," he said, now making his voice solid and commanding. "Let's go." He turned the music back on and walked toward me. He stood next to me and faced the mirror. "Now!" he yelled, and he took off.

I was already behind in speed. I took in a quick, deep gulp of air and started. I tried to catch up. I tried hard. But I just couldn't catch up to the beat. I closed my eyes so I couldn't witness in the mirror how absolutely ridiculous I looked next to this magnificent man. But then, in trying to do the side jive kicks, I kicked too hard and too far to my side and got off my center of balance. I nearly twisted my heel on the blasted stiletto. I tried to right myself but I went too far to the other side and basically ended up on the ground, flat on my butt, my legs splayed and knees bent. I opened my eyes and looked in the mirror. I looked like I'd sat down to go to the bathroom and completely missed the toilet. I looked so absurd I couldn't help but laugh.

But unlike Pepe, Sasha did not laugh with me. The expression on his face was a look of disbelief mixed with anger mixed with disgust. The last upset me the most. He wasn't Pepe. He wasn't a Latin man to whom dancing was a soulful release, a cultural expression that he longed to impart to his American students. He was Russian, and dance was his career, his calling, his life. I remembered from ballet how intensely serious Russians took their dancing and how fiercely competitive they were. This competition was extremely serious to him. To do well, and eventually God-willing, to win, was his life's passion, his life's goal. He needed me to help him achieve that. My heart pounded so hard I could almost hear it as it hit home to me how unsure I was that I could do that, how immensely insecure I was about my abilities. But he'd trusted me. And he wasn't stupid. He believed I had it in me. And I was failing him.

"I'm sorry," I said, immediately picking myself up off the floor and dusting off my hands and the back of my leotard. "Let me try again."

He said nothing, but simply nodded, and went back to the iPod to restart the music.

I took a deep breath and held my hand to my chest, now nervous and trying in vain to stop my pulse from quickening. I told myself to try, try, try to get it right for this man who I was falling for. He'd invested a lot in me—a lot of his time, money, and belief. I couldn't let him down. Or myself. It was my life's passion to be a dancer once too. I knew how it felt. And now was my chance to make good on that with the greatest ballroom dancer in the world. He was giving me everything, and I was throwing it away with my silliness.

"Okay, ready," he ordered, then began calling the steps out. "Triple step, triple step, rock step, triple step, triple step…"

As I began, I realized he'd slowed the music considerably.

I could do this. I focused on myself in the mirror initially but it made me nervous to see myself next to him. So, while keeping my eyes open, I forced myself to focus more inwardly, concentrating only on becoming one with the music, on putting my foot to the ground on the proper beat and making sure my muscles moved the way he and Greta had taught me. I soon got into a rhythm. And it felt okay. It felt like I was getting the basic on time, anyway, and my body had a fundamental understanding of what it was doing.

"Okay, okay," he said. "Nowhere near perfect but we move on for now. Now we do the jive kicks."

These were harder—what I'd messed up before. The footwork was smaller and faster and the steps had to be way tighter and the leg movements sharper and more precise. I looked back at myself in the mirror, afraid I'd trip again if I physically or mentally closed my eyes. I just couldn't get the flick of the kick to look right.

"No, no, they should be like a snake's tongue, snapping at something. Needs to be quicker and sharper. Don't jump so high, Rory, it's slowing you down. Your movement needs to be directed down, not up. No bouncing."

I concentrated hard on the downward movement, on not jumping or bouncing, and inwardly closed my eyes, trying to envision a snake snapping its tongue out, envisioning my leg as the snake's tongue. But I glanced at his image in the mirror and saw panic in his eyes. Panic that I wouldn't be good enough in time. And it threw me. Then I really screwed up.

"No. No. These are horrible. So sloppy," he said, turning off the music.

"Do you mind if I take my shoes off to practice. Until I get the speed down, I mean?" I asked.

He threw his arms up. "Rory, I've already turned the speed—"

"I know, I know. And thank you. That's helped a lot. But I think I need to get the movement right without the heels—"

"I really don't want that. You'll get used to doing it that way and it's wrong. You have to wear the shoes in competition. I don't want you to practice it wrong. Remember, it needs to be right in your muscle memory. Okay, come on, we do it together. Stay close

to the ground and flicks with a small bounce, no jump."
He spoke a kilometer a second.

We faced the mirror and he stood beside me.
He counted the beats and we did the footwork in sync.
He counted slowly.

"There. That's perfect," he said without smiling.
"See, I knew you could do it." There was an accusatory
tone in his voice, as if I'd been playing games before.

"Yes, I'm fine in slow mo—"

"Now, we go at proper speed," he said, slicing
his hands through the air as if to silence my dissent. "If
you can do, you can do. You know. Speed doesn't
matter." As he walked away from the stereo and back
to me, the music came on at lightning speed.

I closed my eyes and heard the music,
envisioned the snake snapping its tongue.

"Okay, go," he yelled.

And off I went. I tried hard to keep up the
speed, not allowing myself to glance at myself in the
mirror, or him. I felt my leg action was proper, but I
was a smidgeon behind the beat.

"Come on," he yelled, calling out the steps.
"You can do it."

I literally closed my eyes, trying hard to keep up.
Soon, all the kicking with my left leg began to bring a
dull pain back to my injured knee.

"Come on, you're doing it!" he yelled, excitedly.
I could hear his smile.

But the dull ache was getting stronger. Hurting
myself wouldn't solve anything. I stopped. He moaned
loudly. I reached down and grabbed my knee, placing
both hands around it and rubbing.

"Sorry, I need a break," I said, kneeling and putting my nose to my knee, not daring to look at him, not wanting to see his immense disappointment.

"Here, let me see," he said softly, kneeling down before me, his tone now much more sympathetic. He slowly removed the bandage.

When he had it off, he looked at my knee as if he were examining something very precious. He rubbed gently over the kneecap, then down the calf, massaging my muscle very gingerly.

"Here, sit," he said as he began unbuckling my shoes.

After he had them off, he gave me a mini foot massage, which felt unbelievably good after wearing those hideous things, but ticklish as well. I squirmed a bit, and laughed when my natural reaction was to pull my foot out of his grip. He looked up at me and smiled ever so slightly. He was trying hard to relax and take care of me and it melted me. He massaged up my calf again and returned to my knee, now inspecting it like a doctor. He caressed the skin over the kneecap again for a few moments, then massaged up my thigh. He moved his face down toward the knee, and rubbed his nose over the bone. I wanted badly to lie back and pull him on top of me. Soon I felt his lips on my knee, on the top of the cap, then on the side, then making their way up my inner thigh, spreading wet heat straight in the direction of my sex. He stopped when he got to the elastic of the leotard. He looked up at me with puppy dog eyes, as if the cloth was preventing him from spreading his kisses any farther up.

I opened my mouth to plead with him to continue but in a split second he'd crawled on top of me and was kissing me slowly and deeply, his tongue exploring my mouth, his lips widening to take in everything. I was so mesmerized by the kiss, I didn't even feel the spaghetti straps of my leotard coming down until I felt my nipples exposed to air. He pulled his lips away from mine to look at my bare chest.

"You're so very beautiful, Rory," he said, cupping both breasts in his hands and kissing me again.

I felt the crotch of the leotard getting wet just as he pulled away briefly to take the leotard down my legs and off entirely, the elastic-waisted skirt coming down right along with it.

He threw the clothes aside and crouched down above me, balancing himself on his arms as he looked my body up and down with hungry eyes, his disposition so completely changed from ten minutes ago.

"Sasha," I whispered, suddenly feeling very bashful. I hadn't yet seen his face while he looked at me naked since I'd been blindfolded before. It was embarrassing but at the same time made my sex ache all the more—throb, was more like it—with want.

"Yes, Rory," he said, wicked smile having fully returned.

I wanted to tell him to take off his clothes but for some reason I didn't. I kind of liked being naked in front of him while he was still clothed. It was weirdly exciting. And my being on display and the way he looked at me with immense desire in his eyes, along with his telling me I was beautiful, made me feel like even if I wasn't Arabelle, and never would be, it didn't matter. He wanted me. He did or we wouldn't be here. This man could have anyone he wanted, after all.

I didn't know what to say. I lifted my knees and crossed my ankles around his back. "Come here," I said, wrapping my arms around his back and pulling him down onto me.

He allowed himself to be lowered, and I felt his erection. I moved my legs farther apart, into a straddle split above him. He kissed me deeply again as he moved atop me, the iron-hard bulge—still wrapped in his pants—thrusting between my legs without penetrating me, making me ache more and more for him.

Now I would have insisted he take his pants off but his tongue completely filled my mouth. His hips were placed so firmly over mine I couldn't reach around his front to undo his zipper. So I reached around his back, trying unsuccessfully to tug down at his waistband from behind. When it wouldn't budge I grabbed the gloriously firm cheeks of his ass and kneaded my palms over them, rubbing and rubbing and rubbing. If I couldn't get his pants down I'd get my feel! I giggled as I felt his glutes flex and I bent my knee and raised my leg so that my toe was at his waistband. I began to dig my toe under the material in another attempt to get his pants down when suddenly he bounded up into a standing position, taking me with him. I squealed as he lifted me and I bounced at his waist. Giggling, I rewrapped my legs around his back and hugged him tightly as he walked toward the staircase, holding me.

Again, he carried me upstairs. But this time we didn't stop at his bedroom door; he carried me through to the bathroom, walking around the shower corner, and over to the steps that led to the bathtub. A far easier way to get down to that gloriously deep tub than by sliding from the shower.

"You must soak," he commanded, seating me down gently on the top tier of the porcelain. "There is Epsom salt and bubble bath. I will be back in a few minutes with champagne."

*Ooh, wonderful, charming fun!* I tiptoed over to the faucet and turned the water on, steaming hot, and plugged the drain. When there was enough of a puddle, I poured the Epsom salt in, then waited for the tub to fill a bit before dousing the water with a big helping of thick pink bubble bath, that, according to its price tag, was bought at The Hustler store on the Sunset Strip. Hmmm, I wondered what else he'd bought in there. When the tub was about halfway full, I turned the cold on a bit to cool it down, and, after testing it with my toe, climbed in, sliding under the celestial, giant bubbles. I tied my bun up higher on the top of my head. I felt around with my hands to locate the little love seat area on the second tier, where the bubbly water came up just past my boobs.

After I turned the water off, I heard a knock at the door.

"Who is it?" I joked in my sexiest voice possible.

The knob turned and the door slowly opened to reveal Sasha standing stark naked holding a glass of champagne in each hand. I couldn't help but bob up and down excitedly under the water. So excitedly, I nearly swallowed a bubble.

"I see you're in the love seat," he said, walking toward me, his penis seeming to grow with each step he took toward me, which made me shiver with excitement.

He knelt and handed me a glass. I tried hard to concentrate on taking the stem of the glass rather than his erection now pointing toward me. "Thank you," I said with a giggle and blush.

He knew right where the steps were, even when the tub was completely opaque with dark pink bubbles. Okay maybe I had overdone it a bit with the bubbles. It had been so long since I had a bubble bath, though. He walked down, his now fully hard penis disappearing under the water. He found the love seat as well, no problem, and sat right beside me, his hip touching mine.

"Mmmm," I said, taking a sip of the champagne while feeling his soft silky skin against mine.

He took a sip and sat still for a moment looking forward, something seemingly on his mind though I couldn't tell what. He sank down a little more into the seat, and propped himself up with his elbows on the tier above. He nudged my good knee with his leg and caressed gently under the water. I lifted my leg and placed it atop his, my opening lightly touching his thigh.

He took another long, slow drink. "Feeling better?" he said after a pause, now looking at me, one eyebrow cocked.

"Mmmm, much," I said, taking another sip, then licking the sweet taste from my lips, wondering what was happening with his erection and why he was so mellow and not jumping on me.

He chuckled. "You're so cute," he said, turning slightly toward me and cupping my chin with his right hand.

"Cute? As in, like, a little puppy?

He laughed. "No, not like a little puppy." He continued caressing my face with his fingertips. It felt blessedly good, comforting. I drew my cheek toward his touch. "As in sweet. And beautiful, oh so beautiful.

And…I am limited in my English, Rory. I just don't know all the words for all that I am feeling." He then began speaking in Russian.

I had no idea what he was saying, of course. But the way he raised his eyebrows and looked at me intently, peering deeply within me, his words sounded soft and loving and romantic, then turned more sexy and seductive.

"Tell me what you're saying!" I said, turning toward him and lunging more closely, particularly from the waist down. Now I could feel his erection. It was iron-hard and enormous. "Tell me, tell me!"

"I told you, I don't know the words." His eyebrows shot up, his lips twisted back into that wicked grin that made me want to throw myself on top of him.

I couldn't take it anymore. I did just that— climbed right on top of him, bending my knees and spreading my legs to surround his hips. I'd forgotten that I was still holding my champagne glass, and as I jumped some of the liquid went flying, giving both of us a little shower.

"Oops, sorry," I said with a giggle, placing the glass to my lips and taking a long swig, nearly emptying the cup so the liquid would be less likely to fly again. I spread my knees farther and moved my pelvis toward him; I could feel the tip of his penis at my entrance. I reached behind him to place my champagne glass down on the tile so I could lift myself fully onto him. As I did so, my nipples peeked up out from the bubbles. His eyelids, which had been half closed, shot open the second my breasts rose from the water.

"Here, here." He grabbed the glass from me. "I can't see these beauties well enough," he said as he poured the rest of the champagne down my chest.

The liquid was cold and made my nipples perk up even more as it quickly dissolved any bubbles that had been covering them.

"Hey, that was cold!" I laughed, slightly embarrassed. Ugh, would I ever get over my 'my boobs are too big' issues?

He pulled me toward him and moved my body up so that my left nipple was the same height as his lips. Then he took my nipple in his mouth and licked the perimeter, then tongued the hard center more firmly, sucking gently. He then tongued his way across my chest to the other nipple and did the same. It seemed like he had to open his mouth quite wide. Oh, I needed to get over my breast issues!

I closed my eyes and tilted my head back, just reveling in the feeling, the tiny sparks of pleasure that began flying through me, filling my entire belly. He sucked a little more aggressively, though still gently, as he cupped the other breast with his palm and teased the nipple. I arched my back and breathed deeply, pulsing my hips into his center, my wet opening throbbing, pushing into his abdomen. I felt the tip of his penis and, as I lowered a bit, I held onto his shoulders to steady myself as I arched farther back while taking him fully inside me. I slid up and down. He was huge; far bigger than any man I'd ever been with. I couldn't help but giggle. He pulled my chest closer to him as I threw my head back even more.

"Here," he said, after taking his mouth off my nipple. He nodded toward the opposite side of the tub. He said something in Russian, seeming to momentarily forget I couldn't understand.

But I felt him rising to stand. I rose and stood before him, the water waist high. He stood as well, the bubbles barely covering his erection which peeked out at me from the top of the suds, teasingly, making me want to grab it and pull it toward me. He extended his hand toward me, in the same manner as when he invited me into closed dance hold on the dance floor. I giggled at the resemblance and took his hand as he guided me across the tub toward the shower area.

"Right here," he said, extending his hand.

I walked to where he motioned, then felt around with my hand. There was another seat but this one was longer and more oblong, like a regular bathtub. I lifted my leg and sat down. This seat was higher than the other. The water barely covered my pubic hair.

"Lie down," he said, turning me sideways.

Oh, I could extend my legs all the way down and lie back. The sides were actually quite wide. There was a lot of room on this love seat. And the back of the tub was rounded, so I could lay my head back. It was like a bed.

"Perfect," he whispered, standing over me with his huge erection, looking down, looking all-powerful, with the wicked smile that always sent both chills and thrills down my spinal cord.

The water was shallow enough here that when I breathed deeply my nipples peeked out. He placed his finger over my lips and ran the tip over my chin, then down my neck, between my breasts, over my belly, and all the way down to my clitoris. I spread my legs farther, laid my head back on the edge of the tub and closed my eyes, rocking back and forth as he pressed down on the hard nub of my clit, then stroked gently up and down before parting my vulva and stroking my insides. He continued massaging my clitoris with his thumb while adding a finger to caress my outer folds.

"Sasha!" I bent my knees so they were jutting out over the water, on each edge of the porcelain. I gripped the outer edge of the tub with one hand and reached toward him with the other, indicating I wanted him inside me.

In an instant he climbed over me, wove himself between my legs and thrust inside me, hard and far, filling me completely. His thrust was more aggressive than the first time, but the water and my extreme inner wetness really necessitated that. I longed for his fullness and I pushed my hips up just as aggressively to meet his. The water began to pour out of the side of the tub, into the shower. The more he pumped, the more we rocked, the more of a waterfall we created.

It wasn't long before we drained the love seat dry. Water began to fill it from the rest of the tub, creating a double waterfall effect, one into the big tub's smaller love seat and one from the tub down into the shower. The water trickling down two ways was incredibly sexy. I had the feeling of becoming even more wet, though that wasn't possible at this point. I felt the first spasms of my orgasm coming sooner than I expected and I lifted my knees even higher until my toes curled over the edges of the love seat. I arched back more and moaned loudly, knowing no one could hear me inside the porcelain walls of Sasha's secluded mansion in the hills. Kind of the singing-in-the-shower effect, though, because the more I moaned, the more my pleasure outbursts seemed to echo. It seemed like Sasha could tell I was ready to climax because his movements became more rapid and fluttering, until he released three bursts of heavy pumping, timed almost to the nanosecond with my, by this point, near-screams of ecstasy. Definitely the most vocal, earth-shattering sex I'd ever had. By a landslide.

# CHAPTER 8

"Rory, Rory." I heard Sasha's gentle whisper above me.

I slowly opened my eyes to see his deliciously long-lashed sapphire blues streaming into mine. He was shirtless, and propping himself over me with his elbows. He balanced on one arm so he could brush the hair out of my eyes. His locks were a wavy, wild sexy mess. Mmmm, what a wonderful way to wake up. I felt the tip of his hardening penis on my inner thigh and instinctively bent my knees and spread my legs.

"Nope," he said, quickly jumping off the bed and throwing the covers completely down to expose my nakedness.

It was cold. I instinctively crossed my arms over my chest and crossed my legs. "Hey!"

"Sorry," he said, "but you insisted I wake you up at six. It's already six fifteen. Come on, sweet, time to rise and shine."

*Ugh, yes, Monday morning.* I needed to start spending weekend nights here. I had to be at work in two hours. Crap. I quickly sat up and when I did, got an immediate rush of pain to my head. Then I remembered the champagne I drank—three glasses, as it ended up—the most absolutely amazing sex I'd ever had, multiple goes at it, until the bubbles melted and the water grew so cold we had to leave that glorious tub, making our way to his throne of a bed where there was more champagne, more toe-curling, scream-inducing sex.

I had no idea what hell awaited me at the office. Well, with Gunther as a boss it could be hell or it could be absolutely nothing. I guess I did have to go in and find out. Though how I wanted to stay here. "Okay. Thank you," I groaned, forcing myself to get completely up. I stood in front of him naked, as he stood before me, the same. We were both so groggy. But that wily smile of his slowly began to spread across his face.

"Stop it! Don't make me want to call in sick again!" I shouted, pawing at his face.

"I did absolutely nothing of the sort!" He laughed. "You stop it!" He took my pawing hand and slowly began to kiss it, licking each of my fingers.

I closed my eyes, getting lost in the sensation, wanting badly to spend my day with this man instead of moody, angry Gunther.

Suddenly Sasha stopped. "Come on, it's getting late. Gunther may have you work on the case you like so much today, with the innocent client."

Oh yes, I hoped so. That would definitely be a fulfilling day.

He laughed. "Your face completely changed expression. You have this excited look about you now."

*My mind-reading man.*

"Thank you for the motivation. You know me well," I gushed, taking his arms and wrapping them around my back. "Promise me we'll pick up tonight where we left off," I said, giggling, nuzzling my nose and lips into the silky skin of his chest. I needed one last whiff of his oaky, musky, cinnamon-y scent and one final feel of those rock hard, protective pecs to keep me hopeful throughout the day.

"Mmmm, I don't know about that, my sweet."

I moved my head back and looked into his eyes. *Say what?*

"Tonight after I pick you up, we will start again with the routine. Greta will be here. We must focus, as we have not done the last several nights." He looked at me admonishingly, but his raised eyebrow and curled lip indicated he took more than half the responsibility for our mischief and wasn't sorry at all for those little extracurricular excursions. "But, yes, okay, we will start with a little one of these," he said, taking me into his arms and pressing his lips to mine, giving me a full, deep kiss that seemed to last a good five minutes.

Okay, that would get me through the day!

"Mmm, where are my clothes again?" I said, still holding him as close as I could to me, rubbing my head into the crook of his shoulder, not wanting to leave.

"Where they always end up. On the practice floor."

\*\*\*

"Rory, I want to ask you something. Quickly, I know, because you have to go to work," Sasha said, caressing my knee.

We were sitting in his car in front of my apartment building and I was just about to get out. "Uh-huh," I said.

"I just got a cancellation tonight and was wondering if you could come over early to rehearse? I mean not as in leave work early, but as in skip the studio early. We are missing so much valuable practice time lately, I wondered if you would mind missing some of your group classes this week and instead just come straight to my place after work every day to rehearse with Greta. And with me as well, of course, when I get home from the studio."

I wanted nothing more than to spend as much time as possible with this man. I would miss Rajiv and Paulina and some of my other studio friends for a while, though.

"Not for the rest of the month or anything. Just to make up the time we've missed," he said, reading my thoughts. "You have the keys. You may come over anytime and use anything you like—the bath or hot tub to soak your knee, the ballroom for practice, the weight room for working out."

*Weight room?*

"I'll have to show you the weight room. I think I may have forgotten. The pool as well for laps. Swimming is actually very therapeutic for many dancer injuries."

I nodded. I remembered this. My nods became more rapid and I grew bouncy. "I would love to!" I giggled.

"Good, good," he said. "I will be home by seven. Greta will begin choreographing our Blackpool routines tomorrow night. So tonight will likely be our last night alone, of regular prrrractice," he said. "For a while, anyway."

The way he said "alone," combined with those rolling r's, made the muscles in my womb spasm. It wasn't easy pulling myself out of his car.

\*\*\*

I managed to make it to work only half an hour late, though I have to say I showed up in a state of bliss over how quickly everything was happening between Sasha and me. My whole body tingled. Throughout my entire commute, I kept feeling like I had to pinch myself.

"Late night?" Gunther said, looking up at me as I stood in the doorway to his office, holding my notes on Jamar's case.

*What?* I'd showered and changed. How could it be that obvious?

"What? Oh no, I just, I just don't feel tremendously well. I may be coming down with a head cold or something," I said, rubbing my temple.

"You're sick a lot, Rory," he said, shooting me a dubious look.

I'd only taken off one sick day in the six months I'd been here. I shook it off. "Well, hopefully it's nothing. Anyway, here are my notes on the Jamar Jackson case. I reviewed all of the case file and the videotaped—"

"Yeah, I'm not ready for that right now, Rory," he snapped. "I think you tried to talk to me about it Friday too. I'll come for it when I'm ready for it. Believe me. Go find something else to do." He shooed me away with his hand again.

Ugh, looked like Sasha was wrong about my day being full of meaning. At least my work day. I nodded and left.

After I placed the memo in my drawer, I walked around the office, asking the other partners for work, since I'd finished Gunther's other research on Friday. No one had anything, save the guy with the wills. Another boring day.

Until five o'clock rolled around. I was packing my bag, getting ready to leave, when Gunther appeared at my door.

"You got in a half hour late today," he said.

"Oh…" He'd caught me off guard. "Right. Well, I don't have anything to do. I've finished the wills Edward gave me and I don't have anything else. I can definitely stay for another half hour, though." But not much longer than that, I thought.

"Actually now would be a good time to go over the Jackson case," he said.

*Ugh, seriously?*

"Great," I said, retrieving my notes and memo outlining the contents of the file from my desk.

I followed him to his office, handed him the notes and sat in the chair opposite his desk. He began reading through them. I twiddled my thumbs, waiting for him to finish, to ask me questions. I waited, and waited. "Do you want me to come back when you've finished?" I asked, noting the time. It was now six. I'd likely be late for Sasha.

"No, wait."

I waited for twenty more minutes, thinking I should text Sasha, letting him know I'd be late. But how to get out of Gunther's office and to my cell phone?

Just then Gunther looked up. "Okay, so why do you think this guy's not guilty?"

"Because he has no criminal record and the co-defendants do. He's young, way younger than the co-defendants. He's not in school, has no school records. And he just seemed...from watching the videotapes, he just seemed slow. Like he wasn't getting things. And the D.A. had the upper hand with him. Totally the opposite of the co-defendants' taped statements. They were so much more—"

"So?"

"So...I think the others took advantage of him. I think he's slow—"

"What you think, the way someone seems, those aren't real, they're not legal...they don't work in a court of law, Rory. You should know that. I can't do anything with that. There's nothing solid here for me to argue he was taken advantage of by them." He harrumphed, throwing the notes down on the desk.

"Well, I've tried to call the mother, but so far I haven't been able—"

"What good will that do?"

"She can tell us if he has a history of retardation. I also want to talk to his bro—"

"You always have to go about things the hardest way possible, Rory." He shook his head and rolled his eyes.

He made me vomitously nervous, and angry. He made me doubt myself. Maybe it was stupid of me to even try to get ahold of Jamar's family. But wasn't that all we had?

"Go on, I'll have to figure out a defense," he said, shooing me away again.

It was seven when I got back to my office.

*Sorry again, Gunther problems again. On way now*, I texted Sasha.

\*\*\*

"I'm really excited for Greta to start choreographing for Blackpool! I'm really excited to get our routines and have something specific to practice and just...this will just be so...good."

We were in Sasha's ballroom, beginning our practice two hours later than expected. I felt like crying, and chose to babble instead. I was nervous Sasha would be mad, and was mad at myself for allowing Gunther to get me so out of sorts. To both put me on the defensive so and to keep me at the office so late when that really didn't seem necessary. It seemed for the past several weeks now I was spending days with nothing to do and being flooded with work right when I was supposed to be training with Sasha. My life was making no sense to me.

"Yes. Me too," Sasha said, raising his eyebrows. "Having specific moves to practice will be good for honing problem areas. And choreographing is fun." He smiled. It was a genuine smile, the one with the boyish dimples. He didn't seem angry about Gunther.

He held his arms open for me, inviting me to dance. I placed my left hand on the "musckle"—as Bronislava called it—of his strong, sexy bicep, placed my right hand into his left, and we started a rumba basic.

"Jeez, you are very tense, Rory," he said. There was urgency in his voice. He shook my right arm with his left, still in handhold, making a kind of waving effect. "Try and let go of the tension of the day or you can seriously hurt yourself. It will make your muscles less flexible, makes you more susceptible to injury."

I knew this. But easier said than done. "Maybe I need a massage," I ventured.

He stopped shaking out my arm, released me, stood back and took a deep breath. He closed his eyes, and when he opened them again, he looked at the clock. He closed his eyes again, and when he opened them this time, he looked me straight on, a wily smile flashing across his face. Wow, he really didn't seem mad about my job!

But what exactly was I suggesting? We really needed to be serious tonight; I felt sure he thought the same. I couldn't end up staying over again. A back massage from Sasha was not the answer as much as I wanted it to be.

"You really want massage?" He eyed the zipper of my sky blue cover-up top.

"No," I said flatly. "We need to practice and I can't stay overnight again and that's what that would lead to and..." I started to feel a pulsing sensation between my upper thighs, thinking of him unzipping me. I had to stop. "No. I'll unwind while we're dancing. Come on."

"It's not like we will get much done tonight. It's so late already." There was a weariness in his tone, but I couldn't detect any anger. "It's important for you to relieve your stress. I'm serious," he said, sounding as if he was trying to convince himself along with me.

"No." I grabbed him, positioned us back into handhold, and started the basic footwork, necessarily pushing him back a bit when I took a step. "I'm not back-leading," I insisted. "I'm just trying to get you to start dancing so we don't waste any more time and I can relieve my tension through dancing. And, so that, um, you can stop looking at my zipper."

Now his wily smile completely overtook his face, increasing the pulsing in my inner thighs severalfold. "What is wrong with me looking at your zipper? Does the zipper not want to be looked at? Is the zipper self-conscious?"

"The zipper is very self-conscious. She does not want to end up in a discarded heap on the floor," I said, trying not to crack up over our goofy conversation.

He turned his lips down and gave me faux sad puppy dog eyes. "Oh poor zip—"

But I had to cut him off. This could not go where it seemed to be headed tonight. It was Monday. Way too early in the week. "Seriously," I began, slapping playfully but meaningfully at his hand which was currently fingering the bottom of the cover-up. "If you touch that zipper I'm worried I'll get no sleep, I'll be late to work again, Gunther will get pissed, and it'll only cause more stress. So no zipper action. Let's dance."

He gave me one last cockeyed, loopy smile then looked away and sighed. "Okay, okay. Zipper will remain...unmolested."

"You and your words." I smiled and shook my head at him.

"What words? I like English." He squinted at me and reached for my hand.

He began moving his feet and I closed my eyes and tried to lose my thoughts in the muscle memory of the movement, in his body guiding mine.

"Rory," he whispered after a few basics. "I do worry about your tension. You are so pretty." He briefly leaned in, breaking our proper dance hold, and ran his nose along my cheek.

I thought he might kiss me and I prepped for it, deciding that a kiss would be fine. Good, actually. *But it must stop at that.*

He continued whispering. "You are so soft, so beautiful...for this, this job you have."

Wait. What did he just say? I stopped mid-step and looked at him.

He seemed surprised. He frowned, looking very confused.

"I can't be pretty and be a lawyer? Is that what you just said? That sounded like what you just said," I blurted out, a little over-hysterical. I'd had a Russian friend in a class at Hastings and she was always complaining about how sexist Russian men were. I'd thought Sasha was different.

His eyes widened.

"Don't you have women lawyers in Russia?" I went on.

He remained open-mouthed, not speaking.

"Well women can do anything we want here. We're not limited by stupid sexist notions that we should just sit around being soft and pretty and not destroy our fragile constitutions."

I broke away from him and stepped back, wondering why he wasn't responding to me.

Mom's reasons for forbidding me to continue ballet were that she thought it made me too body-focused, and would limit my life choices. She'd blamed my dad for my obsession with my body that led to my anorexia. I never could see it—because I don't ever remember him calling me fat. Quite the contrary. But she did and that's all that mattered since she had control over me—body and mind—at that point. She said Daddy's labeling me the pretty one and Jackie the smart one at such young ages molded our opinions of ourselves and solidified in our minds our limitations. I didn't know if Mom was right, but I never was as good as Jackie at school—I trailed behind her from high school through law school. After I left dance, I was forever in my sister's shadow.

"You think I'm too stupid to be a lawyer?" I could hear the panic in my voice.

Sasha was such mesmerizing, passionate, fiery perfection. I never stopped to consider how different our cultures might be in terms of gender roles, that they might create an impasse.

Sasha's frown deepened. He shook his head several times and looked up at the ceiling, throwing his hands up.

"Well? Are you going to answer me?"

He put his hands on his hips. "Only if you can tell me how anything I said prompted that question. Or the insult against Russia."

At first I didn't know what he was talking about regarding the second sentence. I couldn't remember now all of what I'd said.

"Of course we have female lawyers, Rory. It's kind of a big country, and we are not Third World," he continued.

*Oh, yes.* I'd forgotten that I'd asked him whether they have female lawyers. He was right—it was a nonsensical line of attack. I was relieved he found it an insult, though. "Well, good. I didn't mean to insult you. But I felt insulted by your comment that I was too pretty to be a lawyer. That…that's a sexist thing to say." My voice lost power as his pupils bore into mine, chastising me.

"Rory, I said absolutely no such thing. I don't even know how you interpreted my words to mean that."

"Yes you did. You said your job is too intense and you're too pretty for it. Or something like that."

He continued shaking his head.

"You did! I heard you."

"I said…I don't know exactly what I said before I was interrupted but I meant that your job seemed to cause you a lot of distress and that I hated seeing you that way. That's all I said, Rory."

"That's not all you said!" I couldn't believe he was denying the 'you're too pretty' remark. "You specifically said 'you are too pretty to be a lawyer.' Okay, you might have said you're too pretty for all the tension your job creates or something like that. But it's the same thing. It implies I can't handle stress because of the way I look somehow."

He continued to stare at me for a few moments, then threw his hands up and sighed deeply. "Okay, I might have said the remark about you being pretty alongside the remark about my being bothered by the tension." His eyes then darted up and to the left as if he had a thought. "It is possible that I used the word pretty when I meant soft or nice, but if you heard pretty, I believe that's what you heard. In any event, I did not mean that you are too stupid to be a lawyer because you are pretty. I would never say that."

The intensity of his gaze and those penetrating pupils were making it hard for me to maintain my tough composure but I was determined to have this out. "Okay, good. I'm glad you would never say that. But…you think I'm too soft to be a lawyer?"

One eyebrow shot up. "I don't…I think you can be whatever you want to be. I think you're a very good lawyer. As I said to you the other night, I think you are a very compassionate lawyer who sees the humanity in her clients…"

That's true. I remembered that, and how sweet it was and how wonderful it made me feel. What was I doing?

"I just think," he went on, "that this job is very stressful for you and you are not handling it well. I think you are letting it wear you down. From what you tell me about the judges and the lawyers you work for and the clients as well, it seems you have to have somewhat of a hard personality to deal with these people. A hard, hard…" He picked at his skin. "A hard body. Outer body. Thick skin!" He added excitedly, remembering the term in English.

I couldn't help but laugh, but immediately felt tears well in the back of my eyes. Yeah, I was not handling my job stress very well. Maybe I did need to be a "harder" person. Maybe I was just not cut out to be a lawyer and my whole education was a waste. I nodded, feeling the tears invade my eyes. I blinked, hoping he wouldn't notice.

But of course he did. "No, no, no, I didn't mean to upset you," he said, reaching out for me. I let him wrap his arms around me, letting the tears flow once my face was embedded in his chest. "Please just forget this whole conversation. Let's just continue to dance. What we do well together. Okay?"

*What we do well together?* Did he actually just say that?

"Deal," I said, my tears drying, my head still ensconced in his protective pecs.

We danced several rumbas, in blissfully—albeit improper for competitive ballroom—super-close handhold, in peaceful silence. But I could feel him tensing a bit toward the end. Was I not doing something right, I wondered? I didn't want to ask. Oh, I just wanted to feel at peace with Sasha, and leave it to Greta to correct my technique issues.

"Okay, I have something to say now. May I?" His tone was polite, imploring.

"Yes," I said, taking a breath and bracing myself. "But, you know, I am just…I'm just melting into you. I know I'm not doing it properly, I'm not concentrating on my technique. I'm so—"

"No, no, it's not that. Not that at all." He released a little laugh.

I sighed in relief and held my head back so I could look into his laughing eyes. "What, then?" I smiled back.

His smile dissipated and he took a moment to think. "I feel that you made an assumption about me because I'm Russian and I wish you wouldn't do that. I don't make assumptions about you because you're American."

I was a bit taken aback. I didn't know what he was talking about. "I don't understand. What assumption did I make?"

"That I am backward. That I would think women shouldn't be in professions because all Russians must think that way."

*Oh*. I guess I was guilty of making that assumption, because of what my Hastings friend had told me about Russian men. I laughed nervously. "Okay, you're right. A Russian girl in my law school class complained to me once that her boyfriend was sexist, as were all Russian men. Her words, not mine," I added defensively when I felt him tense again.

"So this one girl who I've never met makes a general statement… Where was she from, anyway? And how old was she that she knew every single Russian man so well?" His jawline clenched and his biceps tightened.

"She was from Moscow and she was my age. Sasha, calm down. I know she didn't know you—"

"Are you still friends? What was her name?" He sounded as if he'd been betrayed.

"Katya. No, she was just in my study group. I haven't talked to her since we graduated. Since second year, actually. Sasha, seriously, calm down. I'm sorry I let her influence me. I'll make a conscious effort to forget everything I ever heard her say." I laughed nervously again. I felt like there was something seething below the surface that I didn't understand.

He took a few full breaths. I patted his arm softly. I certainly hadn't meant to start another fight.

"Well, I wish you would judge me by what I say and do and not by some stereotype someone else plants in your head."

I harrumphed. But he was right because I'd listened to her. "I already told you I wouldn't. Can we be done with this, please?" My tone was more snappish than I'd intended, and I didn't want to set him off again. "Please?" I said more playfully, batting my eyes up at him, then tracing a peace sign onto his chest with my fingertip.

He exhaled. "Yes, after one more thing." His eyes had lightened but his tone still retained an air of seriousness. "I would appreciate it if you would not mimic my accent. I am trying to speak English well and it doesn't help to be reminded of my shortcomings."

"What! You mean the rolling r's?"

He nodded. "If that's what you call them. Russian way of pronouncing is different, so it's hard to make your mouth move in a certain way—"

"But I love those! I was never ridiculing you. I think they're so sexy!" I was stunned he'd been offended. I actually hadn't even realized I'd ever mimicked him to his face, only in my own mind. But he had read my mind on several occasions, so I shouldn't have been surprised.

He considered this, his eyes darting around the room for a few seconds. When they returned to me, his frown had softened and his lips curved into a very slight smile.

"I can't believe you thought I meant it in a bad way! They're so hot!"

"It wasn't that I thought you were rr-r-r-rrridiculing—" Now he was trying hard not to trill his r's and the result was that they were even more pronounced.

I couldn't help but crack up.

Thankfully, after rolling his eyes, he laughed. But then his straight face immediately returned and I was laughing all alone which was no fun. This was serious to him.

"Why is this such a big deal to you, that you have no trace of a Russian accent? Seriously? It makes you different, it makes you stand out."

He thought about it a moment then shrugged. "Maybe I want to stand out for some things. Like dance. But…" He shook his head and looked around the room again. "I don't see what's the point of standing out for things you can't control. Things that are equated with being backward and… Maybe I can't explain. Just not this." There was a sadness in his eyes.

"It's not backward!" I couldn't understand why he was associating being Russian with being backward, or why he thought I was doing that. "Why would you say that? I can't speak any of your language, with or without an accent."

He raised his eyebrows and nodded. "True. But...I can't explain." He shrugged. "Let's, let's drop it. Okay?"

"Okay, why don't you teach me some Russian and then you can crack up over my pronunciation."

"What would be the point of that?" He laughed with a bemused frown.

"I made you feel bad. So you can laugh at me."

"But you say it was unintentional. And I believe you."

"Yes, it was. But..." I really wanted him to teach me some Russian anyway. It would be fun. "Come on, just teach me some Russian. Just teach me to say something!" I playfully punched his bicep again and bounced up and down on my heels in excitement.

"Why? I don't understand." His frown deepened, though he laughed.

"Because I want to learn your language! Come on, teach me. Just one sentence!" I bounced higher.

"Okay, okay," he said, giving in.

"Thank you." I rubbed my nose along his cheek.

"Okay, *ya umnaya ee krasivaya zhenshchina.*"

"That's huge!" I shrieked.

"No. It's very simple sentence. We'll take it in parts. Repeat after me."

"Okay, I'll try. Your language is a lot more complicated than mine," I said.

"No. It's really not," he said firmly, but still laughing.

I'd heard many say English is the hardest language to learn to speak. But I was enjoying giving him a hard time.

"*Ya*," he began. "Come on, that's easy. It's the German word for 'yes.' Russian for 'I.'"

"Okay, *ya*."

"*Umnaya.*"

"*Unmaya.*"

"No, the m is before n. *Umnaya.*"

"Okay, *umnaya.*"

"*Ee.* That's just the word for 'and.'"

"What are you having me say!" I asked.

"Not yet, just repeat."

"*Eeee.*" I said, elongating the vowel because it was fun. He laughed.

"*Krasivaya.*"

"*Krasss…*"

"*Ivaya. Krasivaya.* I know you can say that."

"*Krasivaya,*" I said trying to roll the r like he did. He chuckled again.

"Good. *Zhenshchina.*"

"That's a hard one."

"No, it's not. Stop playing. *Zhen-sh-china.* Just take it one part at a time."

"*Zhen-sh-ch?*" I questioned. The two consonants sounded odd together.

"Yes, *Zhen-sh-china.*"

"*Zhen-sh-china.*"

"Good, now put it all together. *Ya umnaya ee krasivaya zhenshchina.*"

"I am never going to remember that long sentence without writing it out."

"No, I don't want you to do that. Feel the way it sounds on your tongue."

"Back to feeling and not seeing again," I said, teasingly.

"Yes, that's my point. You use one sense way more than all the others. Way more."

I guess I did. "Okay, *ya umnaya eee…*"

"*Krasivaya zhenshchina*," he said, finishing.

"*Ya umnaya eee krasivaya zhen…*"

"I know you can do this," he said, frustration beginning to taint his tone.

Oh I didn't want that. He frustrated so easily sometimes. "Okay, okay. *Ya umnaya eee krasivaya zhenshchina.*" It was easier once I took each syllable at a time, like he said.

"Very good, and it's true," he said, giving me a short but ever-so-sweet kiss on the lips.

"Okay, now what did I just say? I'm really horny and…I want you to come on my…"

"Rory! Would I have you say that? Seriously?"

I stood a shoulder's length away and looked at him squarely. "Mmmm, probably not."

He shook his head. "For all that we've done together, you don't know me very well."

His mischievous smile I'd so missed was returning. I wanted to jump on him. But first I wanted to know what he made me say. "Okay, so what was it? What did I just say?"

"Believe it or not, you just said, 'I am a smart and beautiful woman.'"

"Aw, really?" I blushed. "That's so sweet, Sasha."

"Yes, really."

I nuzzled my nose into his cheek and took his hands and wrapped them around my back. "Okay, so now every time you think I'm laughing at your rrrr's— and I never am—you can remember that I had such trouble calling myself a woman." I giggled. "That I had such trouble with everything but the 'I' and the 'and' actually. And those I probably didn't pronounce completely right either."

"It's very hard to speak another language," he whispered, rubbing his lips along my forehead. "But you did very well." His lips began trailing down my nose to my cheek.

Mmmm, I liked that. But I wanted to learn more Russian. "Teach me something else," I squealed with another little bounce.

"Something else? Why?" he moaned without looking up.

"Because I'm having fun learning Russian! Come on!"

He took a breath and lifted his chin. He looked up and to the right, in thought mode again. "*Ya tebya lyublyu.*"

"Oh come on, you're not serious! That's huge!"

"It's three words."

"Yeah but the second and third one are crazy."

"No they aren't. Not crazy. You wanted to learn. Come on. So easy." He laughed.

"Okay, I got the first word. *Ya!*"

"Very good," he laughed. "*Tebya…*"

"Dubya. Like the way George W. Bush says his middle initial." I laughed.

"No, t, as in TV. *Tebya.*"

"Oh *tubya*. Bathtub."

"Rory, no bathtub. *Tebya*, like rhymes with the name, English name, Ted. There's a movie with Mark Wahlberg."

"Oh, *tebya*."

"Yes, yes. Okay, now *lyublyu*," he finished.

"Oh good lord. *Leeyou*...the vowels together are hard," I whined.

"*Lyublyu*," he repeated.

"*Leeyoubleeyou*," I said, rather proud of myself for getting such a hard-to-pronounce word on the second try. But before I could voice that sentiment, he was on top of me. Literally. We were right next to the couch our things were on, and he'd tossed them off then pulled me down onto it, kissing me so hungrily.

"What did I say?" I asked.

"You guess," he managed, his lips shifting from kissing to sucking the back of my neck.

Those were going to show the next day. I'd have to remember not to wear my hair up to the office. Now his hand was back on the zipper, but not for long. Because soon the jacket was off, followed by my skirt, then my shoes, then my tights. Before he got to the leotard straps, I went for his belt buckle.

"I can't stay the night," I moaned, unzipping his pants and sliding them over his rock-solid ass, along with his underwear.

"I know, I know, I know. That's why we're not going upstairs. See, very close to the door," he said, which made me giggle. He tugged down on my spaghetti straps while I pulled his shirt up and over his head.

An hour later, we were still on that couch. He, running his fingers up and down my arms, in between soft, wet kisses to my neck and lips; me, tracing the lines of his winged thinker, nuzzling my nose into the soft, silky skin of his iron-hard bicep.

"Sasha?"

"Mmmm?"

"I don't want to go but you know I have to."

"I know," he said after a long pause.

"We didn't do much practicing tonight," he said, now standing at my car door in his driveway.

"I know," I said.

"What time do you think you will be able to be here? Or is it futile to ask?"

I shrugged. "Probably futile. But hopefully by six."

"Okay. I will have Greta be here by then. You can start choreographing and I will be home at nine. I need to take a very short trip again. I will be gone Wednesday through Sunday. I will book Greta every night this week from six to nine. You two will get a lot done and we will be together again by Saturday." He said this all really fast, and ended with a long kiss to my forehead.

"A trip? Another show dance with Xenia?"

He nodded.

"Where?"

He took a breath. "Japan."

"Again? Wow, they really love you guys there."

He nodded. "The Japanese market for ballroom dance is very, very strong. You and I will go there someday." He had a weary smile. "As I said, please stay here as you like. Take baths, soak your knee, stretch at the barre, and use the weights and the pool."

"Um, okay," I said, trying to take it all in. He sure went away a lot with Xenia. He sure went to Japan a lot. I tried not to worry.

"Rory?" he said, cupping my chin in his hands.

My eyes had been darting all around in thought. I now looked straight into his.

"I love you," he said.

My eyes widened to the size of golf balls, it felt like. Oh my gosh, did he just say what I thought he had? My heart pounded nearly out of my chest. "I-I-I love you too!" I said with a ridiculous stutter.

"I know. You told me earlier. In Russian."

Aha, that was the second sentence he'd had me say. *Wow!*

He brought my chin toward his face and gave me a long, delicious kiss that banished all my worries.

# CHAPTER 9

"Rory, you need to know something," Greta said to me. She had a sincere, worried tone.

We were in Sasha's ballroom, getting ready to begin our rumba routine as soon as he got home from his last private at the studio. Miraculously, Gunther didn't give me anything last minute so I was able to leave work at five o'clock.

"What?" I looked up at her from practicing my swirling airborne *ronde de jambs* that I so loved.

"Sasha...well, he is very strong and fast. He is an excellent dancer."

"You really think you needed to tell me that!" I laughed.

"Yes, but there is more." She paused, seeming to choose her next words carefully. "He can be very difficult. He is very difficult. In fact...I've never known him to not be extremely difficult with any partner, no matter how romantically involved he is with her. And he has always been romantically involved with all of his partners, except Arabelle. And he has always fought with every one of them. I don't think you have seen what he is capable of yet because you are still in a kind of honeymoon period with him."

"Yeah, I came in on the tail end of his partnership with Xenia, and I've heard all the rumors…"

"The rumors are true, I hate to say. He has difficulty keeping partners because of his extremely demanding nature. And the fact that he is so fast and strong. He is just…he is like fire. I don't really think any woman could keep up with him no matter how hard we try. We are different, after all. We can't move quite as fast. In ballroom there is a saying that the man is the frame and the lady is the painting inside the frame, and of course that's not always true. The man often is just as enticing to watch as the woman. But it's true to the extent that perhaps he is more of the athlete and you must rely more on your artistry. Let him be, what you call…a speed demon, but you create the style, the emotional resonance."

I swallowed, wondering if I could possibly have enough artistry to stand out when dancing with him. My goal thus far had been just to keep up, to keep from getting yelled at.

"Now, my partner, Dean, he was the same way," Greta continued. "He was like lightning. People would scream when they watched him dance. Like he was Elvis or something, the way he moved his hips." She laughed and rolled her eyes. "Yes, he was wild. And I felt like the dirt beneath his feet when I first started dancing with him."

Wow, severe, I thought. And I'd thought I had no self-confidence. But I didn't say that. I just nodded.

"Then I realized if I was going to hold my own I had to create my own style," she went on. "But my partner was a bit different than Sasha. He understood that, and he let me have the freedom to create my own magic. Now, I have tried to tell Sasha this over and over and over again and I think he understands logically but not intuitively. You are going to have to remind him of this over and over. Otherwise, as a couple it will look like you are always trying to keep up with him and failing miserably. And he will be frustrated and eventually angry. Your partnership will say to the world that you can't keep up with him and that he resents you for it."

I gulped. She was a genius. She'd gotten it so right. That was exactly what it looked like when he'd danced with his other partners.

"But I see something in you," she added, softening. "I see a certain potential. Not just as an artist with a balletic background, which makes you stand out from a lot of the other girls. But as someone who can soften him. And I don't know why. I just see that you have a kind of effect on him. I can't put my finger on it."

"Really?" I said, gushing, holding my palm to my chest. *Wow.*

"Yes, but like I said, it's just a feeling I have that I can't explain. The other thing is that the judging is different this year, which I'm sure is why he's taking a chance on someone without a specific ballroom background."

"How so?" I said.

"They're not having the usual judges, which often consisted of various of the couples' coaches, which made it seem very unfair. I mean, if your coach had influence over the other judges, you'd be in a better position to win."

I nodded. "Yeah, that's how my teachers have described to me what the American competitions are like," I said, remembering my conversation with Mitsi at the O.C. competition.

"Yes. But at Blackpool this year they're bringing in new people who know a great deal about ballroom and are former champs, but who don't coach, and who don't really personally know anyone. They don't have any stakes. Since they've never seen you before, it's no big deal. They haven't necessarily seen a lot of the people who will be out on that floor."

"Oh. That explains why he's taking a chance on me." I was a little deflated. But it did explain why he didn't insist on a pro ballroom dancer to be his partner for such an important competition.

"Yes, but he realizes you're a wonderful dancer even if you don't have a ballroom background," she said, grabbing my hand, urgency in her voice. "He wouldn't have chosen you if he didn't recognize your talent. But this is why it's all the more important that you remind him that instead of insisting you be a replica of him—which you will never be—he must give you the freedom to express yourself and create your own style, which you do so very well, Rory!"

She rubbed my hand. I blushed.

"I'm serious. And please feel free to use me as a backup. In fact, put it all on me and tell him that I told you to remind him of this. Repeatedly. I was a world champion, the world champion he wants so badly to be. So I kind of know what I'm talking about." She raised one eyebrow and flashed a sideways grin.

She was definitely a woman who could hold her own. I'd seen it on the videos. I couldn't believe she'd once felt like dirt. I couldn't believe she was giving me advice, and telling me she saw potential in me, in us.

"Okay. I will," I said, head down, still blushing. "Can I, um, just ask you another question about him?"

"Sure."

"He and Xenia were together for a really long time, right?"

"Yes, and they fought together for a really long time. I don't know how they stood it for so long, to be honest."

"Well, he goes away a lot with her. Do you think…"

"Mmmm, no?" She frowned. "You mean, besides show dances?"

"No. Just those. But I mean, they do it a lot…"

"Well, that's a professional demand. The last person you won Worlds or Blackpool with is the person with whom you are invited to dance at these show dances all over the world. This is mainly how top pros make their money. I mean, how do you think he affords all…?" She waved her arm about the room.

"Yeah, I used to think he made his money from the studio until he told me." I laughed.

"Everyone thinks that. Please, the studios pay crap. The wealthy students who compete all the time do put some money in the teachers' pockets, but the studio takes a great deal of it. The pros make their money from the pro comps, their commercial sponsors, the showcases they perform for audiences around the world, and maybe choreographing for TV or the Olympics or something like that. I never did that. Sasha does. But most definitely not the studios," she repeated sharply, following with a cackle and shake of the head for emphasis.

So that echoed what he'd told me. The house definitely wasn't bought with mafia money. But I knew that. I did wonder, though, why he spent so much time at the studio and on comps with people like Cheryl and Luna.

"Well..." I began to ask her but stopped. I didn't want to look jealous and childishly competitive.

"Well, what?" One of her eyebrows shot up dramatically. I wondered how she did that. It looked very cool.

"I mean, I just wondered, because he spends a lot of time at the studio and with his pro/am students. If there isn't a lot of money in it for him, then why does he do it?"

She shook her head. "Sasha's not an American citizen," she said. "Much as he wants to be, he's not yet. So, he needs an immigration visa. He's dependent on the studio for that. Without the studio's employment, he'd have to go back to Russia."

*Gulp.* I certainly didn't want that.

She must have seen the worry in my eyes. "Don't worry, sweetheart," she said, looking sincere.

I looked at her. Yes, I knew the studio loved him. His job was secure. They weren't letting him go. I nodded and went to say as much. But she spoke first.

"There's nothing more between him and Xenia. Believe me. She has another partner. He has another partner."

Oh, I actually wasn't even thinking about him cheating on me with Xenia. The thought surprised and pleased me. Had I actually become more secure?

"You know, now that I think about it," she continued, "I think I know what it is about you that he sees. I mean, besides the talent."

"What?" I practically shouted.

"You have a certain softness about you. Like you're not going to fight with him like the others did. He's mostly danced with Russians. Russian women can really be controlling." She laughed. "Sorry to make a blanket statement like that but it's true. Plus, maybe the American-ness makes you seem more carefree. I think you relax him a bit. I know it doesn't seem that way, but I think you do. That's good. He needs to calm down. But he is going to be mad if he comes back and we haven't even started," she said, glancing at the clock above the bar.

"You're so right!" I said. "But thank you for all of this." I smiled. "You don't know what it means to me." I held my head down, meaning to say *to have a world champion coaching me, giving me a pep talk like this.* But I felt stupid suddenly and the words wouldn't come.

"Of course, dear," she said, squeezing my hand, indicating she understood.

I absolutely loved the rumba choreography she gave me. She totally took advantage of my ballet background and my flexibility. She had me start off with this lovely arabesque *penchée* where I lifted my leg high in back, straight up in the air, while kind of bowing down to him. He was to wait till I'd slowly lowered my leg, then he was to grab me—delicately, of course! And pull me close to him, then spin me away into a series of rapid-fire *chaîné* turns before pulling me close again into a twisty spiral. He was to lunge while I lifted my leg toward him, and wrapped it around his shoulder, so that when he rose to a full standing position, I'd basically be doing a standing split. Then he'd pull me toward him in a slide. *Très* sexy!

"How are we doing, ladies?" Sasha called out, walking in.

I was so engaged in the routine I hadn't heard his car pull up. I still had my leg high in the air, opened toward him—or to the imaginary him. When I looked up at him, it must have looked like an overt sexual invitation.

"Impressive," he said, eyeing the leg from hip to toe.

"Yes, very," said Greta, also looking at my standing leg. Calling attention to the fact I was holding a balance for quite a while of course made me lose it. I swung my leg down and giggled.

Greta showed Sasha what she'd choreographed so far, having me demonstrate my part, while she marked his moves herself. Then she ordered him to dance his part. We started with a couple walks toward each other. But then he sped up the last one, which I wasn't expecting, as Greta hadn't choreographed it as such. He grabbed my hands, pulling my upper body toward him rather fast. He caught me off guard and I didn't know what was going on. I nearly fell into him.

"What's wrong? Why aren't you doing the arabesque?" he said, looking at me, eyes wide.

I looked at Greta, as did he. I felt my mouth open but no words came out. He was already getting pissed and I was already letting him unnerve me.

"I don't think she understood what you were doing," she said. "I didn't lead her into it so fast like that. But it's okay. Now that she knows that's what you're doing, she'll be ready next time. Try again."

At first I wondered why Greta didn't just tell him not to lead me so strongly, to let me shine, as we'd talked about. But the way he did the move did look snazzier. If he gave me time to get it, it would look cool.

We did it again. Now that I understood what he was doing, I knew to bow to him and hold my leg up in back. But he still pulled a little too hard, and I nearly lost my balance.

"I'm just getting used to your strength," I said, trying to stand up for myself by keeping my voice from shaking. Unsuccessfully, I might add.

"It's okay, Rory. No one expects perfection on the first go-round," Greta piped in, giving me a wink.

Sasha exhaled audibly. Ugh, he was annoyed. We tried it several more times and by the last time, I was finally able to control my leg lift and maintain my balance. It was getting better.

"Good. It's really improving," Greta said, echoing my thoughts. "Practice will make perfect. Let's move on for now."

The same thing happened with the *chaîné* turns. Sasha whipped me into them so fast I lost control and went spinning too far away from him. I wasn't focused enough to spot when I turned and got dizzy. I almost fell. It was a mess.

"Okay, so that's going to be a really strong lead too," I said, laughing nervously. Sasha looked confused by my laughter.

"Sasha is strong. I warned you," Greta said.

"I don't understand. It's rumba. It's dance of passion. The man's lead must be strong to emanate passion."

*Is that how people show passion, though?* By pushing each other around the dance floor, I thought? But I didn't want to say it.

"Again, she just needs to get used to your strength. You don't know how strong you are, Sasha," Greta said. "Try again."

We tried several more times, and again it got better but remained far from perfect. I really felt like he was pushing and pulling me too hard. I'd either have to get used to it or find a way to talk to him about it.

I looked at the clock. I had to get going to be home in time for a good night's rest for work. "I'm sorry, you guys, but I really need to go soon."

Sasha exhaled loudly, his nostrils flaring. "I know," he said, the gentle sound of his voice at odds with his demeanor.

\*\*\*

"So I'll see you tomorrow at about six?" I said to Greta on my way out.

"Will do," she said. Then she propped my chin up and whispered, "Remember what I said. Keep your head up, always."

I nodded.

Sasha walked me to my car. I opened the door and turned back to face him. His eyes were big and fiercely serious. "Have a good trip," I said.

"Thank you," he said after a moment's hesitation. "I won't be gone long. It will be Sunday before we know it. And when I return we will work very hard."

I nodded. He was touching my car door, but not touching any part of my body. I wanted him to grab me and scoop me up into a passionate embrace. But it wasn't happening. He was too sober, too focused on the competition and on how much we were currently lacking. Greta was so right about how crazed he'd become once we got going with the routines.

*\*\*\**

I packed myself a little suitcase with clothes I'd need for the next few days for work and practice. I also packed a swimsuit for Sasha's magnificent pool. And, I brought all the DVDs I'd bought at WorldTone.

It was fun and relaxing working with Greta over the next few days. She choreographed really exciting routines for us for all five dances. In jive, I had lots of cutely sexy toe-heel swivels and fun hip-swaying jive walks, and lots of super-charged flirty American and simple spins. In cha-cha, I had a lot of sassy walks around Sasha, using him as a kind of stripper pole in a sexy kind of way, and in samba loads of those beautiful samba rolls in shadow position. In paso doble I had a beautiful multiple pirouette in response to a hot high-jumping turn by Sasha. She also gave me a lot of soulful flamenco taps, my favorite part of that dance. And the rumba was just gorgeous and really used my balletic abilities with lots of slow, sultry arabesques, sexually suggestive but graceful forward and side *développés* of the leg, beautiful swan-like *port de bras* of the arms, and sexy, deep lunging splits that showed off my flexibility.

"You're so awesome! You loaded the routine with all my favorite moves in each dance!" I gushed.

"Yes. I know," she said with that sly, knowing smile of hers.

"Really? How?"

"Because I'm a genius, of course," she said completely nonchalantly.

When I began to stutter a response, caught off guard by her lack of modesty, she burst out laughing.

"Seriously. Sasha told me, of course. How else would I know?"

I was equally caught off guard by this. It dawned on me I'd never actually told him what I liked because I'd been so nervous around him from the very beginning of my first private.

Well, there was his mind-reading sixth sense at work again. So he was kind of watching over me, making sure I was happy and comfortable.

After Greta left, I turned on Sasha's gigantic TV and watched the DVDs I'd bought at WorldTone. I first looked at some of the early Sasha DVDs where Greta and her partner had competed. Her partner was so fun. He did *bachachatas*—these crazy-fast hip-swaying back steps in samba, like a slithering snake approaching prey. The crowd screamed for him even louder than they'd screamed for Sasha. It was sheer insanity. Interestingly, she didn't even try to keep up with him. She merely pointed toward him as if to say "Look at that! Look at my man!" They then switched and he extended his arm to her as she did the *bachachatas*. Hers weren't nearly as fast but she did them with a little up-and-down motion and rounding of the pelvis more than a sideways back and forth like his. So hers looked more like Carnival samba, which looked sexier—like something that would look good on a woman but maybe not so much on a man. And with her flared skirt with all the shimmies, the motion of the fabric bouncing this way and that accentuated her movement.

In their rumba her partner began coming toward her with crisscrossed steps. The way he walked toward her had such intention—both the movement and his facial expression. He wanted her. He was in love with her. She looked back at him and slowly stretched her upper body out to the ceiling, then out toward him, as if to say with her body that she wanted him back. Then he spun her out into some of the exact same turns as in our routine. She didn't lose connection with him like I did with Sasha. She stayed with him. He seemed to be gentler with her, but his passion was still there. You could be gentle and passionate. I made a mental note to show Sasha this part of the tape the next time he got crazy with me.

But you could tell by the way Greta's partner looked at her, at her body, the way he touched her, that he was taking care of her, making sure he wouldn't spin her out of control. He seemed to know her so well, how fast she could take it. I also noticed she used his body a lot, touching it, leaning on it, both front and back. This had both a functional effect, since she could use him as a balance, and a narrative aspect, since she was basically saying "I am here for you. I love your body." At one point, she actually ran the nail of her index finger down from the base of his neck to his pelvis. The crowd went wild over this. Could I ever do that to Sasha on a crowded ballroom floor?

I watched some of the later tapes, of the newer couples, after Greta and Dean had retired. I noticed Micaela and Jonathan had the same connection going on as Greta and Dean. You could just tell they were in love. And, as I'd noticed before, Jonathan was not as good technically as Sasha, and Xenia was not as precise with her body movement and swift with her footwork as Micaela, though both were close. The couples could easily have tied, since each had one stronger partner, one weaker. And yet they didn't. Jonathan was gentler with Micaela, seemingly making sure she could take whatever he gave her. They respected each other's bodies and private space. Micaela did some of the balletic movement Greta had choreographed for me. Jonathan would support her fully, waiting for her, for example, while she finished the slow, natural progression of lifting her leg high up in the air. With Sasha and Xenia, in contrast, it looked like he was moving swiftly, dancing gorgeously, but that she was forever trying to keep up, just as Greta had stated. It looked like they were dancing individually, not together. I needed to be Micaela, not Xenia.

Watching the tapes of the pros made me long more than ever to be a truly great dancer. Like Micaela. I was determined to be like her, just as good as she. Watching her drove me to work hard every day with Greta. I learned all five of our routines right away to get the footwork and movement in my muscle memory. Now, I mainly had to learn to dance them with Sasha, to learn whatever tweaks he'd want made, and to add my own style and flair, and better my technique. I made sure to stretch several times per day, both at Sasha's barre, and even at the office, so that my muscles would be as long and lean as possible by the time of the competition.

Staying at Sasha's was an absolute dream. Each morning I'd take a quick lap in the pool. So refreshing; a perfect start to my day. And Sasha was right—far from feeling any pain or weakness in my knee afterward, it actually felt better. Swimming was good cross-training for dance. And every night after Greta left, I took long, luxurious baths in that gorgeous tub of his to soak my muscles so they would stretch more easily.

\*\*\*

Toward the end of the week, Gunther finally had me return to Jamar's case. I was full of nervous excitement. On Friday, I actually made a trip out to the pens in Compton to meet Jamar. He looked exactly the same as he had on the video. He was a pretty big guy—well over six feet, weighed maybe 300 pounds—and had that heavy brow that I could imagine could put serious fear into anyone running into him late at night on a secluded street, just by his appearance. And yet his personality throughout just seemed so at odds with that. He sat hunched over and looked down, almost like he was scared to glance up at me. I'd wondered if his physicality had gotten him into this position. Maybe if the other young men had wanted to set him up to take the fall for them, they knew jurors might be squirming in their seats just seeing him.

"Hello, Mr. Jackson," I said.

He glanced up at me, making brief eye contact, then looked down immediately again as if in embarrassment.

"I'm one of the attorneys assigned to your case and I'm here to help you."

"Mmm, yes, ma'am," he murmured, still peering down.

"Okay, I want to start by asking you about the interrogation. Did the police ever suggest to you that you cased the store for several weeks prior to the break-in?"

He continued to regard the floor. He frowned, but said nothing.

"Um, well, did you ask the police for any meals or to go to the bathroom while they were questioning you?" I waited but his frown only deepened. "Did you ask them for any water?" I continued. "Because you were brought into the precinct at nine thirty p.m. and the time shown on your videotaped statement is seven forty-five the next morning. You must have asked for some food or water." Still no words from him. "Mr. Jackson?"

Finally he looked up at me, but again only briefly making eye contact. Then his head went down right away.

"That's a long time to be awake. Did you sleep at all that night?"

He slowly shook his head. "No, no sleep."

*Oh good, finally some words.* I was beginning to worry he'd forgotten the whole night entirely.

"Okay, and what about the other things I just asked about? Needing to go to the bathroom, eating a meal, water, the police telling you that you'd cased the place?"

He frowned deeper, seeming to think hard. Then he slowly shook his head.

"No? No to what, Mr. Jackson?"

He simply continued shaking his head, more and more rapidly. I wondered if I was confusing him. Maybe I was going too fast.

"Did they give you any water?"

He continued shaking his head but the shaking slowed now.

"And what about food? Did you have anything to eat, or to drink, in all that time?"

He squinted, looking again like he was thinking hard, then slowly shook his head.

"Did the police ever tell you they had your friends in custody and that they were confessing and naming you ringleader before you gave them any statements?" I asked, figuring maybe he wasn't understanding what I meant by them suggesting to him that he'd cased the place.

His frown deepened again and soon he started holding his head in his hands, pressing hard on his temples. He closed his eyes and let out a sigh as if he were in pain.

"Are you okay, Mr. Jackson? Do you have a headache?"

He slowly nodded, still not opening his eyes.

"Do you need aspirin or anything?" I said going for my purse then realizing they made me check it before coming into the back rooms. "I can go out and get you something. Or I can talk to the guards," I offered.

"Nah, nothin' really stops 'em."

"You get these often?"

He nodded. His fingers were pressed so firmly into his temples I worried he was making the pain worse. But how would I know?

"Have you ever been diagnosed with anything, Mr. Jackson? Any medical condition? Were you ever in an accident or anything to cause pain? This just came on suddenly?"

He shook his head, now bending down and holding his head in his lap.

"Miss, I think I'm going to need to go back and lie down?" he mumbled, his head between his knees.

"Yes, of course. But can I just ask, Mr. Jackson, did you have any headache the night of your arrest?"

"Before you go, miss, can you just do one thing?" he said without answering my question. He still didn't look up, was still rubbing his head.

"Of course."

"Can you ask them why I can't see my brother?"

"Is that Darnell?"

"Yeah, Darnell. They said I could see him. That I'd be near him. I ain't seen him. He's my brother. They said I could see him. They said I could see my brother," he repeated.

"Well, is he in this facility? I thought he was already convicted and at a maximum security prison in another city, Mr. Jackson. Is he back here for another case?" I was confused as to why he was told he could see his brother. They never bused people around unless someone was needed to testify at a trial.

"I dunno. Miss, I gots to go. Please just make 'em lemme see my bro." He was now slurring his words.

I worried about that headache. I wondered if it could be a stroke. *But he said he gets them all the time.*

I told him I would investigate the situation and do what I could. On the way out I also asked the guard who I could talk to at the holding facility about getting him medication for what appeared to be excruciating and debilitating head pain.

When I got back to the office I called the number I was given, and left a message on a voicemail. I looked up Darnell Jackson in the prison system online and found out he was housed up north. So, like I thought, not in Jamar's facility at all. I called his prison and tried to place a call to him but was told he was in lockup and couldn't take phone calls for the time being.

I asked when he would be able to take a call or see a visitor and they told me they didn't know. I'd tried Jamar's mother before with no luck, but tried her again, leaving a couple messages for her to call me back.

When the counselor from Jamar's holding facility finally called me back, he had no information on Jamar ever having suffered from any kind of head pain. Nor did Jamar have any medical files, either there or stored anywhere the counselor knew.

"Well, he had a pretty severe headache when I came to visit him. He had so much pain, we had to cut our visit short. Is there any way I can make sure he gets the proper medical care?"

After a big sigh, he said, "Ma'am, we're a holding facility. We have aspirin if he asks for that, and he hasn't. He's got a trial coming up so he won't be here long anyway."

I took that for a 'no.' This must be how it feels to be a social worker, I thought.

\*\*\*

Saturday afternoon was costume day for the mambo team. We loaded into three cars and trekked up and over the Hollywood Hills to Calabasas, to the shop of a costumer named Drucilla.

We were greeted by a young Russian woman who led us down a long hallway, which we had to walk down single file because it was so narrow, through a series of large rooms bearing other young women working behind sewing machines. Finally, at the end of the long hallway we entered a large room. There were huge tables bearing loads upon loads of catalogs, drawn designs, swatches of fabric, and photographs of dancers modeling their costumes. The walls were lined with signed headshots of dancers thanking Drucilla. I recognized several from "Dancing with the Stars," and Mitsi's was there. I looked for Sasha but didn't recognize anything at first glance. I did, however, recognize Arabelle, all the way at the end. I walked down and looked closely at the photo. Oh, she was so beautiful. And those lusciously long, spidery limbs. Her dress was gorgeous. But of course her ballerina body was a huge factor in making it so. It was the same dress she'd worn in the competition in which I'd seen her dance with Sasha.

Soon a very tall woman with a platinum blonde asymmetrical bob appeared at the doorway. "Helloooo," she said, extending a graceful arm toward us. "Welcome. Please seat."

She had a thick Russian accent and indicated for us to grab one of the plastic chairs or sit on the floor. If I had to guess I'd say she was about sixty, though I think by the way her eyes were slanted outward, she'd had some work done and could have been much older. It was clear from the way she carried herself—with perfect posture, slightly turned-out toes, and elegance galore—that she'd been a dancer.

"Now, what do you all look for?"

"We're thinking basic black men's Latin costumes for the guys, with the neckline cut way low, like…" Mitsi began, demonstrating by pointing to her navel. "Is that okay?"

"'Course, 'course!" Drucilla chirped. "And ladies."

"Yeah, we dunno yet. We were hoping you could help?" Mitsi said.

Drucilla looked around at us slowly, taking us in one by one. A frown slowly grew across her face. The frown was likely unintentional, though I totally understood it. We were all completely different shapes and sizes. There was no way the same design was going to look good on all of us. And we were women so of course we all had different ideas about what color suited us. This was going to be a nightmare, I thought. And I was right.

Drucilla first suggested shimmies which tended to hide flaws in bodies by leading the attention to the swinging pieces of fabric. But as Mitsi quickly pointed out, shimmies brought fast attention to flaws in dancing. If everyone's hips weren't going the exact same direction at the exact same time it was going to be uber-noticeable. We all agreed shimmies were a no-no.

So, what about a cute halter dress with a short and sassy skirt, Drucilla suggested. Roxy didn't like her legs so protested the skirt. And Judy thought her arms were way too flabby for a halter.

"I really need some kind of sleeve. Even a short, puffed sleeve. Just to cover the triceps area," she said.

"Puffed sleeves for a mambo?" Roxy said.

"With jagged edges, then. Or just tight," Judy said. "Anything. You know, you could use a sleeve yourse—" she started before Mitsi shushed her.

"Ladies, ladies, please let's not fight. There's a civil way to do this."

"Here, leet me work at it," Drucilla said grabbing a pencil and ripping a large piece of drawing paper from a book.

After a few minutes she held up her idea. The top had tight sleeves that extended to just past the elbow, and a deep scooped neckline. The bottoms consisted of tight capri-length pants. Mitsi nodded her approval.

"But how much space is there going to be between the pants and top? I don't want my midriff showing," Judy said.

Roxy didn't like the scooped neckline. "Everything I have is going to come shooting out of that," she said.

Lilly made it clear she'd wanted and expected the original idea—the shimmies, short skirt and halter, similar to what she'd worn in the competition I'd seen her at in the O.C. It cracked me up how the most Betty White of us wanted to dance in the most skimpy, glitzy costume. You had to love her for that courage.

"I just wasn't expecting to be so covered and…boring," she said, on the verge of tears.

"What do you want, Rory? You're the only one who hasn't piped up, and you look like you have a definite opinion," Mitsi asked.

Suddenly all eyes were focused on me. But all I could think about now was Arabelle. How I could never look like her in the dazzling costume Drucilla had designed for her. Suddenly I began to wonder what I'd wear with Sasha, how much worse I'd look than his former partner alongside him. I knew this was the wrong way of thinking and I tried to shake it off.

"Earth to Rory!" Mitsi laughed, snapping her fingers.

"Oh sorry. I…I dunno. I'm really okay with anything," I managed. At least Roxy and Judy only hated one body part apiece. I was disgusted with my whole package. "A sack?" I found myself uttering.

Everyone laughed, apparently thinking I was kidding. Except Roxy, who seemed offended. "Well, I'm sorry we don't all look like you, missy. Someday you're going to be sss…older, and young girls are going to say such things to you. It happens to us all. Believe me, honey, it'll happen to you…thirty's just around the corner for you, in fact, isn't it?"

*What?* I had no idea what Roxy was on about. I didn't mean I wanted them to wear sacks; I'd only meant for myself.

"Hey, hey," Mitsi said, cutting her off. "Come on, she was making a joke about how ridiculous we're all being. She wasn't insinuating she was embarrassed by you and wanted you to dance in a sack."

Of course I hadn't meant that and wasn't sure how anyone could have interpreted it as such. Nor had I meant to make a joke. "I'm just self-conscious about my whole body. That's why I suggested a sack," I said defensively.

"Oh, please. You expect us to believe that?" Roxy rolled her eyes.

"Ladies, this is out of control!" Mitsi said raising her voice, which was unusual for her. "We're all women, or maybe it's that we're all dancers and used to being on display. In any event, we're all self-conscious nut jobs. Let's just leave it at that and act like teammates, okay?"

In the end, we all okay'd Drucilla's design of the three-quarter-sleeved top with the capri pants, albeit with a high neckline and waistline. Mitsi chose—and we managed to agree on—fuchsia with black trim as the color, reasoning that the flashy shade would make up for any lack of sexiness in the design.

"Okay, measurements," Drucilla said, clapping her hands. Several young women appeared at the doorway, wearing tape measures around their necks like scarves.

"Skinny," my seamstress said, raising her brows as she whipped the tape up, down and around me, then recorded the numbers.

Not really, I felt like saying, but didn't.

Finally, the oh-so-traumatic experience was over and we all walked single-file through the hallway like a duckling family with Mitsi as the momma, toward the exit. I was last in line.

"Oh, hey, fancy seeing you all here," I heard Mitsi say as she opened the door.

A shot of adrenaline burst up my spine, literally making my back raise what felt like inches when I saw who she was talking to. Luna, Cheryl, and two of Sasha's Russian students stood in the doorway, Sadie holding the door open for us. The latter was the only one smiling and I managed to flash her a nervous grin as I passed. I tried hard not to look at Cheryl. But I could see her in my periphery. As I passed, she raised her shoulders and placed her hands on her hips, seeming to brace herself for me to pass by her.

As if I was some threat to her? *What?*

"Oh," she said, tapping me on the back after I thought I'd successfully passed.

I hesitantly turned around, so not wanting to.

"I'm really sorry to hear how about you and Sasha," she said.

I looked into her eyes. Her bottom lip was jutting out and her eyes were turned down at the corners, in her best look of faux sympathy.

"This is L.A. and there are lots and lots of studios in town," she continued. "I'm sure you can find someone else who's just as good...well, maybe not as good, but, you know, close. There's more than one fish in the ocean is what I meant to say." She nodded conclusively, looking like she was doing everything possible to avoid bursting out in laughter.

I was befuddled. Had Sasha gotten back together with Xenia? Had he now decided to compete with her at Blackpool instead of me? If so, how did Cheryl know it already without me knowing? The shock must have shown on my face.

"You'll be fine, dear," she continued. "As I said, you'll find someone else. And for now you have your mambo team. But...you're in danger of losing them."

She waved to Mitsi's back—she was now ducking into her car. I hoped they knew I wasn't in yet and weren't going to take off without me. I said nothing to Cheryl and took off after them, my face burning. I could hear her and Luna snickering behind me.

# CHAPTER 10

After I said goodbye to my teammates and was on my walk home from the studio, I whipped out my cell phone and called Sasha. He answered on the second ring.

"Hello, Rory," he said, sounding a little out of breath.

"Hi," I said, suddenly not knowing what exactly to say. Why was he out of breath, I wondered?

"How are you? Is something wrong?" There was an urgency in his voice, but it sounded like he was trying to hide it, or to calm himself down.

I couldn't hear Xenia in the background. Cheryl's just playing with you, my inner voice said. I didn't want to seem insecure. I decided not to broach my conversation with her.

"No. I'm fine. I just wanted to hear your voice. What about you? Are you okay? You sound out of breath."

"Everything's fine." I could hear him take a deep breath. "Both show dances went fine. We'll be flying out on the red-eye tonight. How is training with Greta coming along?"

"Really well," I said, unable to control the excitement in my voice. "We've made so much progress. We've gotten through all the routines and I really love the choreography she's done. She gave me things to do that I'm good at that look right on me, and she still kept all the basic steps we need. I'm learning so much through her. She's awesome."

"Good. Good. I'm very glad to hear that." He sounded much calmer now.

It didn't seem like he was out of breath because of anything to do with Xenia. I couldn't be sure but it just didn't seem that way. It didn't seem like she was anywhere around.

"I can't wait to see you," I said.

"And I can't wait to see you," he said, his voice now a seductive rasp, melting me. "Our flight is at nine tonight. I will be home tomorrow evening and we can resume prrrractice."

Oooh, I felt he did that rolling r on purpose. My lower abdomen pulsed and I had to catch my breath before responding. "It's a plan. Have a good flight."

"Thank you. I will see you very soon."

The pulsing in my belly turned to hot liquid as I said goodbye. The second I clicked off, I couldn't help but be bothered by the fact that he used the plural in speaking of his flight: "we fly home tonight." Ugh, I needed to stop worrying. He was traveling with Xenia of course, so it made sense they were flying together. Cheryl was full of it. I couldn't imagine anything was going on. Still, I wondered where she got her information. And I wondered why he'd initially sounded so out of breath.

\*\*\*

Greta and I were in the middle of rehearsing the cha-cha routine when Sasha walked in. The music was so loud I hadn't heard his car and didn't realize he was watching us until I spotted his beautiful face in the doorway. I stopped mid-cha and ran toward him.

"No, don't stop. Please. I was enjoying that." He was wearing his leather ensemble and his hair was wavy and mussed about. My favorite look on him. He had that sexy cocked smile and a raised brow.

"Sorry, can't help it." I wrapped my arms around him, pressed my cheek to his, not wanting to get too PDA with Greta there though I couldn't help but wish she wasn't so we could throw off our clothes and melt into each other. As I hugged him I tried to smell or detect any remnant of Xenia. I couldn't.

He pressed his lips to my cheek, then sought my mouth, giving me a long, drawn-out kiss, albeit one with solely lips, no tongue, I'm sure due to Greta. "Okay, I'm going to put on workout clothes. I'll be back down in ten minutes max."

He squeezed my shoulder and gave me another peck on the forehead before he flew up the stairs. He was definitely happy to see me. If he'd just hooked up again with Xenia, he was a damn good actor.

We spent the next couple of hours cursorily going through the routines Greta had choreographed to see if he liked them. He did, for the most part, but had several tweaks to his parts. Nothing that would affect me, which was good because I didn't need anything throwing me off my game, which, as it had developed with Greta, was quite decent at that point, if I might say so myself. Of course it was a completely different dynamic dancing with him than with Greta. Even though we were just mapping things out and not dancing full-out, I had to readjust to his strength and power, had to re-center myself so as not to feel pushed and pulled. At one point in our cha-cha he was supposed to send me out so I could do this beautiful *ronde de jambe en l'air*, and, as with the arabesques before, he pushed too hard and I went out too far and lost my balance and couldn't execute the leg lift. Plus, I was too far from him and he had to tug me back to him or we'd lose contact—a big no-no in ballroom.

"It's okay, it's okay," Greta said, trying to clear the air before it had even been sullied. "It's only the first time you two are dancing the choreography together. It will take some time to work out kinks."

I glanced at Sasha, frightened I might see anger on his face. His eyes were wide and serious, and when my gaze connected with his, I ever-so-briefly saw that deep frustration born of panic flash by. But it was only a flash. He blinked it off and breathed and a relaxed smile took its place.

Part of me wanted to try again to make it right, but part of me knew it could end badly if I screwed up twice, and I really had to go home so I could get to work in time the next morning.

"You know you are more than welcome to stay the night, as always, Rory," he said, without any sexual innuendo. "I mean you may use the bath whenever you like as well, to soak your knee. And the pool for cross-training. While I stay down here and Greta gets me up to speed. Don't worry, I give you my assurance I will leave you unmolested." He sounded like a deliciously dangerous vampire with perfect seventeenth-century English. And at this his cocked smile returned.

*Argh, could he be more frigging tempting?*

"I will this weekend. Starting Friday night," I said with a sad smile. "I need to return to my regular pattern, at least early in the work week." I knew I'd never be sleeping, never getting up in time to be at work at a decent hour if I stayed. And it could be a big week with Jamar's case.

"Okay, do what you feel is necessary," he said, understanding in his eyes.

"You two will be on your own tomorrow night, as I have a prior engagement," Greta said to me on my way out. "I will make sure he knows the choreography inside and out." She gave me a wink, which I hoped meant she was going to have a little talk with him about being patient and gentle with me as well.

\*\*\*

Nothing happened at work on Jamar's case, except that I tried to call his mother, in vain, a few more times. I had a day full of boring wills, which was good because I was able to leave the office promptly at five and make my advanced mambo class. I was back to taking studio classes now—at least the mambos for team practice. I left the studio right after and got to Sasha's at seven. That gave me a couple hours till he got home from his private lessons to take a quick swim, stretch at the barre, and practice the steps again myself. I was proud to say I had the routines totally memorized. Unless he threw something in completely from left field, I was good and prepared.

Still, I had to brace myself when I heard his key in the door lock.

"Oh good, you are all ready for me," he said as his handsome visage appeared in the ballroom doorway.

"I am," I said, though my voice sounded anything but confident.

We started with rumba, as usual, which I was beginning to think was not a very good idea, as it never seemed to get us off to a very solid start. Slow though it was, the movements had to be perfect since the judges had plenty of time to see imperfections. Anything lacking technique-wise would be totally obvious. I knew that all too well from watching his pro/am students. And all of my beautiful tricks—the high leg extensions which ended up wrapping around his back; the splits into his arms; the deep dips and full back arches—all relied on us having a solid connection so I wouldn't fall. Plus, with it being the dance of passion, the partnership just really had to show that we were in love. There was no room for his frustration or annoyance with me or my fear of him.

We got through the first section of slow basics in closed hold. I knew where my feet should go and when. But I knew I was concentrating too hard with my brain, and I knew I'd mess up that way. So I closed my eyes and tried to let his body guide me. I tried to feel his strength so that I could return it, and therefore avoid that sensation of being pushed and pulled around. Then came the series of crazy-fast spins. He lifted his arm slowly, indicating the underarm turn, then once I was halfway into it, whipped me into several more spins away from him, following me with his hand still holding mine. It was much faster than Greta had done it, but, because I knew to expect it, I was forward weighted on the balls of my feet, ready to turn fast on my toes, and had a solid connection to both him and the floor beneath my feet. I kept my center tight, my shoulders down and my posture as upright as I could so as to avoid losing my balance. Amazingly, it worked, as did the subsequent spiral and slow struts around him.

"Good," he said.

But, argh, that jinxed us, because the very next step was a deep, one-legged dip. He took me down faster than I was expecting and I got a little dizzy and un-centered, and when my arms flew behind my back and I lifted my leg I had to grip the floor to remain balanced.

"No touching the floor," he said. "The judges will know that's a mistake. You need to keep your arms straight out, over your head."

"I know, I know," I said, head still upside down in the dip. "You took me into it faster than I've been going with Greta and I got dizzy and had to use the floor for balance." I sounded like a whiny child who'd just gotten in trouble for leaving her toys scattered across the room. I hated that.

"Keep going," he said, now lunging toward me while I did one of the crazy-high leg lifts.

His lunge was far deeper than Greta's and he really had to stretch to keep his fingers interlaced with mine. Of course the deeper his stretch the cooler it looked, but I needed as solid a connection as possible with his hand while I balanced my entire weight on one stiletto and did the splits in the air. I gingerly spread the toes of my left foot inside the tight quarters of the shoe to find solid footing on the ground while slowly lifting my right leg. The imagery was so sensual, so sexual. And yet he looked so dead serious. And I felt panic in my eyes. Would I be able, I wondered, to gain the confidence to make this actually look beautiful and romantic and sultry by the time we performed?

When I had my leg fully extended, he rose from his lunge and came toward me. I was supposed to hook my foot around his shoulder so he could pull me forward in a kind of a one-footed slide. But he did so quickly and it startled me. I leaned back with my left foot, forcing him to adjust the distance he traveled to reach my airborne leg and wrap it around his shoulder.

He sighed deeply but continued.

When he tried to pull me toward him, I was too tense, too weighted on my left foot to allow that foot to glide lightly over the floor. He pulled and the left foot stuck.

"Stop," I cried, not wanting to tear a muscle. I was already in a split. I couldn't stretch much farther.

He closed his eyes, breathed deeply, and unhooked my right foot from his shoulder. When both of my feet were on the floor, he put his hands on his hips. His eyes narrowed at me.

"I was nervous and therefore had my foot too weighted…"

He held his palm toward me. "No excuses now, please. I mean…" He seemed consciously to adjust his expression, raising his eyebrows out of their furrowed frown and pulling the corners of his lips upward into an ever-so-slight smile. "Let's not talk about it now. Let's just continue." He nodded and politely extended his arm to me.

I blinked back tears and walked toward him. He wasn't yelling at me, but it was clearly an all-out effort on his part not to do so. His boxed-in anger was making me all the more on-edge, making me all the more inclined to screw up, making him all the more likely to get angry and frustrated. It was a vicious circle.

We continued where we'd left off. I gently pulled my leg off his shoulder and swept it back behind me in arabesque *penchée*, while he kneeled. This was such a beautiful move. Executed properly, it should look like he was on his knees, ready to propose, and I was bowing down graciously to him. But my standing leg was wobbling because of my nerves and I leaned too far forward and feared I'd tumble over him if I didn't put my back leg down. Suddenly, before I had the leg all the way down, he pushed on my hand, causing me to slide back and land flat on my behind.

"Why did you do that?" I said, a bit stunned.

"Why did I do that?" he asked, sounding equally stunned. "Rory, you need to resist me. That's the way we maintain balance. You didn't push back against me at all. You can't just let me push you around."

At first I was confused, then realized he was right. Again, the force he used was so much harder than Greta's. "I…" I began but realized I was just going to be making excuses all night long if I didn't stop now. "Okay. Again, I wasn't used to your force. But now I am. So now I'm ready for you."

He opened his mouth, then closed it, seeming to realize there was nothing to protest. "Okay," he said, his clouded eyes clearing. "Let's continue, shall we?"

I lowered myself down on top of him, into his outstretched arms, as he raised me above him, still on his knees, with my toes pointed behind me. Another beautiful move, if we could look at each other with love in our eyes instead of terror.

"Pull up through your center," he said. "Your body is not in a straight line and looks awkward."

I looked at myself in the mirror. Okay, my butt looked big but it was tucked in as tightly as I could. I squeezed even tighter.

"No, your shoulders. That's what I'm referring to," he said. "They are rounding, like you're hunched over. Pull up."

"Oh." I held my shoulders back, and raised my arms behind me like a bird as he pushed me out.

"Good, now look back at me but keep your upper body arched."

I did as he said, gazing down at him when he pulled me back toward him. But it felt strange and incongruous arching back while looking down.

"Good!" He sounded genuinely excited that I'd exhibited what he wanted. So I decided not to voice my objection.

He led me into a basic but flashy step I liked, called a fan. He lowered his arm and I shifted my weight by twisting my hips sharply from side to side. It was one of my favorite moves because the hip twist was so sharp and flirty.

"No, it needs to be quicker." He stopped.

"What?" I said.

"The twist, it needs to be faster. You are going too slow."

I'd done it the same way I had with Greta. We were dancing to the same music. Greta hadn't told me I was too slow. And I felt like I was on the beat. "Okay," I said under my breath, deciding it wasn't worth a fight.

Then we came to another move that would be pretty if we could do it right. I stood facing away from him, and went to lift my leg to circle it in the air, but when I began the *ronde*, he pulled back on my arm and I literally fell backward, on top of him.

"What was that?" He was losing his battle to remain calm.

He wrapped his arms around his waist and tried to turn me around to look at him. But I stopped him. I put my hands over his and leaned my head back to cradle on his shoulder, closing my eyes to shut out his frustration, which was swiftly turning to anger. It felt so good for him to hold me even if I was basically making him.

He sighed in resignation, then cradled me, rocking back and forth. "Okay, c'mon," he said after a few moments, trying to pry my hands off his arms. "Rory, we need to practice. We don't have much…" he began in protest.

"No, we need to talk this out first, Sasha," I said, moving forward, releasing his hands, and turning toward him. My voice had somehow acquired assertiveness from somewhere.

Judging by the expression on his face when I turned to look at him, he was surprised too.

"I've been doing this with Greta and everything's been great," I continued. "I have to get used to your strength and power. You push or pull or whiplash me around and I'm just not ready. You have to give me time to get used to you so I can give you proper resistance. Otherwise I'm going to be falling all over you."

"Rory, we have been dancing together for a while now. That's what we are doing. That's why we're going over this."

"No, we haven't been dancing like this, Sasha. We've been doing lead and follow, not a Blackpool routine."

He sighed deeply. "Don't you see it is the same, Rory? We have choreography but you still need to follow me. You still need to sense my weight, my position, do as I lead you. You are still dancing on your own. Not with me."

"Shhh," I said, putting my finger to his lips. He was getting too worked up; he'd never listen if his excitement got too out of control. And I hadn't finished what I had to say. "But it can't be all about me doing whatever you want me to, trying to keep up with you. If I keep trying to resist and push back or whatever, and it's all about you laying the standard and me trying to adhere to it. You're not allowing me to be myself—"

"You are still a beginner. You need instruction!"

This wasn't coming out as all as I intended. It appeared that Greta hadn't talked to him. Or she had and he hadn't listened.

"Sasha, I need you to listen to me. For just a minute. Just listen. The whole time you were gone I watched a bunch of tapes of prior Blackpools. A bunch. I saw all the top couples and especially Greta and Dean and how they moved together, how they worked together. How they respected each other and how their love and respect for each other showed in competition. The man was always faster and more precise, but he gave the woman the freedom to do her own thing and show her artistry. So it worked even if he had greater athletic ability than she did."

"This is not about athletic ability, Rory. I'm not criticizing you because you are not as fast. That's an obvious fact. We can't do anything about that." He threw his arms up, not understanding what I was trying to tell him.

Which was understandable, since what I wanted to say was all coming out in a jumble.

"Sasha, we need to work together. You need to not fight me."

"I don't know what that means. I am trying to teach you to dance, Rory." He was now standing, pacing the room and shaking his head, sweat flying in all directions.

Okay, maybe I should just focus on getting used to his strength, I decided. One point at a time. "Okay, look. Can we just go back to that thing we did at the studio that one day where I leaned on you and you felt my weight? Except this time it needs to be reversed and I need to feel yours."

"You're not ever going to be lifting me, Rory. That makes no sense." He stopped pacing and looked at me dead on.

"I need to get used to your strength. Seriously, come here and hold my hands. Come on."

"This is a waste—" He harrumphed and shook his head like he was listening to a crazy woman, but walked to me anyway. "Now what?" he said, taking my hands into his.

"Just push and pull me."

"Rory, this is ridic—"

"Just humor me and do it. Please."

"Okay?" He tugged on me. I went flying toward him.

"Sasha, not as hard as you can. I mean, as if we were dancing."

"That's what I did," he maintained.

"No, it's not. Do it again."

He did, this time ever-so-slightly less strong. This time I was ready and I pulled back. But his pull was still too strong and I had to step forward quickly lest I lose my balance.

"No, see, that's too strong."

"You said you wanted to know my strength. Now you know. You will get used to it."

"No, that's the problem. Sasha, I'm pulling and pushing as hard as I can and you're still overwhelming me. This is not a partnership, it's a fight. We're not ballroom dancing, we're wrestling."

He laughed. It seemed to be a genuine laugh, as if he really thought what I said was funny. Finally, some comic relief. Even if I hadn't really meant it as such.

"We can't have it look like that to the judges or we have no chance," I continued. "It's not just me who needs to adjust to you; you need to adjust to me and my strength too. Or lack thereof, okay. We need to work together."

His mouth was agape. It was a look I couldn't really interpret.

"I'm serious, Sasha. I watched those DVDs so many times. What distinguished the couples who won from the ones who were only finalists was that the winners were a team. They each respected the other and let each other shine. It wasn't like they were good separately and were trying to outdo each other, or keep up with each other."

My voice was losing steam. The "losing couples" were Sasha and Xenia or Sasha and Micaela. I was directly criticizing him. His eyes darkened. He seemed to know this.

"I'm talking about Greta and Dean as the couple who were taking care of each other on the floor," I added, hoping to alter the focus and deflect my criticism.

He nodded and took a deep breath before speaking. "So now you are an authority? You know more about ballroom dancing than I do because you watched a few tapes? You think you should be teacher?" He put his hands on his hips and rocked back on his heels, as if I were challenging him. He wasn't yelling, but I could tell he was inwardly fuming.

"No, of course not." I laughed nervously. "I'm just trying to say that Greta knows better than anyone what it takes to be a champion. So let's just let her teach. She's a disinterested party. That way we won't resent each other for anything. I thought you guys had already agreed on that, anyway."

"She can't be here all the time, Rory. She can only be here three or four times a week."

"And the rest of the time, we'll just practice the routines on our own, without criticizing each other. Just working together."

"Then how will you learn? You'll only be receiving instruction a few times a week. You need it every day," he said, almost shouting.

I glanced at the clock. It was an hour later than I'd planned to leave. We were just going around in circles. He wasn't listening. Maybe I wasn't making myself clear. In any event, this was just getting worse and I needed to go home and get some sleep before work tomorrow.

Tears began to clog my throat. I couldn't talk. I walked toward my bags, pointing at the clock.

He exhaled loudly and lowered his head into his hands, an action I'd seen him do oh so many times during fights with Xenia and Arabelle and countless others at the studio.

"Sasha, I'm sorry, I just can't deal with you when you're like this," I said, my voice cracking. I meant to say that I needed to go home and resume things tomorrow, but instead I said, "I can't do this until…until you change your attitude."

I ran outside without looking back. I cried the whole way home, tears at times clouding my vision through the long, winding roads. I'd made the decision to be the best dancer I could be, to try with all my heart to win, to help Sasha win. I just didn't know if I could go through with it. I'd fallen for him too hard.

# CHAPTER 11

It was a good thing Gunther had a lot of miscellaneous research for me to do the next day at work because it was busywork that occupied my mind without being stressful, and forced me to focus on something other than my fight with Sasha last night. I made myself concentrate, and worked so diligently that five p.m. actually snuck up on me.

I hadn't heard from Sasha. As much as it pained me to think he wasn't going to change, and our dance partnership—and therefore, relationship—could well be over, I tried to cheer myself up by focusing on having an evening back at the studio. I was still paying for unlimited classes and because I was now advanced, I could take anything I wanted, not only the international-style classes. I could take a hustle or swing class and hang out with Rajiv and get flung around the floor by crazy-fun Eduardo again.

"Oh, look! Welcome back, stranger," Mitsi called out on seeing me in the back row in her bolero class.

"It's really good to see you again," Rajiv said, giving me a hug. "You're…okay, right?" He had a worried look.

But seeing Rajiv only made me think of the Orange County competition, of spying on Sasha while having dinner with Rajiv at Musso & Frank in Hollywood, of all our conversations about the man. *My man.* Of everything that had happened since. I blinked hard and held my head down, forcing myself not to cry.

"Oh no, you're not okay," he said. "Okay, we'll have to get together and talk. I have to leave early tonight, but I'm free tomorrow night, or this weekend?"

"That would be so good," I said, my voice cracking. I took a breath and told myself to snap out of it. "I'll text you later about the time," I continued after I'd willed the tears away.

"Cool. Let me know." He patted my shoulder.

\*\*\*

Next, I decided to brave Bronislava's silver-level samba. It was the third week of the month, but she didn't give me any crap about missing the first two weeks and, hence, not having seen the routine before. I knew the syllabus backward and forward now and could easily do any step she called out. Of course as much as I tried to avoid it, I couldn't help glancing at Cheryl. And when I did so, of course we locked eyes. She actually looked genuinely sorry for me; there was nothing faux about her pout this time. I felt like she'd jinxed me. Nothing had actually been wrong with me and Sasha when I saw her at Drucilla's but after she'd made those nasty, inscrutable remarks, there was. It was like she'd foreseen it or something.

"Oh my lord, he has done wonders with you, honey! Wonders, wonders, wonders!" Paulina wrapped her construction-worker-sized arms around me. "You are like a pro, girlfriend! Well, not like. You are! Damn!"

I laughed but then, again, had to struggle hard to keep the tears at bay. Paulina was squeezing me so hard, I don't think she noticed. I peeked over her shoulder and caught Cheryl's face again. She was looking up at the back of Paulina's head, her face now contorted with confusion.

\*\*\*

"Save me a dance, *senorita*, you must," Eduardo demanded after our hustle class ended. "Tonight is the hustle party, don't you remember?" he clarified when I frowned at him.

*Oh yes, of course.*

And I did save him a dance. Dancing with Eduardo was the perfect antidote. He whisked me around and around, cracking me up with his goofy, faux-cocksure smiles as we did our best John Travolta, strutting toward then past each other, raising our arms in unison when we met like madly flapping swan queens.

\*\*\*

It was pretty late when I started my walk home. But it was Hollywood, so it felt like the middle of the day with all the tourists snapping pictures of the Chinese Theater and name blocks on the Walk of Fame, and hooting at the break dancers and fake Johnnys and Marilyns.

Living in Hollywood was perfect for taking me out of myself. Maybe I'd get sated with it eventually, like James, but right now everything was such a show. It was hard not to be captivated by all the life around me.

But after I passed the touristy part and started up the quiet tree-lined street that led to my block, that eerie feeling I'd felt in the parking lot at my office returned. That feeling that someone was watching me. I looked around, but saw nothing. Nothing out of the ordinary, anyway. Cars parked on the side of the street, lights streaming through bedroom and living room windows. A woman was looking out her window up and down the street, but she didn't look at all threatening. A guy was walking his dog. No one was hiding in the bushes. And yet the feeling was so palpable.

Stop creeping yourself out, I said to myself. *This is ridiculous.*

But the creepy feeling wouldn't go away. I knew what it was: I was just missing Sasha. Oh how I longed for him, to walk down this quaint little street off the main boulevard, hand in hand. I hadn't allowed myself to check my phone to see if he called. And though I wanted to badly, I forced myself to wait till I got home.

But by that point, there was no need. When I approached my apartment, guess who was sitting in front of my door? Just as he had the last time he surprised me with an apology, along with a proposition that completely changed our relationship.

"I thought you would never get home," he said, looking up at me with puppy dog eyes that begged for forgiveness.

And I knew this was going to be good.

"I haven't been to the studio in a long time. I stayed for the practice party. It was fun," I said.

He stood. "I'm glad. It is important to have fun." He'd been outside my front door for a while. He smelled like the outdoors, of pine trees and fresh night air.

"Yes, it definitely is." I unlocked the door and walked in, tossing my bag on the floor and my keys on the counter. I turned around. He stood in the doorway.

"May I?" he asked meekly. It was cute he didn't automatically assume he could just bust in on me.

"Ummmmm…" I pretended I had to think about it.

"Don't worry, I won't stay late. I will let you go to work at a decent hour," he said with a cocked smile that made me just want to rip off his clothes and jump him, and put off talking about the fight to a much, much later time.

Instead I turned the rose-colored ceiling lights on high, to an unsexy bright, and sat down on the sofa. We had to talk sooner rather than later lest we lose too much time practicing. I motioned to the scarlet-padded rattan chair across the couch but he said "Thank you" and sat down right next to me, so close our hips touched.

Why was I not surprised?

"Rory, I'm so sorry," he said before I could say anything. "I…" He leaned in and took my hand, caressing it with his fingertips. "My biggest shortcoming is that I am a perfectionist and I know that makes me very hard to work with. I know that. I just want to win this competition more than anything. And I guess I just freak out when there is an imperfection, however slight. I just panic." He put his head down.

"I've lost a lot of partners. I know I need to calm down. I don't want to lose you. You are everything to me."

Okay, at that I wanted badly to jump sideways onto him, whip my leg around his waist, wrap my body around his. That was really all I needed to forgive him. His assurance that he was being too hard, that everything was not my fault. That I was everything to him.

But he had more to say. "I had very strict teachers in Russia. They were very hard on me. They would smack me hard with a stick if something was jutting out wrong, making the line sloppy, if I wasn't fast enough, or precise enough. They would leave marks on my body. And they demanded I win. Second is never ever good enough in Russia. Second is a failure. That's why Russians"—he paused to chuckle and shake his head—"why Russians are so crazed and competitive. American teaching is so different. It's so much more…casual. You correct but if something is not perfect you let it go. You definitely don't use a stick." He laughed.

"No! Here, that would open you up to all kinds of legal liability," I said, laughing with him.

He turned his body toward me, put his arm around my shoulder, and kissed the side of my face, then trailed kisses from my temple, down to my cheekbone, to the hollow behind my ear, then down my neck to my shoulder. *Mmmm, splendid*—the kisses, and the fact he'd spoken about something that happened to him in Russia for the first time with me. How I wanted to know more.

"It makes sense to me why you want to win so much," I said, gingerly trying to broach the subject of his past. "If that's how you were taught to think, I mean. In Russia."

He said nothing, continued pressing his lips to my skin, now making his way around to the hollow of my neck. Okay, that may be all I get for now, I thought.

"You were never, like, seriously injured, right?"

The kisses stopped. His breath on my neck suddenly felt tense. He lifted his head and looked me in the eye. There was a darkness there that hadn't been there before. "What?" he said.

"I just meant by the teachers. With the sticks." I laughed nervously, worried I'd opened up a serious wound. "You know, here the bronze and silver medals are really prestigious too. I mean, I've looked up all the pros on the TV shows, on "Dancing With the Stars," and most of them never actually placed first at Blackpool. And it's hardly like they're unsuccessful. Would you ever want to do that, be on one of those shows? I mean, everyone should see you. The public. Not just the Blackpool judges. You're too good."

I was jabbering, trying to get the subject far away from where I'd taken it. I had wondered though why he was so hell-bent on winning now that there were other outlets for ballroom dancers. In the past, before the TV shows, I understood why the competitions were everything, when that's all dancers had. But not so much now.

His eyes now strayed from me, focused on something in the distance. His pupils dilated and his irises darkened. He breathed heavily.

"What? What are you thinking? Let me in," I said, wiggling his arm.

Still staring, he began to speak, slowly. "No. I wasn't hurt. Someone else was. I have to win. It makes everything…it makes everything okay. Maybe not okay, but…bearable."

"What? Who—"

"No. I don't want to talk about it. Not now." He shook his head, as if to rid himself of whatever blue cloud had momentarily shadowed over him. "Besides, I just don't want to be on those shows." He spoke more quickly now, back to his regular speed. His gaze returned to me. "They are just…not enough for me. Not now," he said with a burst of laughter that, happily, seemed genuine. "But I appreciate what you are trying to do. That you are trying to lessen the pressure." He squeezed my shoulder, kissed my cheek.

I smiled. I wanted to know so much more, but this line of questioning was clearly too much. I didn't like that black, hazy look in his eyes.

"What first made you fall in love with dance?" I asked instead. "For me it was The Nutcracker."

He laughed.

"I know, big surprise. I think that's most Americans' first experience with dance. With concert dance, anyway. I fell right away for The Nutcracker when, in Clara's dreams, he comes alive and does all that badass sword fighting and saves her from the evil mouse king," I said with a little bounce.

He kissed the crown of my head. "Dancing…when I was little, it was my way of taking out aggression. I didn't talk much. I was shy and withdrawn." He was quiet for a moment before continuing. "But when it came time for dance, I just came alive. It was like no one could stop me, constrain me. I was free."

I began to tell him I understood but a lump caught in my throat. Minus the aggression issues, which

I desperately wanted to know more about, dance made me come alive too. I was shy as a little girl as well. When I was little it was the only thing that brought me out of myself.

But that person, that little girl with the inner fire, was so absent from my adult self. The grown-up self only worried about what others thought of her, whether she was good enough, smart enough, thin enough.

Sasha caressed my cheek with his thumb, which I suddenly realized was wet.

"Hey," he said, gently. "What's this about?"

I hadn't even realized I was crying. I shook my head, unable to get any words out. My whole body began to shake. He pulled me toward him. I cried into his chest. He kissed the crown of my head again and rubbed his hands up and down my arms, warming my whole body which had become cold. We sat like this for I don't know how long. Until I finally caught my breath.

"Sasha, you are still most alive when you dance. That's so obvious," I said, trying to bring the focus back to him since I couldn't seem to control my emotions when I focused on myself. "You're on fire. You're the definition of captivating. People can't look away. Watching you that one night at The Beverly Hilton reignited my passion for dance. Instantly. I knew what was wrong with my life, what was missing. After seeing you I had to go back to it. I had no choice."

He reached around and held my hands, rubbing my knuckles with the pads of his fingers. "You don't know what it does to me to hear you say that," he whispered.

"Dance makes me alive too," I said, nearly choking, my throat constricting again. "That's why…"

He squeezed my hands tightly. "I know. You don't have to say it. That's why it hurts you so much when I'm so hard. It's like I'm stomping out your flame. I'm so sorry."

He wrapped his arms around me again. I cried into his chest a little more and we rocked back and forth together.

When I recovered my breath, I again tried to return the focus to him. "What drew you to ballroom dancing anyway? I mean, there are lots of ballet dancers who dance with this animalistic passion, this abandon. I mean Carlos Acosta, Rudolf Nureyev, Baryshnikov. If you'd become a ballet dancer, you wouldn't even have to rely on a partner. I mean, you would when you're dancing a *pas de deux* with her in a ballet, but not to win competitions and be considered brilliant in your own name."

"Ballet was way too straight-laced for me," he said, flashing that oh-so-sexy cocked smile again. "I wanted to move my hips. I liked the rhythm of Latin, the sexiness of it, the pulsing music. But…I guess you could also say ballroom chose me." The wicked grin disappeared and something in his eyes darkened.

"You mean, you took a class and loved it so much you couldn't stop?" I said, worried I was unearthing some demons.

"No." His tone was flat, his eyes dark and hazy again. "We didn't have ballroom in my school. We had traditional Russian dancing. Everyone learned it. Lots of, I guess what you call, folk dancing. And of course we had ballet. But the traditional Russian dance was mandatory. Those kicks and jumps…they got rid of so much aggression. I went so high on them. I flew. The other kids would laugh, the teachers would scream. I lashed out at the world, my father…" His voice trailed off.

Just as I was about to speak, he continued.

"I was so-so in my other classes. But dance, I could do things that would make people take notice of me. I was a shy boy. Withdrawn. I wasn't very happy. But I was another person when I danced."

I forced myself to resist asking why he wasn't a happy boy, though, of course, I desperately wanted to know. He'd said that part under his breath as if he wasn't sure he wanted me to hear, anyway. I didn't want to open any wounds right now.

"So you initially loved Russian folk dancing and ballet. I get that. I loved ballet and tap as a kid. Actually tap dancing was my first dance, and my favorite."

"Why do I not have problem seeing you as tap dancer?" he said, face brightening. He gave me a loving grin and kissed my cheek.

"So, you said ballroom chose you? How did you get started in ballroom, then?"

He slowly moved his lips from my cheek, as if he was bracing himself for a long story. "Way I remember is, a lady saw me in class, dancing traditional Russian dance, and one day she told me she thought I had talent. She asked me if I would meet with her niece, who needed a partner."

"Micaela?"

"No," he laughed. "She came much, much later. This was still in Novosibirsk. Actually, not Novosibirsk yet, but the small town where I lived."

"Where's that?"

"Siberia. I met Micaela in Moscow. Actually, first time I met her was in England. But we returned to Moscow and competed there. She was already a rising star when I met her. She was a star before I was. A local star, anyway. She…" He exhaled slowly. "She made me a star." At first I thought it was a difficult admission for him, but when I looked into his eyes I saw a peaceful acceptance, a kind of nostalgia.

"You grew up in Siberia?" I don't know what kind of expression I had on my face. I'd only ever heard of it before as a place where mainly poor people lived or where people had been banished under the Soviet regime.

He quickly averted his gaze and squinted off into the distance.

"I mean, wow. I just know it's really cold up there, right? Like the snow will completely cover an entire town? I read that in a novel once. I can't remember the name—oh, Andrei Makine. That was the author's name. Have you heard of him?" Blabbering again. Someone needed to stop me. I just wished I could have interpreted the look in his eyes. "I mean, it doesn't matter. I think his books were banned… Anyway, I'm sorry, I read too much. And blabber. So who was this woman's niece and what happened?"

"You're cute when you blabber." He was still looking off in the distance but he grinned. "And you can never read too much. Ever. I've heard of Makine. Haven't read anything by him, that I can remember. And yes, the towns can become quite buried by snow." He rubbed my palm between his thumb and index finger. "The girl's name was Tamara and she went to a dance school in Novosibirsk," he continued, still looking off into the distance. "I wasn't actually from there as I said. I was from a small town. Novosibirsk is not a small town. But Tamara's aunt brought me to Novosibirsk and put me in Tamara's dance class. Her school specialized in ballroom. It was kind of a try-out. She liked the way we were together and really wanted me to dance more permanently with her niece."

"So Tamara was your first partner?"

"Yes. I moved to Novosibirsk and lived with the aunt, and we continued classes and soon started training by a coach from there. And then there was this big competition in Moscow."

"And you won, of course!" Now it was my turn to peck him on the cheek.

"Not even close. We came in fourth." He still looked into the distance, his gaze again fixed on something beyond the four walls of my apartment.

"But it was just your first, right?" I said, trying to snap him out of it. "And you were really young?"

"Seven."

If I was drinking I would have spit out my drink. "Seven years old? Your parents let you move in with someone else at that age? Was this like a boarding school for young dancers or something? Wow."

Now he looked down, so far his lids hooded his eyes and I couldn't see them.

"I mean, I'm sorry, I didn't mean to get so excited. It's just really cool that your parents let you do that at that age. I don't think mine would have." I knew I'd upset him, but didn't know what else to say. So I rubbed his palm as he'd caressed mine, and buried my face into his shoulder. "I'm sorry for interrupting. Go on. Please. I want to hear more."

After a long pause he continued. "I don't know if I can really say my parents let me. I rather made the decision myself." He tilted his head back so he could look me straight in the eyes. "They, my parents...they grew to accept the situation."

I opened my mouth to say something but he held his index finger gently to my lips. "No more questions about that, okay. My parents. Please." His eyes were wide, his pupils piercing mine, his lips a straight line. I don't think I'd ever seen him more intensely serious.

I swallowed. "Okay, I won't. So go on about Tamara, then?" I pleaded.

"We placed fourth, as I said. I was disappointed. But a woman who ran a studio in Moscow approached me. She wanted me to come and train with her. That was the last I saw of Tamara. I moved to Moscow and stayed with this woman."

I couldn't believe his childhood was spent living with all these different women. So far from home. So different from me. I couldn't imagine.

"I trained with the partner she'd had in mind for me," he continued. "Another of her students, Oksana. When I was fourteen we won the junior division of the Russian national championships." His mouth tightened and his chin rose, almost in a paso doble posturing, as if he were immersed in the competition as he spoke about it.

"Wow, that's so awesome." I gushed.

"The next year Oksana and I went to England for the junior division at Blackpool. That's where I met Micaela." His eyes had that faraway look again, glazed over with nostalgia.

I tried to read how he felt about Micaela but couldn't. "So don't keep me in suspense! Which one of you won?"

He laughed. "It was very close but Micaela won. Remember, I told you she was the star. It's funny but the first time I saw her, I knew she had to be my partner. That time, there was no adult in control. That was all me, my decision."

That fierceness was still visible in his eyes, in the way his shoulders rose and arched back, broadening his magnificent pecs, the way the cords of his neck flexed. But I still couldn't get a sense of how he felt about Micaela herself, just that he had an immense passion to win and knew he could do so with her.

"That's the way I felt about you when I first saw you."

I felt his eyes on me. His gaze had softened; the blind ferocity was gone but his sapphire blues sparkled at me, melting my insides to lava.

"What do you mean? You couldn't have seen Micaela in me!" I laughed.

"No. I was attracted to your..." He looked away, pensively. "Your sweetness, your natural talent, your uniqueness. That you brought something different to the floor. Your beauty, that you remind me of...someone." His voice trailed off, the last word coming out as a whisper.

"Of someone? Who?"

He simply shook his head and looked away, his thoughts now in a faraway place.

"Come on, tell—"

He brought his finger to my lips again. "So I eventually convinced Micaela to become my partner. We ended up winning the junior division."

As he returned his gaze to me, a sly, cocked smile crossed his face.

Now we were up to the part of the story I pretty much knew. But I was still fixed on what he'd said about me. Of course I wondered who I reminded him of—someone obviously important to him—and why. But he clearly didn't want to talk about her. I also wondered what he meant by when he first saw me. That would have been at The Beverly Hilton. But I'd tried so hard to catch his attention all those times in the practice room. Had I won him over before then? Had he pretended not to notice me in the studio?

"When exactly was it that you first noticed me? When I did all those *fouettés*? That's when you left Xenia and danced with me and…made a scene."

"I didn't make a scene," he said, rolling his eyes. But his mischievous smile betrayed his words. "And no, I didn't notice you from the *fouettés*. That was you trying way too hard, not realizing you'd won me over long before that."

He raised his brows, and the hot liquid flowed straight to my lower belly.

"Ugh!" I play-slapped him on the bicep. He'd acted like he'd never seen me before in the studio. "When, then?"

"Ouch," he said. "You're strong!"

He was totally pretending. I rolled my eyes.

"What do you mean, when? At the hotel at your ex-boyfriend's party." The way he said ex-boyfriend revealed everything about what he thought of James.

"Really?" He'd obviously caught my attention. But he was the performer. How had I caught his?

"Of course, really!" he laughed. "You act surprised. How could you not have seen me gaping at you? With that…guy who totally did not appreciate you."

"But what did I do to make you notice me?" Honestly, I remember sitting all shyly in the corner feeling totally cowed by James and Mitchell and Cheryl. And then Philip asking me to dance and slobbering all over me, and me making a complete fool of myself. I could only imagine someone noticing me as an object of pity.

He laughed and shrugged his shoulders. "You were just you. You were so incredibly beautiful. You seemed to have a sad look in your eye. I thought that was the most horrible thing. How could such a beautiful woman be so sad? And then I remember some clown asked you to dance. And you were so graceful and elegant with your beautiful long legs and arms and limber body. When you took the floor you were a swan. You had the balance and posture of a dancer. I knew right away you had ballet training from the way you held yourself with him. I didn't really understand what you were doing there. Usually with these parties, it's all lawyers and businesspeople and they don't have any training or real appreciation for the art and you give them a show. And then you try to dance with them socially and, it's okay. I mean, you know you're other. It's their party. You're only entertainment. You're not one of them. But you...you were different. You were familiar. The way you moved, your face. You didn't fit in. And you just looked so sad. I wanted to carry you away and...save you."

His voice was so soft I almost couldn't hear him, and he was looking off in the distance, totally lost in thought. Save me, I thought? From a bunch of lawyers? He had that haunted look in his eyes again. The same one he had when I first danced with him, and then when I first saw him in the studio. And his mouth was beginning to tighten, as if he was getting angry.

"You seemed kind of startled when you saw me for the first time in the studio?" I said with enough force to lift him out of his reverie. His eyes returned to me, wide and deadly serious.

"What? Oh. Well, Rory. I wanted nothing more, of course, than to teach you ballroom. So I was a bit...taken aback when Cheryl showed up in your place, after you'd won the free package. I really wanted you there. And then I felt like I'd misread you. That you were really one of them and I'd been wrong."

His irises were like the ocean, deep and inscrutable. He looked hurt, wounded, but also as if a storm was brewing beneath the surface. He definitely didn't scare me—I trusted him—but it was eerie not knowing exactly what was going through his mind. I swung my leg over his knee and placed my head on his shoulder. "No, you were right. Obviously," I said, gazing up at him.

"When you showed up, I thought you were playing games. I was angry. I wanted you with everything I had. But you had this boyfriend. I didn't know if you were teasing me...or what."

That explained his aloofness. Of course. I really didn't know he knew I'd won. I didn't remember him being present at the announcement. I'd thought he'd run off with Xenia by then. "James gave the prize to Cheryl and Mitchell. Cheryl really wanted the lessons and I think he was afraid not to hand them over since Mitchell's his boss," I explained.

"He was smarter than I gave him credit for," Sasha said with a smirk.

"James? What do you mean?"

"He was afraid of losing you." He raised his eyebrows and lightly ran his fingers across my cheekbone.

I lifted my chin in anticipation of a kiss.

"You need to sleep," he said instead. "You are so tired, my dear." He kissed me on the forehead and nudged me to lift myself, which I did, albeit very hesitantly.

I had no idea just how late it was but I knew I'd be getting very little sleep.

# CHAPTER 12

"Everything is okay now." This came out of Greta's mouth more as a statement than a question.

We were back in Sasha's studio—of course I was—under the chandelier.

"Um, I think," I said.

"It looks like you took my advice and stood up to the man. Well done, dear," she said, patting my shoulder.

*Hmmm, I guess I did.*

\*\*\*

Sasha was back to his professional, hyper-serious self. But he was managing to behave himself. I could feel him tense up with frustration at some points but he merely took a step back, breathed deeply, and looked to Greta for advice. Sometimes she would correct me and sometimes she would say she saw nothing wrong. And sometimes she would even correct him, telling him to give me a little more time to get my leg up; perhaps we should extend the move out to six beats instead of four, and the like. She worked with us as a team, in other words, valuing input from both of us.

But two nights later, she had a prior commitment. We were on our own. We would either end up falling back into our old tug-of-war pattern, or have mad sex. I was determined for it to be the latter. But not if I had to give in to him.

We were progressing through the last quarter of the rumba routine, where again I wasn't ready for the amount of force he used, or his timing in pushing me out and immediately pulling me back to him. I lost my balance and went flying toward him, smacking into his chest. Instead of continuing, as we had been doing when a mistake happened, he stopped. Uh-oh, I thought, afraid to look at his face and thus opting to keep my head lodged in his chest.

He took several long, deep breaths, his pecs rising and falling, his heart pumping. I could tell he was trying to shake it off. After a few seconds, his pulse slowed and I felt his lips on the crown of my head.

"Okay," he whispered.

*Oh good.* From here I happily went into this very lovely backbend, which required a deep arch. I took it down as far as it could go, then I was supposed to lift my leg in back of him as he dipped me. It was a very beautiful move, but I somehow wasn't close enough to him and he had to lean over too far to dip me and my leg ended up going straight back instead of straight up. It wasn't as pretty, plus if someone happened to be dancing next to us on the dance floor, I might kick them.

"Sasha, my back leg isn't in proper position and this feels awkward."

"You are too far away from me. I can't dip you properly without losing my own balance," he said without anger in his voice. "I am glad you can tell when something feels wrong," he added, trying to be conciliatory. I thought.

"Okay, so when you pull me into you, I need to end in a certain position. Let's work with it and figure out how I can get close enough to you so you don't have to over-stretch."

"Yes, that's a good idea. Here." He pulled me into him, aligning my pelvis to his hipbone.

Funny how sensual this would feel, I thought, if we weren't concentrating so hard. Then he swung me out and reeled me in toward him, aiming my pelvis at his hipbone. But he pulled hard and I didn't resist enough. Bone smacked into bone.

*Ouch.* I stepped back, rubbed my crotch and took a breath. Sometimes I felt like a rag doll. But by this point, I was realizing it was futile to say that. "Let's try again."

"Yes, let's."

We weren't fighting! We were agreeing!

But this time he overdid it with the gentleness. He hardly pulled me toward him at all. This time I had to take several tiny steps, making it look like I was tiptoeing toward him. I looked like a toddler trotting into her daddy's arms. Not exactly the sexy look we were trying to convey.

He had his sly, cocked smile back on. I put my hands on my hips. "Very funny," I said. "Is there possibly, you know, a middle ground?"

We tried several more times. We finally got our crotches aligned correctly. But now I was off on the timing when I did the pretty leg lift.

"Try to begin the *développé* on your way toward me. Align the right side of your pelvis with my hip so that you can start lifting your left leg before you even touch me."

Funny how such a romantic dance had become a geometry problem.

He pulled me toward him and I bent my knee and began bringing my leg up before my pelvis hit his hip, as he'd just suggested. But I was so focused on his hip, on trying to make sure the outer right edge of my pelvis made perfectly direct contact with his, my leg ended up there instead of around him. When I heard bone crack bone—this time my knee with his hip—I panicked and moved my leg over. But I lost balance, standing one-legged as I was, and my leg ended up swinging in the wrong direction, ending up smack dab in his crotch.

"Uh," he cried out, taking several steps backward.

Since I had nothing to balance on, I stumbled, but didn't completely fall. "Sasha! I'm really sorry," I yelled when I realized I'd kneed him. But I also couldn't help laughing. Now he had very good reason not to push and pull on me too aggressively.

He unbent himself, stood upright, put his hands on his hips and squinted at me. But there was a hint of sexy playfulness in the squint.

"I'm sorry," I said, trying hard to stop laughing, though my efforts were having the opposite effect. Pepe would have been keeled over on the floor laughing his ass off. "Can you imagine if that happened during the compe—!"

"Rory, please, don't even joke about that..." He shook his head and looked away. He was being semi-playful, semi-serious now, so a big change from his former can't-take-any-semblance-of-a-joke-during-dance-practice self.

"Oh, Sasha, I'm not. I'm just having a moment of levity."

He looked all around the studio, shaking his head and throwing his hands up. "A moment of...okay, a moment, a moment of levity is okay, especially if it is followed by many moments of very intense work."

He was trying so hard.

"I know, I know," I said. "We only have three months. Yes, backbreaking work coming on now. Okay, let's just take it from where we left off. We're almost done with this routine."

His lips turned up at the corners. He looked as if he was smiling against his own better judgment. He extended his hand toward me, the way he normally invited me into closed handhold. We took it from there, the next step being a simple natural opening out where we stood side by side, one arm wrapped around the other, the other stretching out, then he threw me to the opposite side where we did the same. When pulling me in, I was supposed to go past him into a series of three spins on my own as if I were leaving him momentarily. Then he was supposed to do his gorgeous rumba walks toward me as I waited with opened arms. But once again, he pulled me into him too fast and I went torpedoing far, far away, having to do double the amount of spins I was supposed to or I'd have lost my balance, forcing myself to stop too quickly. Because I spun too many times, I ended up way too far away from him and put us totally off beat.

"Rory, what happened?" he said, annoyance returning.

"I know I sound like a broken record. But…you spun me too fast and I lost—"

"I know." He lowered his gaze to the ground.

"I just don't understand why by this point in time you are not used to my—"

"I…okay, I will try hard to remember your…fragility." He took a deep breath.

He was trying. But fragility? I wasn't exactly a china doll. Now I was getting annoyed.

"Come on, let's try again." He extended his arm to me once again.

But I didn't go. I stood with my weight on one foot and put my hands on my hips.

"What?" He looked confused.

He had to give me a little more credit. But I didn't know exactly what to say without sounding defensive, which I just wasn't in the mood for anymore. Not around him. Not during dance, anyway. I'd had too much of that with James, and my legal career.

So I decided not to say anything, but to show him what I was made of—not sticks, not porcelain, not solid muscle. I took a deep breath and grabbed the bottom of my dance top. Tonight I wore a cute sky blue halter dance top with a built-in bra and a pair of form-fitting black yoga pants.

"What are you doing?" he said.

I really don't know, I thought. Trying hard to banish all negative body thoughts from my mind and focus instead on how Sasha had devoured said body in the past, I grabbed the fringe-y bottom of the top and, in one fell swoop, lifted it up and over my head, shaking out my hair as I pulled it completely off.

He stood there open-mouthed in response to my now toplessness. I couldn't blame him. What was I on?

I took another deep breath and grabbed the top of my jazz pants, along with the thong underneath, pulling them down, letting both fall in a pool at my ankles. I looked down at my feet in the puddle of black. I reached down, almost mechanically, and picked up my clothes. I walked past him, not even looking at him, though I could see out of the corner of my eye his jaw had now dropped nearly halfway down his neck. I took my clothes to the front area, placing them neatly on the couch. I walked back to him and, again mechanically, placed myself in closed hold with him. I tried hard to pretend this was perfectly normal and I did not feel weird at all being completely naked except for the Latin stilettos.

"Rory, sweetheart," he began, finally able to talk. "As much as I...we need to practice for a little longer."

"I know, that's why I left my heels on," I said nonchalantly.

"But I can't concentrate with you like this," he said with a hearty laugh.

"Please try, Sasha. I just want to see how this goes. As an experiment. Just the rumba."

"Is this how we're going to dance at Blackpool?"

"Maybe in our minds."

He rolled his eyes.

"Oh I just want to see how it goes. I have a theory. Okay? Come on, please try, Sasha."

"Okay," he said, clearing his throat and placing his arms back in closed position. I could see the cocked smile in his reflection in the mirror. He wasn't mad. He was letting me play.

We started. And it worked just as I'd thought. No mistakes. He was much gentler in the way he handled me. No pushing, pulling. He even caught me and pulled me into him at the end of the series of spins we'd formerly screwed up. It wasn't in the choreography, but was actually more romantic. Then he pushed me away from him, gently again, and did his lunge while I did my high leg-lifting *ronde de jambe*, which should have been rather embarrassing given my naked state. But, weirdly, I was focusing on actually doing the movement as full-out and perfectly as possible instead of my imperfect body. He pulled me toward him and I slowly lifted my leg. I caught him glancing ever so quickly at my now visible vulva, then looking immediately back to my face. He'd screw up the balance and drop me if he lost concentration. I extended my leg completely, and he touched my ankle gently and hooked my heel over his shoulder. Then he slowly walked backward, gliding me across the floor. This was one of my favorite moves and it felt so perfect, so beautiful. He was really taking care of me on the dance floor, not letting me falter. The rest of the routine was similarly flawless—the best practice we'd had.

"I was right!" I squealed as he slowly lifted me from our final dip. "That was so—"

But I wasn't able to finish my thought as he pulled me toward him and I fell into his embrace, his lips pressing firmly into mine, then opening so his tongue could plunge into my mouth.

After one very deep kiss, I looked into his deep ocean blues, and could tell from their twinkle he was smiling genuinely.

"You're right. You win," he said, holding me even tighter this time, tonguing my earlobe.

I cackled wickedly. "You better believe I will never let you forget you said that. I know the key to making Sasha Zakharov a better partner!"

"Well, at least for Rory Laudner."

Another concession. I was on a roll!

"Maybe it's time to go upstairs now," he whispered, tracing the shell of my ear with his tongue, an action that, alone, made me swoon.

"Yes, I don't think we should practice the other dances like this. My boobs would be all over the floor in jive."

"We don't want that. We want them right here," he said, fingering my nipples.

He carried me upstairs in a cradle hold, the same way he had on that first amazing night, when I was blindfolded. He put me down on the bed and, kneeling over me, tore his t-shirt up and over his head while I unzipped his pants. I pushed him over onto his back while I took his pants down past his rock-hard glutes, then straddled him. I massaged his glistening biceps against the silky sheets and bent my head down to kiss him, feeling his throbbing hardness right at my opening. But before I could take him fully inside me, he tore his arms from my grasp, bucked himself up, and tossed me over him and onto my back, the bedsprings bouncing like a trampoline. I giggled and placed a still-stiletto'd foot over each of his shoulders. He began moving his mouth down from my lips to my belly, stopping to lick at the hollow of my neck, each nipple, my belly button, and finally my clitoris, darting into my wet folds, all before I could even wonder how he'd reversed the position so masterfully—getting from me being atop him to him atop me so quickly, so acrobatically.

"Hey," I began to complain, playfully of course.

"Mmmm?" he moaned questioningly, his tongue still darting around my labia.

"You don't always have to be on—"

His tongue, expertly circling the pebble-hard crown of my clit, placing just the right amount of pressure, compelled me to release a long, loud moan. Needless to say, I was unable to finish my sentence.

In one fell swoop, he released his mouth and climbed fully atop me, sent my legs back up and over my head, and plunged far and fast into me. It was fun being so flexible! I think the position opened me more, allowing him to fill me more completely. I threw my head back, and moaned even louder. It's a good thing we were in his mansion in the sky and not my tiny apartment; I probably would have sounded to a neighbor like I was dying.

"Russian man!" I teased, after we'd both climaxed and I'd finally caught my breath. Some of my breath, anyway.

He lay next to me now, holding my right hand with both of his, caressing each finger from root to the tip. He turned his head to look at me, raised one eyebrow, and shot me his ever-so-sexy crooked smile. "Now, let's please not bring race into this," he said after catching his breath.

"You mean nationality," I said.

"Whatever. Semantics," he said with a laugh. "Why did you say that anyway?"

"My Russian friend in law school that I was telling you about, said that Russian men were totally dominant and they always had to be on top." I giggled, but as the words left my mouth, I remembered our last conversation in which I'd mentioned her. That hadn't gone so well. "Not that she was right," I added quickly. "I mean, generalizations are always silly. She'd just know more than I would. Or had. Or—" I didn't know if I was making this better. I decided to stop. "Oh I'm just joking anyway!" I smiled as sweetly as I could.

"Many a truth is said in jest. Didn't Shakespeare say that?" He still wore that sly, sexy smile.

*This one!* He never ceased to amaze me. "I guess he did. It sounds like something he would say!" I said, wondering if I should know this.

"Yes, this is the Russian friend who said all Russian men are sexist. Someday I will have to have a talk with her," he said, still playfully.

Thankfully. And good, he was letting me off the hook apparently for not knowing a quote written by the most famous writer in my language.

"So, to be dominant is to be sexist?" he asked.

"Mmmm, no. Not necessarily. I mean, not unless you're like, you know, stifling the other person."

"Stifling? Do I stifle you?"

*Hmmm.* Not in bed. I was kidding about that. But on the dance floor? Hello? We'd ended our practice on a good note, though. I didn't want to spoil that by broaching this subject again.

Before I answered, he rolled onto his side, facing me. He released my fingers and placed both hands around my waist. Then, in one motion, he picked me up and lifted me over his body, placing me atop him. Damn, this man was strong!

I spread my legs into a straddle split, trying to maintain our acrobatics, which I was totally enjoying. I'd never had sex with a dancer before, now that I thought about it. All lawyers, or business majors and the like in college. Boring, I now realized! I lowered my lips to his, suddenly unable to control my giggling for some reason.

I placed my hands over his glistening biceps again and resumed where we'd left off. He thrust up and into me as I sat up and arched my back. As he filled me, I threw my head back and breathed deeply. Soon I felt his hands on my breasts, his palms rolling over each pebbled nipple. My eyes closed, I felt him shift and soon one hand was on my left breast, fingering that nipple. On the other I felt his tongue. He was now sitting up, pumping into me harder and harder, filling me more and more. His aggressive thrusting sent electric charges up and down my spine. I bent my knees and lifted myself slightly, then allowed myself to fall to the side, pulling him over onto me.

I spread my legs again into a straddle split. He followed my lead, positioned himself squarely between my legs and resumed that intense thrusting. I bent my knees and crossed my legs over his back. He reached under me, wrapped his arms around my back and kissed me deeply. We were completely entwined in each other.

"I sensed that's the way you liked it best," he said after we were again lying beside each other, trying to catch our breath. "That is why."

It was true, actually, now that I thought about it. I did enjoy his large, protective body over mine. "Okay. Well then, you sensed right," I said, giggling again. We would have to have the artistic expression discussion another time. Assuming, of course, he kept being a control freak on the dance floor.

\*\*\*

I was late to work again. My cell phone alarm went off the same time as usual but of course I wasn't at home or with my clothes and work things. I kissed a groggy Sasha on the way out, and asked him to tell Greta I'd be about an hour late tonight to make up for work.

"Mmm hmm," he said, his eyes narrowed, his smile crooked.

I so wanted to crawl back in bed with him.

Despite the fact I still arrived before normal business hours—before nine, that is, when we were expected to be in—Gunther was pretty annoyed.

"I'll work late to make it up," I told him, unsure why he was so pissy since I hadn't had much work to do in weeks now. It almost seemed like the fact that it was now obvious I had a life set him off.

About two hours after I started my next boring assignment—drafting yet another will—Gunther appeared at my door. "I have a big project, Rory. I know you just got a will but I need you to put that aside and focus on one of my cases today. I have a brief due on Monday and I have several complicated issues that need researched. I need you here late tonight and over the weekend."

I took a gulp. I had not only my regular practices with Sasha and Greta, but the big month-end studio party at which the mambo team was set to perform. Plus, I'd promised I'd be there all day Saturday for last-minute rehearsal. I'd invited Sam and Rajiv. I couldn't back out. The team wouldn't be able to perform absent one member.

"I can work a little late tonight and Sunday afternoon?" I asked more than said.

"You're telling me you can't be here at all on Saturday?" he said more than asked, as if he already knew what my answer would be.

"Um…" I mentally went through my schedule. We were booked with Greta tonight from nine o'clock on, and tomorrow morning again at eight so I'd have time to get to the studio by eleven and practice until the six o'clock party. "I can work till about eight thirty tonight…"

"I just asked you about tomorrow," he said sternly.

"I could come in very early in the morning but I have to be somewhere by eleven?" My voice was squeaky, knowing how freaked out Sasha would be if I cancelled both tonight's and tomorrow's coachings, which I really didn't want to do anyway. Blackpool was not that far away. I knew Gunther couldn't force me to work overtime—it was against the law—but not agreeing to work at least part of a weekend day certainly wasn't going to put me in the firm's greatest graces.

"But if it's research, I could work from home!" I said, trying to be more enthusiastic. "I've never had a problem accessing Westlaw from home. So I could spend a few hours Saturday morning and Sunday morning as well." I nodded, feeling like I'd made a good balance. Working from home was always much easier anyway, since the subway didn't run very often on weekends and traffic, particularly during afternoon and evenings, was horrible.

"If you can only work the morning on Saturday, then I need you here through the night," he said and walked out. "I'll email you the assignment within the hour," he called out from down the hall.

I still wasn't completely sure he'd okay'd my working from home on Saturday and Sunday. In any event, I'd have to cancel with Sasha and Greta tonight, at least. Maybe I'd be able to fudge working at home on Saturday, and put in extra time on Sunday instead.

I texted Sasha. *I'm really sorry but Gunther's being a pain again and needs me here all night. Some crazy last-minute research for a brief due Monday. I can't come tonight. I'll see you tomorrow. Sorry again.*

*You can't come tonight at all?* he texted back.

*I don't think so. His words were 'through the night.' I'm sorry. I'll be there tomorrow morning at 8*, I texted, even though Gunther was expecting me to be working at home at that time. I think.

*Through the night? Will others be working with you? I don't want you there all night alone. We both know what downtown is like on the weekends.*

*I assume Gunther will still be here too. Otherwise he wouldn't know when I left.*

*Tell me the second he leaves, Rory. Promise me.*

As much as I liked to be independent, Sasha was right. Downtown was dead late at night and all weekend. *Will do*, I texted back.

# CHAPTER 13

Gunther did have a lot of research but I actually got through it fairly quickly. I'd finished a good portion of it by Friday night at eleven thirty, when he finally left, careful to eye me in my office before doing so. I flashed him a nervous smile as he passed, then immediately called Sasha to pick me up. The office was completely empty, as was much of downtown.

"Good. You can come down now. I'm across the street," Sasha said.

"What?" I ran across the hall to peek at the street through Gunther's corner window. Yep, there was the Porsche. "How long have you been there?"

"Since my last private ended about two hours ago."

"Sasha!"

"I didn't want you waiting here alone. I mean it, Rory. It's a ghost town around here and skid row is not that far away."

I couldn't imagine any homeless people were going to come looking for me, but his overprotectiveness was sweet. I hadn't really experienced that feeling that someone was watching out for me since my dad passed.

I practically skipped to the car, my heart beating faster with each *jeté*-ing little step I took. I couldn't wait to hop into that car and get my hands all over him! He'd be a little annoyed that we missed tonight, but I'd assure him again that I'd make it up—in more ways than one!

But on my way to the Porsche, that ridiculously irrational feeling that I was being watched swept over me again. Again, I looked around. Again nothing. This had to stop. I didn't know what it was about, but I was beginning to feel as nuts as Mr. Warren, my paranoid former client.

I put the crazy thought out of my head and hopped into the car, back on cloud nine.

"What have you been doing out here all this time?" I squealed after a gloriously long kiss.

"Mmm, making phone calls, doing things on my iPhone, people-watching, neighborhood-watching. It is pretty dead around here after nine."

He started the car and we pulled out into traffic. Suddenly, from out of nowhere a blue Nissan swerved around us, honking like mad.

"Hmm, where'd he come from?" Sasha said under his breath.

The mad honking made me glance at the driver. We were directly under a streetlight and I caught a glimpse of his beady little eyes in his rearview mirror as he glared back at us. Oh my, it was Gunther. I knew it. And he seemed to glare mainly at me.

At first, all I could think was that now he knew I'd left right after him; he knew I didn't "stay all night" as he'd commanded. Then I wondered what he was doing. Was he sitting there waiting to see if I'd leave? I'd left the office a good ten minutes after he did, and then Sasha and I were in the car for a couple minutes kissing before taking off. What was he doing for, what, twenty minutes? Did he watch me skip outside and get in the Porsche? No, it was just a coincidence. He wasn't that obsessed with my life. I hoped.

Maybe I had sensed properly that someone was looking at me. But I'd had that feeling as well down the street from my apartment building. Surely he hadn't ever been there. No, I was definitely imagining things with that. Still, very freaky that I got that eerie feeling, and then Gunther, in fact, was nearby.

Gunther never had specified whether I could work at home over the weekend and I hadn't asked again. I simply chose to interpret that to be the case as per our last conversation. As much as I'd already done on the assignment, if I worked from home over the weekend, sans commuting time, I should easily be able to finish it all in just a couple hours on Sunday morning anyway; no need to work Saturday. That whole conversation in his office was a waste of time.

\*\*\*

I ended up nearly falling asleep in the Porsche. I hadn't realized how tiring my workday was. Just arguing with Gunther was nerve-racking, aside from the actual work. I'd wanted to run home and get my things so I could spend the night with Sasha but he insisted I get a good night's sleep for the practice and team performance tomorrow. I knew he was right.

But once my head hit the pillow I was wide awake, my head nearly exploding with what if's. What if

I totally forgot the routine out of nerves and just stood there, having no idea what to do? What would everyone in the studio think of me, Sasha, Pepe? What if I totally teabagged Pepe and hurt him and the whole studio erupted in laughter at his expense? What if I'd gained weight and the costume was now too small? What if it was so tight there was a malfunction and it ripped in an important place? What if I hurt my knee again on the pot stir? I took some melatonin, drank some chamomile tea and tried to calm myself down. I was being ridiculous. I'd been on my way to becoming a professional ballet dancer and I was freaking out over a dress rehearsal at my ballroom studio in front of other amateurs.

*Seriously, Rory. Get a grip!*

\*\*\*

"Good morning," Sasha said, kissing me on my way in. I wrapped my arms around him.

"I missed you last night," I said, taking in the freshly shampooed scent of his hair, thick and still wonderfully wavy from the lack of gel as of yet. I nuzzled my nose in his neck.

"Believe me, the feeling is mutual," he said, transferring his kisses to my cheek. "Even though it's been all of eight hours since we last saw each other." He laughed. "Mmmm, okay, we have to get to work. Greta's here and waiting."

"I know, I saw her car."

But neither of us seemed to want to let go of the other. He finally unlocked himself from my grasp and held my hand, walking me into the studio.

"Remember the last time we danced rumba," I whispered in his ear. "Pretend it's exactly the same!"

He frowned briefly, then rolled his eyes and looked away, but I could see his lopsided, devilish smile.

"Okay, lovebirds, are we ready?" Greta called out, sounding and looking her usual regal self as we walked onto the pine floor.

Somehow, believe it or not, we did dance the exact same way we had last time. Albeit not naked, of course. Sasha was strong but gentle, and even though we were practicing in front of Greta, there was a passion I hadn't felt before. It wasn't just coming from the nature of the rumba, the movements, but it was more internal, more real. I felt like we really lost ourselves—for the first time while actually rehearsing for Blackpool, not messing around and not off the floor. It felt incredible. It felt beautiful.

"Wow," Greta said. "What happened? That was a thousand percent better." She must have seen the coy smiles on our faces because she immediately held her palm toward us, saying, "Okay, don't tell me, don't tell me. It looks incredibly good, though. You guys are on your way."

The other dances didn't go quite as well, though they got off to a good start. Next we went over cha-cha. We weren't as practiced on that as the rumba so there were some flubs but they were minor and easy to correct. The samba was messier since it was a faster dance and I began having problems keeping time, which I'm sure was because I was getting tired. I knew the beat and could feel myself off it. By the time we got to jive, I badly needed a wake-me-up.

"I'm sorry, can I make myself some coffee?" I asked Sasha after my jive kicks were so sloppy I nearly tripped both myself and him. He looked disappointed, but nodded. "I had to work really late last night," I said to Greta by way of explanation. "Sorry."

"Not your fault." She shrugged. "I heard you have a bear of a boss."

I listened to them talking softly to each other while I was in the kitchen. I couldn't tell exactly what they were saying but I heard the words "it's hard" and "not a full-time professional" and "lawyer" from Greta. My stomach sank. They were obviously talking about me. How I was holding him back with my job. I was. There was no doubt about it. If things continued this way, if Gunther kept this up, we just wouldn't have enough rehearsal time.

I made the coffee black, no sugar or cream, so it was dense as possible with minimal calorie intake. It woke me up somewhat. But not quite enough. No amount of caffeine would be a substitute for a good night's sleep. The morning was somewhat of a waste because I knew the routine down solid and Sasha was finally being more gentle with me. Today's problems were all mine, and happened simply because my mind and body were fatigued. If we were really going to have a fighting chance against the world's top professionals, who trained full-time, I at least couldn't work so late at night. I had to keep my day job to Sasha's hours. Even then, since I was a latecomer to the world of ballroom, I still put us at a disadvantage by only being able to train at night.

After Greta left, I was planning on continuing practicing with Sasha for another hour before we both had to go to the studio. But instead he led me upstairs, not to his bedroom, but to a guest bedroom beside it. This room was smaller but had a window with a beautiful view, overlooking a canyon. How many rooms did this place have, I wondered, realizing I'd never been given an official tour of the whole thing.

"Nice room, but, um, what are we doing in here?" I asked.

"You're so tired, Rory. I think you need to sleep before you go and do this crazy team practice. If I put you in our bedroom, you know what will happen and you wouldn't get the proper rest."

I giggled, my heart momentarily stopping at his use of the term "our" for the master bedroom.

He didn't laugh back. "Seriously. Rory, training when you're tired can too easily lead to injury." He laid me back on the plush comforter, resting my head on the pillow. He continued to hover over me, massaging my neck and shoulders.

"Mmm, you're so good to me." I could feel myself drifting off.

"Rory," he said, his hands now kneading the muscles of my biceps.

I opened my eyes. "Mmm hmm?"

He took a breath, closed his mouth again. "Never mind. You get sleep."

"What?" I asked, eyes opening wide. "You look worried. What's wrong?"

"No, no, nothing to worry about. Nothing at all."

"Would you just say it, please? Just tell me what's on your mind." I took a deep breath. "You want me to quit the team, right? It's taking up too much time?"

"What? No," he said.

I exhaled. *Oh good. Because I so don't want to do that.*

"No, I know how much fun you're having," he continued. "I can tell even though you take it seriously, it helps relieve stress for you. Plus, any kind of Latin dance is generally good practice. No…" He stopped and took a breath. "My prrroposition was for something else."

This word and his sexy rolling r's were becoming the theme of our relationship. I would have giggled again if his brows weren't furrowed so. If that worry wasn't so apparent in his eyes.

"Just something for you to think about," he continued, being cryptic.

"Okay, what?"

His eyebrows were raised. He took a long inhale, his eyes darting around the room before settling again on me. "Rory, your job stresses you out so much. And from the way you talk about it, it doesn't seem to make you very happy. I just thought…maybe you could take a little break from it while we trained. And go back to it after Blackpool. I mean, if you decide you love it enough to stay with it."

*Wow.* That was a loaded prop for me. I was almost positive the firm wouldn't give me that much time off. The competition was still over two months away. I definitely didn't have that kind of vacation time. And how would I pay my bills, even assuming they gave me the time off unpaid?

"Just something to think about. You have too much going on today. Don't worry about it right now."

I guessed he could see the panic, the worry in my eyes. Law jobs were fiercely competitive. What if they fired me for asking for the time off, thereby making it clear I wasn't so happy there? And if I left, I didn't know how that would look on a resume. I'd had such a hard time getting this job. I also wasn't sure I actually hated the work. It was more the firm, the people—Gunther—I couldn't stand. I felt for Jamar and cared about his case. We could really have an innocent client on our hands who could be wrongly convicted of something extremely serious. Assuming Gunther was still letting me work on that case. He hadn't in a while.

"Seriously, don't worry, Rory," Sasha said now with laughter in his voice. "I shouldn't have even brought it up today. Just rest."

"No...I-I-I-" I stuttered.

My mind started to wander to Blackpool's Winter Gardens. I thought about the videos I'd seen of the couples, how I'd feel when I was actually there. I knew how fierce our competition was from watching those videos. I knew they'd be even more intimidating when I saw them in person.

"You are worrying way too much. Get some sleep. We will talk about it later, after your performance is over. Which I'm very much looking forward to." Sasha smiled and kissed my forehead.

I tried. But it was hard to stop thinking about his proposition long enough to get a whole lot of actual sleep. It was very attractive but I wasn't sure whether I wanted to put my law career on hold at this early date and how I could even afford to. But I couldn't dance forever; a dance career was pretty much over by your mid-thirties, if even that late. This had started out a hobby, but now I wanted to see it through. I wanted nothing more than to win with Sasha. But how would I juggle both?

***

Despite my continuing lack of rest, team practice went pretty well. We were now at the point where there were no major mishaps, although we still weren't perfectly in sync in places and we weren't always completely in line during formation changes. But good enough to try it in front of an audience tonight at the party. Said Pepe, anyway.

The costumes had come in from Drucilla. Mitsi brought them for us to try on. If there were problems with anyone's, she said, we simply would all wear jeans and t-shirts tonight to perform in, and get the costumes altered. I was surprised when I tried mine on. It was actually a bit loose in the butt and chest. Hmm, she must have taken my measurements wrong. I asked Mitsi for her opinion.

"Yeah, you have been losing a good amount of weight," she said. "I've been noticing that."

*Really?* It didn't feel that way.

"But the costume still looks good. I think it's fine."

I was so excited to see Samantha that evening, I nearly knocked her out, rushing her.

"You look gorgeous, Rory!" she said, petting my fuchsia costume. "But skinny. You're losing weight, right?"

"Really? Mitsi—one of the teachers—just said that. I dunno. Anyway, I'm so glad you're here! Thank you so much for coming."

"Are you kidding? I wouldn't miss this for anything!"

I introduced her to Paulina. "So nice to meet you, dear. A friend of Rory's…well, you know the saying." She turned her attention to me. "Whoa, look at you! What's happening tonight? You look simply fab, my dear."

"Thank you! The mambo team is performing our competition routine."

"You're on the mambo team too? Wow, you really have been bitten by the ballroom bug! But, I mean, it's nice to see someone with such talent realize it, dear. Truly. Have you seen her dance lately?" she said to Sam.

Sam shook her head. "No, but I will soon, and can't wait!"

"Well, she's simply amazing. In, what? A few months? She's dancing like a consummate pro! Well, I mean, she's dancing with a pro—the best in the world, I.M.H.O. But seriously, I've never seen anything like it." Paulina shook her head in mock disbelief.

Suddenly, I saw out of the corner of my eye, Cheryl's nasty glare. Funny, she was actually standing quite close to us but I hadn't noticed her, probably because of Paulina's extravagant attention. Cheryl was wearing a very sexy magenta dress—not dissimilar in color to our team dresses—that appeared to be made of Lycra, so tight-fitting I wondered how it didn't cut off her circulation in various places, and slit up the right side to the hip, with the vee neckline plunging to nearly to her waist. It appeared to be laced with rhinestones, or something sparkly. It looked like a costume but I knew Sasha wasn't performing with anyone tonight.

*Hmmm.* When we locked eyes, I shot her a nervous smile. She responded with her usual lift of the chin and toss of the hair, followed by an abrupt turn in the opposite direction as if my smile was simply too boring. Well, she seemed to be done feeling sorry for me. Maybe she realized Sasha and Xenia had not gotten back together or whatever it was she thought had happened that didn't. I was so done trying to figure out the emotional cycle of that one.

"Paulina! You're too sweet," I said, returning my attention to the person who far more deserved it.

"She thinks I'm just saying it to be nice, poor deluded girl."

Sam was giggling, clearly dazzled by Paulina, who was decked out in a gorgeous floor-length cinnamon red ballroom gown.

"Look at yourself," I said, running my fingers along the beautiful organza. "I'm so glad you're dancing with Maurizio tonight. Watching the two of you is breathtaking. I didn't get enough of you at the comp."

"Well, thank you, dear. I've been at it a whole lot longer than you, anyway. Ballroom's something I can do halfway decently, at least."

"Much more than halfway decently, Paulina." I laughed.

I also introduced Sam to Eduardo, insisting he must save a hustle dance for her, being the most mad-fun disco partner I'd ever had.

As I hugged her again, I saw Rajiv giving someone behind me a professional but nervous-looking smile and nod. I turned around. Sasha's ocean eyes connected with mine and sent an electric bolt charging from my center to my toes, just like the first time I ever saw him. Something told me that man would always have that effect on me, no matter how close we became. Since he wasn't performing, he was dressed in dance workout clothes—the black Latin pants and a tight white t-shirt that showed off his delectable pecs and biceps. Pecs and biceps that were all mine now, thank you very much! Without taking his eyes off me, he grabbed a glass of chardonnay from the table. He had a plate of cold cuts and veggies in his other hand, from the snack table. My natural impulse was to run over, hug him and bring him over to meet my friends. But he simply nodded at me politely—the same look he'd just given Rajiv, albeit with a sly twinkle in his eye.

He turned and sauntered toward the door, his gaze flashing ever so quickly to the side of the room on his way out. I looked to the place where he'd glanced, to see Cheryl, eyes darting back and forth between him and me. I knew Sasha didn't want to make a scene and still preferred for very few people to know he and I were an item or were training together professionally. I knew, even though he was no longer my teacher here, it was still in the back of his mind that the studio manager might think her no-fraternizing policy had been violated. Of course she couldn't prove it, but I understood Sasha's need not to have to deal with any nonessential B.S., especially with Blackpool so close and the immigration visa a possible issue. Still, I didn't like having to hide our relationship anywhere.

"Wasn't that Sasha?" Samantha asked a little loudly.

I hadn't told her about his desire to keep our relationship a secret here. I hadn't thought about telling her; for some reason I just assumed she wouldn't make a scene.

"Yeah, he just came to get some food before his last private lesson," I said. "But you're coming over to my place after the party, right?"

"Of course."

"I'm just going to introduce everyone to him there."

She had an extremely confused look on her face which made me feel very stupid. When I agreed to keep our relationship under the radar in the studio I'd overlooked the time when my friends would be here, to watch me dance with a team, at a party. Now I had to explain.

"Yeah, it's…I mean, complicated. Basically, he just doesn't want to broadcast that we're dancing together here. I mean, just here."

Now she looked completely befuddled. "Rore, I mean, I definitely want to see your place and all, but can I just ask why he wants to pretend you're not involved with each other here?"

"He just doesn't want the studio owner to think we violated the no-fraternizing policy," I said.

"But you didn't. You didn't get together till after you ceased to be a student. That's what you told me anyway, Rory," she responded, her eyebrows rising.

"Of course it's true!" I said. "It's just, he doesn't want to open any potential Pandora's boxes, you know? Not right before the biggest competition in the world, where we both need our complete focus. Plus, I dunno, the studio might think he took a client away and might try to sue or something." The latter part I added, feeling put on the spot. He'd never told me he had to sign a non-compete clause or anything.

Sam was still frowning. "But that happens all the time, Rory. People meet in the studio. Whether they're teachers or amateurs or students or whatever. They realize they're good together and start competing professionally."

"Maybe other studios are just different," Rajiv said. He was trying to help out and it was nice. I didn't like feeling so on the defensive.

Sam harrumphed and gave Rajiv an evil eye. But an evil eye that somehow seemed playful. That's odd, I thought, given that they didn't know each other very well. But before she could say anything more, the door opened and in walked none other than Kendra. I nearly jumped out of my costume.

"Kendra, Kendra!" I called, waving like a loon. A smile spread quickly across her face and she practically ran toward me. We hugged like two long-lost family members.

"How are you?" she said. "You look amazing! And thin."

"So do you!" She was wearing an electric blue body-clinging dress with high-heeled, shiny black Mary-Jane-style tango shoes. "You look gorgeous, actually!"

"Thanks," she said with a bashfulness that was very un-Kendra-like.

I introduced her to the others and asked her if Josie was coming. "No," she said, the magic in her eyes sadly fading. "She probably won't ever be back here, Rory."

"Oh no, the thing with Luna never got resolved?"

She shook her head.

"What happened?" Samantha asked.

We explained the costume debacle and Luna's outrage at the Orange County competition.

"Luna just has connections, at least in that competition," Kendra explained. "And it's a big comp for this studio. So it's kind of either, you know, Luna or Josie."

"Connections and money," I said.

Kendra smirked.

"I still don't understand how they enforce these no-copying-costumes rules. I mean, they don't know for sure Josie even saw Luna's costume beforehand, and they definitely can't prove she copied it."

"Rory, you're such a lawyer," Kendra said, laughing. "These competitions don't exactly work like a court of law."

"Yeah, but they should—"

"Hon, give it up!" Kendra said. "I appreciate your sense of fairness. Really, I do. But at this point Josie just doesn't want to be where she's not welcome, you know? She's perfectly happy to transfer to another studio. It's not like there's a dearth of them in Hollywood."

*True.* Okay, I'd stop being such a lawyer about it.

"Anyway, what's up with you?" Kendra said, batting her eyes at me, totally changing tone. "I know you're dancing with the team, but I heard you and Sasha are training for Blackpool with Greta? Spill, girl!" she squealed.

"Where did you hear that?" I asked, whiplashing my head back in Cheryl's direction. But she'd gone. I didn't see her anywhere now. Thankfully. After what Kendra just told us, Sasha and I certainly didn't need any trouble from Luna's principal cohort.

"You know me! I have my sources," she said, raising her eyebrows. "So, what is he like? Are you guys really going to Blackpool? Are you an item?" She was practically screaming.

I was so excited, I almost didn't care who overheard. Still, I glanced around briefly. No sign of Cheryl or Luna. "Yes!" I chirped, doing a slight Lindy hop with a jive kick. "It's soooo hard, but we're training. We're doing it. I'm so excited! I want this so badly!"

"Awesomeness! When is it?"

"Two months away. OMG, we have so much to do. But I'm loving every second of it." Once I vocalized this, I realized its truth. Hard as Sasha was on me, I was so much more fulfilled by working with him to achieve this goal of his, this goal that was now mine as well, than by my job.

"And...what about the item part?" Kendra's eyes shot up nearly to her hairline.

"Yes! Yes. Everything is going...yes, well, very well." I was tomato-red. I could feel it. My eyes began watering.

"Rory, I'm so happy for you!" Kendra threw her arms around me, and as she did, I spotted over her left shoulder, Cheryl's lovely face looking right at me. Her skin blanched, her lips first made an open O, then became tightly pursed as her eyes narrowed and her nostrils flared. Her eyes too began to water and she blinked hard then slowly turned away, now looking almost wounded.

"Thank you," I said to Kendra, trying to remain calm. I should text Sasha and tell him she clearly overheard, I thought. But just then the D.J. announced our soon-to-come performance, and that the mambo team members were to assemble in the back room pronto. It would have to wait. I mean, did he really care, anyway? The whole thing was kind of childish.

"Oooh, you're on!" Kendra said, backing out of our embrace and patting me on the back.

"Break a leg!" shouted Rajiv. "I mean, wait, what is it you say to a dancer? French shit or something?"

I cracked up.

"I remember from the comp. It's *merde*, right?" said Kendra.

"What?" Samantha said.

"That's what ballet dancers say to each other as encouragement. It means 'shit' in French. No one knows why or how it got started, but that's what they say. I taught it to them at the Orange County competition," I said to her.

She shrugged. "*Merde* sounds good to me."

"*Merde, merde, merde*," they all said, making me laugh so hard I momentarily forgot about Cheryl.

When I got to the back room, everyone—or at least all the women—were on the verge of nervous breakdowns, each one delineating in excruciating detail every possible thing that could go wrong. Hadn't they done that last night like I had, I thought? I apparently hadn't gotten all the butterflies out of my system though, since now my nerves were completely aflutter.

"Seriously, you guys. It's just the studio. Just your friends. This is the best and easiest time to get over your stage fright, right?" Pepe said.

We did the routine one more time and everything was definitely not perfect but nearer perfection than it had ever been.

"See. You guys rock. Nothing to worry about," Ron insisted.

And then we took to the ballroom floor, center stage.

"Performing in their very first competition at the University of California at Irvine in only two weeks' time, I present to you Mambo Caliente, Infectious Rhythm's very first mambo team!" the D.J. boomed.

"Go, go, go," said Ron, both cheering us on and commanding some of us once and for all to conquer our fears.

But everything was wrong from the get-go. First problem was, they dimmed the lights so much we couldn't see where to go to get into place. Pepe led me around in the dark, literally feeling out for where the other dancers were, not wanting to make us look stupid by shouting "Turn on the lights!" The lights suddenly flashed on and the music simultaneously began. It took me a couple seconds to get acclimated, though. Thankfully I was dancing with the pro, who began leading me right away. If it wasn't for him, I definitely would have been beyond lost.

Even with Pepe leading me, I was literally turned around. Every time we'd rehearsed, we'd been facing south, facing the mirror. We were now facing north because that was the way they'd set the stage up; with our backs to the mirror, toward the audience. I tried my best to follow him, dizzy as I was getting.

There seemed to be a lot of whispering. I couldn't tell whether it was coming from the audience or the team. The music was fast and there was definitely no time to look around.

"What are you doing?" I heard someone say.

"You're blocking me," said a man whose voice I didn't recognize.

Ugh, we seriously had to deal with audience upstarts at a time like this, I thought?

We prepped for one of the first tricks, a difficult one where Pepe had to spin me out and stop me abruptly, then lower me into a split, which I was to lift myself out of using the strength of my legs only, before continuing on with the lightning-fast basic.

More cacophony came from the audience. Shut up, I thought. I tried to look out but saw only a blinding light.

"Just keep up with me. Don't worry about them out there," Pepe whispered, gently squeezing my hand. "I know you can do it."

He went to spin me out but I got confused and initially went the wrong way.

"This way," he tried to say under his breath. But his voice sounded like it boomed over a microphone.

I spun the opposite way quickly, then made it down into the splits just in time with the beat.

The lights shining down on us, the noise from the audience, the rapid movements of my teammates – everything seemed to blur. I was in the splits and I began bringing myself back up by squeezing my thigh muscles together as tightly as I could while sliding the back leg in. I must have been off time because Pepe began pulling me up. But my back foot came into contact with some kind of object. It took me a second to realize that it was someone else's leg. My first thought was that one of my teammates had gone the wrong way, as I'd been inclined to do, and now we were in kind of a pretzel. Pepe was looking straight ahead, not down, which was proper. But it meant he couldn't see what was happening to my left leg. I couldn't get it untwisted with the other person's foot. It felt like my ankle was twisting at a bad angle. I kicked my back leg up with all my might to release my ankle and ended up flying forward, falling onto the other leg, straight onto my right knee. My bad knee.

I heard a lot of oooohs and ohhhhhs coming from the audience. And one or two actual screams.

"Ouch, you stepped on me," someone yelled. "You really, really hurt me." It took me all of two seconds to realize it was Cheryl's voice. "Can't you see where you're going?"

"Don't worry about it. Just keep going," Pepe whispered as he quickly pulled me up and, skipping a few steps, caught us up to the rest of the team. But when I began doing the basic, I realized my knee was really hurting. I had to step very lightly on the toe, not pressing down at all on my heel.

"Are you okay?" Pepe said.

"No. I thought I was but my knee is really hurting," I whispered without actually stopping.

He continued with the basic footwork instead of doing the more intricate moves, like we were supposed to at this point. "Tell me if you need to stop. We have the pot stir and snake coming up. You think your knee is going to make it?"

"We can try."

"You sure?"

"Look at my hand. It's bleeding," yelled Cheryl.

"No. But I want to try," I said, trying to extricate her voice from my brain. Why was it not surprising she'd been the one to make me fall? I wanted to prove to her I could still rock, damn it.

"Okay, here goes," Pepe said, pulling me in toward his body, which I wrapped around and slithered down.

"I can't believe she did that to me." Cheryl again.

Her voice definitely brought on the adrenaline. I completed the whole move that had originally caused the knee sprain without even grimacing. I even did it well. No, that was an understatement. I rocked it.

I didn't really feel the pain until the routine ended and we were taking our bows. I went to do my curtsy with the right knee bent and the pain just surged through me. The leg actually buckled and I fell right there, all over again.

*Oh, no. This is bad.*

Sasha and Rory's story continues in "Fever, Book Three."

# Acknowledgments

I would like to thank Julia Ganis, my brilliant editor, Robena Grant, my wonderfully gracious mentor from the Los Angeles chapter of Romance Writers of America, and my amazing friend and reader, Elizabeth Donatelli, who all were so generous with their time and whose advice and critiques were absolutely invaluable in making this a better book. For words of wisdom on early drafts and overall much needed emotional support, I would like to thank writers Laurie Ellen Horowitz, Katrin McNevin, Margeaux Klein, Kathy Fielding, Maxine Nunes, and Tara Tyson. Thank you as well to Kristine Marsh for help translating Russian into English. This book began in Laurie Horowitz's Monday night fiction group at Beyond Baroque in Venice Beach, and I am extremely grateful to everyone in that class for their support, inspiration, and encouragement.

## About the Author

After working for many years as a criminal appeals attorney in New York, Tonya Plank now lives and writes in Southern California. A former amateur ballroom dancer, she wrote the dance blog, Swan Lake Samba Girl. Her first novel, Swallow, won several awards, including gold medals in the Independent Publisher and the Living Now Book Awards, and was a finalist in ForeWord's Book of the Year and the National Indie Excellence Awards.

When not writing, she enjoys taking road trips with her rescue dog, Sofia, devouring Mexican food and Cadillac margaritas, sweating to dance-based workouts, cuddling up with her cats and a good book, and of course seeing dance performances of any kind. Her favorite places in the world are Lincoln Center in New York City, the Pacific Coast Highway from Laguna Beach to San Francisco, and the Best Friends Animal Sanctuary in Kanab, Utah.

To connect with her, please find her at www.tonyaplank.com where she tries to blog regularly. For information on her upcoming releases, sign up for her newsletter: www.tonyaplank.com/newsletter.